So... her mind, a softness, almost a warmth, that eased the lingering pain of the vision.

"You won't remember my face," the man murmured in that deep, sexy voice.

"Of course not." Like she could ever forget that face.

He wasn't beautiful. Such a word implied a degree of softness, and there wasn't one soft thing about this man's features.

"I'm dreaming, remember?"

The growl that rumbled in the man's throat sounded more pained than threatening. The softness brushed her mind stronger than before, sending a shiver of pleasure rippling through her blood.

His scent teased her nostrils, increasing the pleasure playing with her senses. The feel of his body pressing against hers sent heat coursing through her veins.

Heaven help her, this guy was actually turning her on.

By Pamela Palmer

OBSESSION UNTAMED
DESIRE UNTAMED

Coming Soon

PASSION UNTAMED

PAMELA PALMER

OBSESSION UNTAMED

A FERAL WARRIORS NOVEL

AVON

An Imprint of HarperCollinsPublishers

This is a work of fiction. Names, characters, places, and incidents are products of the author's imagination or are used fictitiously and are not to be construed as real. Any resemblance to actual events, locales, organizations, or persons, living or dead, is entirely coincidental.

AVON BOOKS
An Imprint of HarperCollins*Publishers*
10 East 53rd Street
New York, New York 10022-5299

Copyright © 2009 by Pamela Poulsen
Excerpt from *Passion Untamed* copyright © 2009 by Pamela Poulsen
ISBN 978-0-06-166752-7
www.avonromance.com

First Avon Books paperback printing: August 2009

Avon Trademark Reg. U.S. Pat. Off. and in Other Countries, Marca Registrada, Hecho en U.S.A.
HarperCollins® is a registered trademark of HarperCollins Publishers.

Printed in the U.S.A.

10 9 8 7 6 5 4 3 2 1

*For my parents, Stew and Pat Palmer,
for your love and encouragement,
and for instilling in me the belief
that anything's possible*

Acknowledgments

Thank you to my editor, May Chen, and all the wonderful people at Avon Books who've made this book possible. And to my agent, Helen Breitwieser, for too many things to name.

To Laurin Wittig and Anne Shaw Moran, wonderful writers and dear friends. I couldn't do it without you. And to Anna Campbell for making me laugh and keeping me sane.

To the wonderful and talented men and women of the Washington Romance Writers and the Virginia Romance Writers. And to my 99er sisters for laughter and tears and an accidental friendship that bonded us for life.

To my real-life hero, Keith, for always being there, always supporting me, and always doing the grocery shopping. To Kelly, my wonderful daughter and shopping buddy, and to Kyle, my son and go-to guy for all things magical or fantasy-related. Thanks, pal.

Chapter
One

Five millennia ago, the Therian race of shape-shifters joined forces with their magic-wielding enemies, the Mage, to defeat and imprison the High Daemon, Satanan, and his vicious horde. They succeeded, but at a terrible cost, both races forced to mortgage the bulk of their power. All but one Therian from each of the ancient lines lost the strength of their animals and the ability to shift. Only nine shape-shifters remain.

They are the Feral Warriors.

Their duty is to protect the race, to hunt and destroy the dangerous, mindless, Daemon dregs called draden. And, most importantly, to guard the Daemon blade, in which Satanan and his horde are imprisoned, for the Daemons' return would bring hell to the races of the Earth.

* * *

The Feral Warriors were in a world of hurt.

Tighe lifted his face to the night wind, trying to cool the frustration lodged beneath the surface of his skin as he traversed the rugged, rocky woods high above the Potomac River.

The Mage had lost their freaking minds and were apparently *trying* to free the Daemons. After sacrificing so much five millennia ago to imprison them, Tighe couldn't fathom why, but there was no denying at least one Mage, the witch Zaphene, had been determined to free Satanan. Zaphene was dead, but she'd left a hell of a legacy.

One of the Ferals, Vhyper, was missing. The Daemon blade itself was gone. And one of Zaphene's creations had run off with half of Tighe's soul. Literally.

Where the Mage witch had come by the magic to split souls, no one knew, but she'd done so to make clones of the Ferals. Clones who would raise the Daemons from the blade in the real Ferals' stead, since the real Ferals weren't *stupid* enough to want that plague freed again. *What were the Mage thinking?*

A growl rumbled deep in his throat as he climbed the last of the stone outcroppings onto the cliffs above the river. The night was clear, the brightest stars little more than a dull glow, thanks to the damned humans and their incessant need to battle back the dark.

His clone was, by all indications, currently wreaking havoc on the human population. Tighe and two other Ferals had been tracking him for three days as he'd left a path of dead between Great Falls, Virginia, and nearby Washington, D.C.

And while, yes, the clone's deadly rampage needed to be stopped, Tighe's stake in his capture was a lot more personal. He needed his damned soul back. No one knew for sure how long he could survive with it split like it was, but the consensus was, *not long*. At least not with his sanity intact.

Dammit.

Which was why he returned to Great Falls and Feral House each night instead of remaining on the trail of his clone. He'd seen what could happen to a Feral with a split soul, and it wasn't pretty. Hell, it gave him nightmares. He was determined to hold on to his sanity, even if every Feral watched him as if he expected to have to lock Tighe up in the prison deep below Feral House at any moment.

Wulfe stepped onto the rock beside him. "Any sign of draden?" Wulfe was the biggest of the Ferals, a monster of a man close to seven feet tall, with a face that looked like it had once been used as a cat's scratching post.

Tighe released his frustration on a huff. "Not yet. They'll come." Then he'd rip their hearts out, as he did every night, and release some of this gut-eating frustration. Enough to feel relatively safe returning to the hunt for his clone in human-infested D.C.

"I'm surprised Lyon let us take you out without a leash," Jag drawled behind him.

A growl rumbled in Tighe's chest. The idiot wasn't satisfied until he had every Feral ready to rip his throat out. And Tighe was in a foul enough mood to accommodate him.

"Shut up, Jag," Wulfe snarled. "The last thing he needs right now is your needling."

The last thing he *needed* was everyone treating him like he was filled with gunpowder, a lit fuse dangling from the corner of his mouth. He was *fine*.

But the burn in his fingertips gave the lie to that little assertion. He struggled for control, struggled to pull back from the feral rage engulfing him. Under normal circumstances the feral state was merely a place of lost tempers and healthy fighting. The place halfway between man and beast, where human teeth elongated into fangs, claws erupted from fingertips, and human eyes no longer looked human. A place where a hawk and a tiger could access their wilder natures yet fight on equal footing.

But these were not normal circumstances. Thanks to the rending of his soul, he didn't know how much longer he'd have the strength or control to pull himself out of that state again.

He fought against the fury engulfing his body, clenching his teeth even as he willed himself calm, but it was too late. Claws unsheathed from the tips of his fingers. Fangs dropped from the top of his jaw. Daggerlike incisors rose from below as a backload of dammed-up rage ripped free of his control. In a rush of feral anger, he lunged, tackling Jag to the rocky ground.

In a haze of bloodlust, he felt the slash of claws

and the ripping of flesh as Jag went feral, too. Blood spilled into his mouth, both his own and Jag's, tasting warm and fine. His vision hazed in a wild bloodlust that had him suddenly longing to sink his teeth into Jag's neck and rip out the bastard's throat for real.

His logical mind recoiled. He was losing it. He could almost see the dark, swirling waters of chaos lapping at his sanity. As his sane mind clawed its way back from the precipice, Wulfe wedged himself between the two warriors, jerking Jag out of his grasp.

Tighe slowly struggled back to his controlled, human, form. As his claws and fangs retracted, Wulfe balled up his fist and hit Jag in the jaw with a hard right hook.

Jag went sprawling. "What'd you do that for?"

"You can be such an ass," Wulfe snarled. "Do you *want* to see him locked up? *Now?* Would it be too much to ask you to *not* hasten the destruction of one of our strongest warriors?"

Jag scowled and pushed to his feet. "Fuck you."

"I'm not heading for destruction," Tighe growled, standing and adjusting his ripped shirt so that it continued to hang, *barely*, from his body. He wouldn't let it happen. He *refused* to let it happen.

But he couldn't deny he was shaken.

"Let's kill some draden, then," Wulfe said.

Tighe compressed his mouth and nodded. They hunted draden by waiting for the little fiends to smell their Therian energy, energy the Ferals emitted in their human forms. It wasn't much longer before a faint dark cloud appeared over the cliffs across the river.

"Incoming," Wulfe said quietly. The draden had found them.

Wulfe yanked off his tee shirt and unzipped his jeans, tossing his clothes onto the rocks. Jag stripped out of his camouflage pants and army green tee. Tighe did nothing. He was one of the Ferals who possessed the ability to retain his clothes when he shifted. A handy trick, especially when he hunted among humans.

The dark cloud of draden moved quickly toward them over the gleaming river, a smudge against the stars and the shadowy distant cliffs. A *huge* smudge.

"Holy *shit*." Jag whistled low. "Is it just me, or is that five times the usual number?"

There had to be hundreds coming at them. Maybe more than a thousand. Holy shit was right. They'd known the draden were multiplying faster than usual, but the evidence was alarming. If they didn't get them under control, there wouldn't be enough Therian energy for them to feed on. They'd turn on the humans.

And if that happened, they'd decimate the population in no time, without the humans ever knowing what hit them.

"Then let's get 'em, boys," Jag said.

"I'll take first bait." Tighe pulled his knives. One of them had to remain in his human, or Therian form, or the draden would fly off. But as *first bait*, he would absolutely be fighting for his life.

In a sudden, heart-jarring instant, a veil of darkness dropped over his eyes, swallowing everything. Tighe's blood went cold.

He couldn't see. "*What the hell?*"

"What's the matter?" Wulfe asked beside him, as if nothing were wrong.

Shit. His pulse began to pound in his ears. This must only be happening to him. His vision was gone. Totally. Was this the first step to losing his sanity?

As quickly as his sight vanished, it reappeared, but his relief lifted and plummeted in the same instant. He wasn't actually seeing. Like a movie lighting a dark screen, a scene appeared before his sightless eyes.

A harsh, bright light lit a rough room, nothing but half a dozen washers and dryers on a cement floor. A public laundry room. Two heavyset women worked, one shoving wet laundry from the washer into the dryer, the other standing before a nearby table, folding clothes. The standing one glanced toward him, her expression at once appreciative and wary.

"Hi," she said cautiously.

Suddenly, her face grew in his vision as if a camera lens were pulling in close. Her eyes widened with terror as the room lurched dizzily. As if he'd attacked her and taken her to the ground.

Was this a premonition, *heaven help him,* of what he was to become?

Behind him, the other woman screamed, piercing his eardrums.

"No!" His victim threw up her hands, the terror in her eyes churning up rancid memories buried deep in his mind.

Memories of another time, another place.

His gut knotted until he thought he'd be sick. But he couldn't deny the evidence. It seemed he was finally doomed to become the very thing he'd been accused of being all those long, miserable years ago.

A monster.

FBI Agent Delaney Randall strode up the front walk of the Potomac Side Apartments in southwest D.C., her hand fisted tight around her notebook, her gut burning with a need to find the bastard who'd killed more than a dozen women and children in the past three days.

To stop him before he killed again.

It was late, nearly 10:00 P.M. The last three murders had taken place in that general neighborhood, and she'd spent all day canvassing the nearby apartments, interviewing residents, searching for clues. Someone had to know *something*. She was bone tired, but she wasn't quitting until her body refused to move another inch.

Not while the murderer was still on the loose.

And, unfortunately, that could be a while. Even with more than a dozen victims, there was no real evidence. So far, there had been no witnesses and no DNA left at the scenes despite the teeth marks on the victims' throats. Even the cause of the deaths was a mystery. It was as if God had pointed His divine finger at each of them, and said, "Time's up."

The breeze blew loose tendrils of hair into her face as she strode up the front walk of the apartment building. A man in a polo and khakis walked toward her, the streetlight illuminating a nice-looking face. White male, late twenties, not visibly armed. Her brain clicked a mental picture, filing him away as yet one more suspect.

He flashed her a bleached smile. "Evening."

But Delaney had already logged him, and her gaze had moved on to the pack of smoking teens sitting on the front steps ahead.

"Bitch." The muttered word carried to her from the man she'd just passed.

Her gaze jerked back to him, her hand lifting to hover at her waist, a hairbreadth from her gun. But the man never looked back as he strode away purposefully.

Bitch, he called her. As if she had time to flirt when yet another scumbag was prowling the streets, hunting innocents. *Moron.*

She ran up the steps, past the teens, and tried the door. Locked, as she'd suspected. Through the glass, she saw a balding African-American with tufts of gray hair over his ears running with an awkward gait toward her. The building's super, she supposed. She'd called a short while ago and asked him to meet her here.

As he neared the doors, the mix of agitation and fear on his face became apparent. Her instinct for trouble kicked into high gear, her pulse speeding up, the fingers of her right hand flexing. Had she stumbled on a domestic situation in progress or finally hit the jackpot?

The instant the man opened the door, a keening cry high in the building raised the hairs on the back of her neck.

She flashed her badge and pushed through the doorway. "Agent Randall, FBI. What happened?"

"I called the cops, but they aren't here yet."

"*What happened?*" Her gun was in her hand now, senses on high alert.

"A lady dead in the stairwell. Her kid just found her."

Her kid. *God.*

"How? Who did it?"

"Don't know. There's no blood."

Without waiting for further explanation, Delaney ran for the stairs in the middle of the building, following the sound of the crying.

But as she neared the third floor, the stairwell became so clogged with people she could hardly get through. She holstered her gun, and barked, "FBI!" The nearest residents parted for her to pass, eyeing her with varying degrees of curiosity, wariness, and relief.

Pushing through the crowd, she finally reached the source of the wailing. A little girl of no more than seven lay across the prone and lifeless body of a woman, the teeth marks that had become the trademark of the serial killer in a perfect oval on her neck.

Delaney's jaw clenched hard.

"Momma!" Tears streaked the child's brown cheeks, her dark eyes wells of fear as she rose to pat her mother's face. "*Momma.*"

Delaney's heart clenched as the child's fear flowed into her, echoing deep in her soul. She remembered that fear all too well. And hated, *hated*, the bastards who caused it. Thirteen people, now, that they knew of. Thirteen *females*. Seven of whom had left motherless children behind.

As she called in the murder, she pressed her palm to the top of the little girl's head. "I'm going to get him." The promise was too softly spoken for the child to hear, but the words imprinted themselves on Delaney's heart.

Death was part of life. She accepted that. Right or wrong, it was man's nature to fight and to kill. She understood deaths caused by war, even the misguided inner-city drug and gang wars. Wasteful as those deaths were, there was some testosterone-laden male sense to them.

But there was *no* sense to attacks like this. None. She'd dedicated her life to stopping them. To stopping the evil that caused them. And this son of a bitch was at the top of her list.

Through the babble of voices and crying, a fresh scream sliced the air, echoing up from the bowels of the building.

Delaney's blood went cold.

She pushed her way back into the crowd but had only managed to descend a couple of steps when an overweight blonde appeared at the bottom of the stairs.

"He's got my sister! He's got my sister!"

"Where?" Delaney shouted.

"Laundry room," the woman cried. "The basement."

"I'm FBI. Get up here and stay here."

"You got to save her. *Save her!*"

As the woman dissolved into hysterics, Delaney scanned the crowd still standing between her and the blonde, then pointed at the two toughest-looking males. "You and you. Keep everyone back and send the cops down when they get here."

The pair nodded soberly and parted the crowd for her to pass.

By the time she pushed through the metal door into the basement, she was alone. No sound reached her ears except the dull thud of her boots on the cement floor.

No screams. No crying. No woman begging for her life.

Delaney held her gun aloft, her heart thudding as she eased down the hall to the wide, brightly lit doorway. Pressing her back to the wall, she peered around the corner.

A huge, muscular man with short, sun-bleached hair looked up from where he knelt beside the prone and lifeless body of a woman who could have been the twin of the one who'd sent her down.

She had him.

With both hands she lifted her gun. "*Freeze*. FBI! Hands in the air!"

The man rose with an ease that belied his size, staring at her, not with the eyes of the guilty but the cold eyes of a hunter spotting prey. Green eyes without humanity. Without mercy.

The eyes of Death himself.

A bead of sweat rolled between her shoulder blades. She was far from short, but this guy towered over her, his shoulders broad, his body lean and strong beneath the navy blue dress shirt and too-short khakis he wore without shoes. No way was she risking hand-to-hand combat.

A chill slithered down her spine. "Hands in the air, or I shoot!"

He moved so suddenly, so quickly, she barely got a shot off before he was on her, knocking her to the ground. Her head slammed against the cement as her gun went flying, jagged lights streaking her vision.

She'd hit him in the chest. Point-blank. He should be going down, dammit. She tried to fight him, but he was as strong as a bear as he pinned her to the floor.

His head dipped. As she felt his cold mouth open on her neck and the press of his teeth into her skin, she struggled against her immovable assailant, a scream of fury filling her mind.

Too soon. Too soon. She'd left too many killers walking the streets.

She didn't have time to die.

*Chapter
Two*

Still deep in the vision, beneath the harsh, bright lights of the public laundry room, the sound of footsteps had Tighe looking up from the body of the dead blonde into the face of a stunning, dark-haired beauty. Dressed in a no-nonsense navy blue suit, the brunette was tall and leggy, her hair pulled into a casual knot at the back of her head, the gun in her hands pointed at his heart.

A strange sensation pummeled the inside of his chest as he stared into her fierce, determined face. A feeling of connection gripped him. Almost a recognition.

"*Freeze.* FBI!" she shouted at him. "Hands in the air!"

He leaped at her as he had the other one. The

gun fired, but if she hit him, he couldn't tell. He couldn't feel anything, could only hear the sound of her thudding heart and the slam of her head against the cement floor as he took her to the ground.

Their gazes met, and in the brown depths of her dazed eyes he saw not fear, but fury, and recognized the soul of a fellow warrior. Then he dipped his head to rip out her throat.

Tighe? Tighe!

He came back to the night in a rush, desperately swallowing the bile that tried to rise in his throat. Even as the stunning, dark-eyed beauty chiseled herself into his mind.

She can't die.

Tighe! Wulfe's voice echoed in his head at the exact moment fire slashed through his flesh like a thousand tiny knives ripping him out of his vision and back to his dark reality.

The horde of draden had found him.

Instinctively, he lifted his knives and began attacking the creatures, little more than floating gas beneath heads shaped like hideously melted human faces. They would steal his life if they got the chance. Beside him, his jaguar and wolf companions leaped and snapped at the attacking fiends.

Sweat rolled down his temples as the woman's face, *those eyes*, swam in his memory. *Mistake.* His gut fisted with horror over what he was destined to do even as the draden tore at his flesh. He fought them off, the blood running in small rivulets down his neck and back.

What would drive him to attack a human woman? *Two* women?

But he knew. That chaos he'd seen swimming at the edges of his consciousness would overtake him before they found his clone, just as it had Wulfe before they'd destroyed *his* clone. Like Wulfe before him, he was destined to become locked in a feral rage, lost to the violence that would transform him into an unthinking, unreasoning killing machine.

At least Wulfe had never gotten free of the Ferals' prison. He'd never harmed anyone in that state.

"Wulfe, whatever you do, *don't let me go feral and escape.*"

Not going to let it happen, *buddy*, Wulfe said mentally from his wolf form. *Shift, Stripes. I'm taking over as bait.*

It's too soon.

The huge wolf turned into a man in a shower of sparkling lights. His friend looked at him grimly. "*Do it.*"

"Damn," Tighe muttered. He must look as bad as he felt. In a harsh rush of power, he pulled on the energy and magic deep in his body and shifted into his animal form, his vision a quick flash of light. Raw, primitive joy surged through him as he shifted into a fifteen-foot Bengal tiger.

The draden released him with a high-pitched squawk. Tighe went on the attack, scattering and destroying the little fiends alongside the jaguar. Wulfe, standing naked in the moonlight, came under attack from the ungodly throng, digging out their hearts as fast as he could, before they sucked the life force out of him or ripped him to shreds.

"You okay?" Wulfe asked. Tighe didn't have to ask who he was talking to.

An answering growl was his only response.

I see the sire. The jaguar leaped, snapping his jaws around the largest of the draden, swallowing its beating heart to destroy it, dissolving the creature in a puff of smoky energy. The sire, or leader of the swarm, was the one who directed their flight. Kill the sire, and the rest would remain right where they were, lost and leaderless, making them easy marks for the animals, whom they couldn't feed from and wouldn't attack.

Wulfe shifted back into his animal and joined the slaughter of the disordered swarm.

Tighe caught one after another of the little demons in his massive jaws. Neither the hearts nor the creatures themselves had any real taste, for they weren't flesh and blood but made almost entirely of energy.

We've got company. Jag's voice sounded in his head.

Tighe swung his massive tiger's head in the direction Jag was facing. Sure enough, two teenaged boys stood in the woods not twenty yards away, watching a sight that must be unbelievable to them. Humans couldn't see the draden, but they could sure as hell see the huge tiger, wolf, and jaguar.

Tighe gave a mental groan of frustration. Damn humans, always getting in the way. Fortunately for them, draden only attacked humans if there were no Therians for miles around. Still, the humans were a problem.

Jag, come with me, Tighe said. The two cats possessed the ability to change the size and, to some extent, the forms of their animals at will. While Wulfe continued to fight the draden in his wolf form, Tighe and Jag shifted into what most humans would see as house cats, then circled behind the two boys.

"Where'd the tiger go?" a youthful voice asked.

"Dude, is this for real? I thought it was the weed."

As Jag closed in on one, Tighe moved behind the other. As one, the two Ferals shifted into human form and rendered the youths briefly unconscious with a quick application of pressure beneath their ears.

As Tighe knew they would, the draden followed his and Jag's now-Therian scent. He pulled the switchblades from his pockets and tossed them to Jag, then knelt on the ground beside one of the boys. Wulfe joined them, and as the draden swarmed, the two Ferals, one man, one wolf, covered Tighe as he called on the ability all Ferals possessed to some extent, though his was undeniably the strongest.

Tighe gripped the face of his captive. "Open your eyes." When the boy did, Tighe looked deeply into those glazed irises. "You saw nothing in the woods tonight except a couple of dogs. When I tell you to, you'll go home and never venture into these woods at night again. And you'll flush the weed and swear off it for good, you little punk."

As the battle raged around him, Tighe rose and moved to the second kid, performing the same bit of mind control. When both boys' minds were successfully clouded, he told them to go, then shifted back into his animal and rejoined the fight.

Hours later, they were still destroying draden when the nocturnal fiends began to take off as they always did an hour before sunrise. In all that time, the Ferals had only managed to destroy half the swarm.

"This is bad," Wulfe muttered, shifting back into human form and grabbing his clothes.

Tighe couldn't deny it.

As they headed for home, Wulfe turned to him. "What happened to you as they descended, Stripes?"

"I don't want to talk about it." But he was going to have to tell Lyon.

Goddess forbid he get loose and become that . . . *thing.*

"Bleed," Lyon said, striding forward as Tighe walked into the dining room of Feral House a short while later.

Tighe glowered at the Chief of the Feral Warriors, but thrust out his left hand, palm up. Lyon made a short, shallow cut in the center of Tighe's palm, nodding when the slice welled with blood as his clone's would not have.

The thought that the draden-based fiend that wore his face could sneak into Feral House gave him chills.

Though it annoyed him to have to submit to someone's knife every time he walked into a room, the alternative was worse. Much worse. The clone could potentially kill one of the Ferals. Or Kara, Lyon's mate and their Radiant. No one was willing to take that chance.

But knowing what he was to become, he feared the clone might no longer be the greatest danger.

Lyon closed his switchblade and greeted Tighe properly, offering his right arm. The two men slapped forearms as they grasped one another just below the elbow in the traditional greeting of the Ferals.

"You're going to have to lock me up, Roar."

Lyon's gaze narrowed. "Why?"

He told him about the premonition. "I'm not going to turn into that monster. And I will if you don't lock me up."

"You will if we don't catch that clone in time." Lyon's amber gaze bored into his. "But we will, Stripes. We're going to catch him. *With* your help." He clasped Tighe's shoulder. "We're spread too thin right now to give you a vacation in the prisons."

Tighe growled. "Vacation my ass."

Kara entered the dining room and joined them, her pert, blond ponytail swinging as she slipped her arm around the waist of her much larger mate. As Lyon pulled her tight against him, she met Tighe's gaze, a sweet smile lighting her blue eyes.

"Hi, Tighe."

His own ready smile slid into place with an ease

born of deep affection for this slip of a woman who'd shown more strength in the past days than all the Radiants who'd come before her over the centuries, combined.

"Hi, yourself." Tighe held out his arms to her, pleased when Lyon released her, and she gave him a quick, badly needed hug. He closed his arms around her and held her tight, absorbing the closeness as much as her sweetness.

At any given time, there was one Radiant, one Therian woman through whom the Ferals reached the great stores of nature's energy and the power they needed in order to shift into their animals. They'd nearly missed finding Kara. She'd been raised human, thousands of miles away. Their energy had been flagging, their ability to shift gone when Lyon finally managed to locate her. And thank the goddess he had. They'd never have defeated the witch Zaphene without Kara's power, courage, and surprising talent with radiance.

He tightened his hold on her. Lyon was a lucky man to have been chosen her mate, an honor Tighe had secretly hoped would go to *him*. Kara was a sweet Therian beauty, as kind as she was courageous.

No man could do better.

As he looked down at her, his eyes began to tingle as they did whenever he was about to go feral. Or when he was in the presence of a beautiful woman.

He alone among the Ferals had that little problem. For the others, feral was feral. The eyes, the claws, the fangs came as a package deal. Not so, Tighe. His claws and fangs only sprouted when he was ready to fight, but his eyes were another matter. If his body stirred with interest, his eyes shifted, the pupils growing until they blocked out the white, their color changing from their natural green to the golden orange of his tiger's.

It was a major nuisance, necessitating dark, wraparound sunglasses whenever he was in human public, day or night. Tiger eyes were damned hard to pass off as human. And the humans needed to think he was one of them. If there was one agreement between the immortal races, it was that the humans continue to believe they were alone.

Lyon growled. "Your eyes."

Tighe shrugged and grinned at his chief. "She's a beautiful woman, Roar." He winked at Kara. "Do you want me to put on the shades?"

Kara's soft trill of laughter eased the craziness inside him. "It's not like I don't know why you wear sunglasses in the house." She pulled out of his embrace and returned to her mate, looping her arm around Lyon's waist. "I'm flattered, Tighe, and head over heels in love with my lion." She grinned. "But you know that."

Tighe laughed. "Yeah, I noticed. Lucky bastard."

The growl that came from Lyon's throat held a note of hard satisfaction. "You need to get one of these for yourself."

"A mate? Hell no." He winked at Kara. "Not unless I can have yours."

At the teasing words, Lyon tightened his hold.

Tighe shook his head. "I never thought I'd see you like this, Roar." The pleasure he felt that his friend had found his one true mate after all these centuries was bittersweet. Tighe remembered all too well how love could transform a man, clearing his vision and changing his world. And how it could destroy him.

Lyon smiled, his gaze dropping to Kara's sweet face. "Sometimes you have to risk your heart."

Tighe prayed Lyon never felt the cutting pain from the other side of that double-edged blade.

"Let's eat." Lyon turned Kara toward the large formal dining table that sat in front of the wall of windows looking onto sunlit woods.

Foxx, Paenther, and Wulfe were already seated, but as he approached the table, each rose and greeted him.

Foxx, who'd only been with them a couple of years and was genuinely twenty-three, nodded to him, his shaggy red hair falling in his face. "Tighe."

As Foxx returned to his seat, Paenther, Lyon's second-in-command, grasped his arm, his intense black eyes boring into him. The warrior, three-quarters Native American, had the bronzed skin and black hair and eyes of his human ancestors. A tribal tattoo snaked up his neck, while across one eye slashed the claw marks that marked him as a Feral Warrior. Dressed head to toe in leather, vibrating with a fine rage long ago burned into his soul by the Mage, he was a man whom others gave a wide berth. Except those few who knew him well.

Paenther, alone, never asked him how he was doing. But his friend's deep concern came through in the too-tight grip on his wrist and the length of time he held the greeting.

"Find him," Paenther said, his voice low, but tight. "I wish I could help."

Tighe shook his head. "We'll find the clone. You and Foxx find Vhyper and that blade. Of the two tasks, yours is by far the more important, B.P. If I die, another Feral will be marked. You won't be down a man."

That black gaze never wavered. "You're not expendable, Stripes. *Find him*. I won't lose you, too."

Tighe found his grin. "Then I'll find him." The smile died as quickly as it was born, worry closing around his heart. "I'm doing my best, B.P." But he was seriously worried his best was going to be too damn little. And too damn late.

"*News.*" Wulfe's deep voice echoed off the walls of the dining room.

Tighe turned to the newly installed flat-screen hanging on the wall behind him. And froze.

"The killer some are calling the D.C. Vampire struck again last night in southwest. Jeanine Tinnings was slain in the same mysterious manner as at least ten others in the past three days." In the middle of the screen was a photo of a laughing blond woman holding a chubby-cheeked toddler.

The air left Tighe's lungs as if he'd been sucker punched. He was staring at the face of the woman who'd been folding the laundry, the first of the two women he'd thought he'd killed. Or *would* kill.

She was already dead.

The hard knot of dread slowly dissolved in his chest. He wasn't going to kill her.

Ah, *shit*. That meant there would be no saving the other one, either. The dark-haired FBI beauty with the warrior's eyes must already be dead, too.

Which meant . . . Chills rushed along the surface of his flesh. "It wasn't a premonition," he said out loud.

Lyon's gaze swung to him. "What wasn't a premonition?"

"I saw her die last night. Through the eyes of the killer. I thought I was seeing the future."

Paenther looked at him with surprise. "You're starting to see through your clone's eyes."

Tighe nodded slowly. "At least when he kills."

"This is the break we need." Lyon's eyes began to glitter. "If you can identify where a murder is taking place, we may finally have a way to catch that son of a bitch."

The crushing weight of the two deaths lifted from Tighe's shoulders, but the relief was slight. The women were still dead even if he hadn't been the one to kill them. And there was still a strong likelihood he'd end up as crazed and deadly as he'd feared. As Wulfe had. Little by little, he'd lose control until he finally tumbled into a feral rage from which he couldn't escape.

Until then? It seemed he was doomed to watch the terror of the dying through the eyes of the one desecrating his soul.

Chapter
Three

As the sun rose over Washington, D.C., Tighe slammed open the door of the safe house and stormed inside, his fingers and teeth tingling with the need to go feral and rip something apart. Anything.

Frustration bled from his brain, down into every cell in his body.

They were getting nowhere. *Nowhere.*

"Easy, Stripes," Hawke said behind him as he and Kougar followed him in the door. "Stay in your skin, buddy."

Tighe strode to the refrigerator of the small row house on Capitol Hill, grabbed a Budweiser, and drank it down with one long pull.

Once the residence of a Therian family, for years

the house had served as a safe house for Therians caught too far from the enclaves at night. Nocturnal creatures, the draden only fed at night but were capable of passing through untreated glass to reach their Therian victims.

The glass of Therian homes and cars were treated with magic to keep them safe from draden penetration. Safe houses were scattered throughout the areas most often frequented by members of the race. Last he heard, there were nearly a dozen around the D.C. area in addition to the five actual enclaves.

This particular safe house was only four blocks from the apartment building where he'd watched the dark-eyed beauty die yesterday morning. For twenty-four hours, the three Ferals had roamed the area, both in their human and animal forms, searching for the clone. In their animal forms, they should have been able to smell him, but they'd gotten nothing. Worse than nothing.

Even the visions were useless. That first one had been so clear he'd really thought they might help him. But only in that one, when he'd watched the dark-eyed beauty die had he seen the death as if through the eyes of the clone. Ever since, he'd seen little more than vague faces contorted with terror. Nightmarish wisps with garbled sound. No details. Nothing to tell him where the killings were taking place. Nothing to help him catch the bastard.

He slammed the empty Budweiser can on the counter so hard that he crushed it.

Hawke lifted one dark, winged brow.

"I'm in my skin!" Tighe snapped, reading his friend's expression all too well. "You can't blame me for being frustrated."

"No one's blaming you, buddy. We're watching you. But we're not blaming you."

"Great." Watching him lose control, minute by minute. Tighe reached back into the fridge and pulled out three more beers, tossing one to each of his companions before turning on the old television in the corner to see if there was any news. He had a morbid need to know the identity of the dark-eyed woman he'd watched die. So far, there'd been nothing about her in the news. Maybe because she was FBI.

Already, she was haunting him. He'd barely gone an hour without thinking about her, without her face rising into his mind's eye, those rich mahogany eyes flashing with fury and fire as she'd met her death. Why he was so obsessed with her he couldn't begin to guess. Yeah, she'd been beautiful. And a fighter, which was admirable enough. But she'd been human. And he didn't give a rat's ass about humans.

Especially dead ones. And with their short, fragile lives, they were all basically the walking dead.

Damn, but he wanted this to be over. He wanted his soul intact so he and his companions could concentrate on the true threat, the apparent Mage plot to free Satanan and his Daemon horde. If there *was* a plot. They didn't know what in the hell was going on.

Hawke's brows drew down. "What's with your eyes, Tighe?"

"The black streak?" He'd noticed it in the mirror that morning, a single black streak cutting across his green iris from pupil to outer ring. "Beats the hell out of me." Frustration simmered inside him, refusing to be distracted. He slammed his fist on the counter. "Where is that son of a bitch clone? For all we know, he could be halfway to Texas by now."

Kougar gave a pull on his Bud, his pale eyes shining over his mustache and goatee. "I wouldn't put it past him. The bastard's different than the other clones. Smarter."

Hawke nodded. "He may be evolving."

"What do you mean?" Tighe asked warily.

"If I'm right, he's going to become smarter and more clever every day until he's nearly your equal."

"Goddess forbid. While I degenerate into a raving lunatic."

Hawke shrugged. "He was the only one who escaped the battle when they were all but defeated. Then he ditched your Land Rover in McLean and stole the cars of each of his victims, one after the other, making him impossible to follow. That's clever. As is the fact that he's staying away from the Therian compounds despite the fact Therian energy is his natural food. He's having to kill human after human to feed himself because he knows the Therians are watching for him."

"Yeah, and maybe he just enjoys the killing," Tighe grunted. "If I could get another real vision, maybe we could stop . . ." As if Nature heard his plea, his sight went suddenly black. "It's happening again." As he was swept into another place, he grabbed for the kitchen counter and held on.

Confusion clouded his mind as he stared into the face of the dark-eyed beauty who'd been haunting his thoughts all day and night. *She wasn't dead*. He watched her in the mirror of a public bathroom, as if through her own eyes. She leaned in closer and pulled open the collar of her white blouse, revealing an oval of red welts on the otherwise-flawless olive skin of her long, graceful neck.

Teeth marks.

The clone had attacked her, yet *she hadn't died*. How was that possible?

Praise the heavens and Earth.

He scowled at himself for the relief and, hell, *joy* rushing through him. She was human, for heaven's sake. *Human.*

Yet there was little about her that reminded him of Gretchen. She was tall where Gretchen had been short. She was dark where Gretchen had been fair. And even in the vision her eyes burned with fire, the same fire that had lit their depths as she'd faced the clone. While Gretchen's eyes would, in his memory, always radiate with fear.

There was a fury simmering inside this woman that he sensed was as much a part of her as her brown hair and high cheekbones. He didn't have to hear her thoughts to know she wanted to catch the creature that had attacked her.

But it wasn't going to happen.

There was no way the Ferals could allow human

law enforcement to get their hands on that thing. The moment they realized he didn't bleed, it was all over. For centuries, the Therian and Mage races had been careful to hide their existence from the humans. The mortals had become too numerous, too powerful. Yet their fear and hatred of the things they didn't understand was as great as ever. The moment they learned of the immortal races among them, they'd turn their considerable cunning and weaponry toward eliminating them.

They'd end up destroying the only ones who could save them.

The woman grimaced suddenly, her face contorting in a pain she quickly masked. Shards of agony bolted through her eyes as her body went tense as a wire. She grabbed for the sink in much the same way he'd grabbed for the kitchen counter a moment ago. As if she feared she'd fall if she didn't.

Suddenly, a second vision overlaid the woman's face in his mind's eye. An old woman this time, with terror in her eyes as her face became a blur and her wrinkled neck loomed large.

"Oh, God," the dark-eyed beauty gasped, and suddenly she was the only one he was seeing again. "What did he do to me?" she whispered to her reflection. "It wasn't enough that he almost killed me. Now I'm going to have to watch him kill others?"

Tighe's scalp tingled as the meaning of her words became clear. *She was seeing the murders. She was getting* his *visions.*

"Agent Randall?" A second woman appeared in the bathroom mirror. An older woman of Asian descent rushed toward the beauty. "Delaney, what's the matter?"

"Nothing," his vision-stealer said brusquely and straightened, the pain and emotion disappearing from her expression as if they'd never been. "I'm fine."

Tighe blinked as the beauty disappeared. He turned to find Hawke watching him expectantly.

"What did you see?"

Tighe shook his head, reeling at the implications. Staggering from the inexplicable need to find the woman.

"Someone's stealing my visions."

"What do you mean?"

He met Hawke's piercing gaze. "One of the two women I watched the clone attack didn't die. The FBI agent. I just watched her as *she* saw the next murder. I saw snatches of it, but nothing useful."

"Interesting," Hawke murmured.

"I saw the bite marks on her neck. I know it's the same woman." As if he could forget the face he'd been staring at in his memory for twenty-four hours straight.

Hawke's eyes got that faraway look they always got when his mental gears started moving at the speed of light. "She probably had backup. If her partner shot the clone as he was sucking her life force, he may have inadvertently exhaled some of his own back into her at that moment of impact, then fled without finishing the feeding."

Tighe scowled. "Are you telling me she has some of my soul now, too?"

"No. Not your soul. A soul can't be split without serious magic. But I think she may have acquired a touch of your clone's life force. Just enough to make her only 99.9 percent human."

Tighe groaned. "Just enough to screw up everything."

"Probably."

"Grab your laptop, Hawke, and start hacking. I need an address for FBI agent Delaney Randall."

"We going after her?"

"Not we. *Me*. I'm going alone. The Feds already know what I look like."

Kougar plucked at his goatee. "Kill her. Get her out from between you and your clone."

His gut twisted as he met Kougar's pale gaze, as cold as any assassin's. Not for the first time, he thanked Nature this warrior was friend and not foe.

"Rest assured, that clone is going to die," Tighe said. "And no one, *no one*, is going to stand in my way."

But he remembered too well his furious thought when he first thought he was destined to kill her.

She can't die.

Chapter
Four

Delaney pressed the elevator button in the FBI field office, her head pounding. Six aspirin over the course of the afternoon hadn't done a thing to help, as if mere aspirin could relieve the tension of knowing that at any moment, in her head she could be watching another murder take place. Three so far this afternoon. *Three.*

Each more painful than the last.

What had that bastard done to her?

If she had to acquire superpowers, why couldn't she have gotten X-ray vision? Or maybe the ability to fly? Visions of death were so *not* on her wish list.

No, that was a lie. She'd take anything, even this god-awful sight, if it helped her catch the killer.

Unfortunately, none of the murders she'd seen so far had given her a single lead to go on. And each time she got one, she saw less. And hurt more. She'd nearly passed out from the last one.

"Leaving already?"

Delaney's gaze swung to her boss, who was walking past with a Georgetown Hoyas coffee mug in his hand. Phil Taylor was in his fifties, with a body that was no longer fit, a mind that was as sharp as ever, and eyes that saw way too much. Which was annoying as hell sometimes.

"It's after seven, sir. You know this is working late for me these days." She smiled at him, trying to paste a look of serene innocence on her face. "I took your lecture to heart. I'm a fifty-hour-a-week worker these days. Not a minute more."

Phil chuckled. "And I'm the Easter Bunny. Come into my office for a minute before you go, Agent Randall."

Delaney didn't bother to muffle her groan as she fell into step beside him. Phil knew she hated his fatherly lectures. He was a good guy, and genuinely interested in the mental and physical well-being of his agents, which made him an excellent boss. But she was sick to death of his warning her to put her job in perspective, get a life, etc., etc. She was the only one he hounded to be a little *less* dedicated. Then again, she was the only one he'd found still at work when he'd come into the office at 2:00 A.M. three mornings in a row.

She wasn't in the mood for another lecture. Not tonight. Not when her superpowers could hit again at any moment. Another groan vibrated in her throat. Now wouldn't *that* guarantee her an appointment for psych eval?

"You don't look good, Delaney." Phil closed his office door and went around his desk.

"Gee, thanks, boss." As he took his seat, Delaney perched on the edge of the chair across from him as if she only had a minute.

Phil waved his hand. "You know what I mean. You've got circles under your eyes. You look pale."

"It's early spring in D.C. Everyone looks pale."

"True, but not everyone was attacked by the D.C. Vampire, though at the rate things are going, that might yet change. You were damned lucky to have lived to tell the tale, Delaney."

"I know." Just before she'd passed out, she'd heard the crack of a gunshot and felt her attacker jerk and flee. Someone had shot the bastard and saved her life, though her savior hadn't come forward. None of the residents claimed to know who had done it, though she suspected one of the tough guys she'd put in charge might have followed her down. The only person she'd been able to thank for her life was the EMT who'd administered CPR and gotten her heart started again.

By the time the cops and Feds had arrived on the scene, there'd been no trail of blood to follow. Not a drop, even though she knew she'd shot the killer as he lunged for her. She *knew* she had. As had her savior. So why wasn't there any blood? It made no sense.

It was almost as if the man *wasn't* entirely human, which was ridiculous of course. Vampires weren't any more real than the Great Pumpkin. The only reason the killer had been dubbed the D.C. Vampire was because of his habit of leaving teeth marks, though decidedly human teeth marks, on his victims' necks.

But the fact remained, nothing about the murders made sense. And she seriously hated mysteries.

Phil steepled his hands in front of his mouth, tapping his forefingers on his upper lip. "I want you to take a couple of days off."

"It's Friday. Taking a couple of days off at this point in the week is traditional, sir."

"Smart aleck. Two days in addition to the weekend."

"Un-uh. No way." As if making her stay out of the office fourteen hours a day wasn't bad enough. "I received a clean bill of health, remember?"

"We don't know what he did to you, Delaney, but your heart stopped, in case you've forgotten. I've been keeping an eye on you today, and you're not looking good. Whether you like it or not, you *need* a few days to get your equilibrium back. Go visit family." He winced as if he'd forgotten she didn't have any. "Or just leave town. Get away from this place."

"I'm fine. I'm working normal hours, taking weekends off, all the things you told me to."

"Yeah, sure. And what are you doing with all that free time? Tell me that."

She smiled sweetly. Innocently. "Scrapbooking."

Phil gave a bark of laughter. "You're stubborn, Randall. Anyone ever tell you that?"

"You. All the time."

"I've always liked that about you." His expression turned serious as he leaned forward, resting his forearms on his desk. "You're one of the best agents I have, Delaney, but I worry about you. You're determined to catch them all, and you can't. Nobody can."

Delaney rolled her shoulders uncomfortably. "I don't have to catch them all. Just the ones I'm after."

Phil shook his head. "Stubborn, stubborn." His expression softened. "A four-day weekend, Delaney. That's all I'm asking. If you're bored, call Mary. Since our youngest left for college, she doesn't know what to do with herself. I'm sure she'd be delighted to meet you for lunch or some shopping. Sleep. Eat. Maybe even read a book. Do something that has absolutely nothing to do with the D.C. Vampire for four days." He nodded once, sharply. "That's an order."

She gave him a wry look that held a hint of a smile. "You're a pain in the ass, you know that?"

His expression softened the way her father's used to after he'd scolded her, right before he told her he still loved her. The liar.

"I wouldn't be doing my job if I weren't." Phil waved his hand toward the door. "Now go home and turn on the television. And make it a comedy. When you walk in here Wednesday morning, I want you looking like the living again instead of the half-dead."

Delaney made a face at him but didn't say any more as she rose, lifted her hand in a brief farewell, and left. Taking a long weekend might actually work to her advantage. Maybe if she weren't so tired, she'd start seeing the visions clearly again, without the accompanying migraine.

Then, if she could just figure out *where* the next murder was taking place, she might be able to get there in time to stop it. Or at least, in time to catch the murderer.

That son of a bitch was going down.

As she walked to her car, she prayed she'd get another vision soon. But as she slid her key into the ignition of her Toyota SUV, her head exploded with pain. *Too soon.*

The keys dropped to the floor with a jangle as Delaney grabbed the steering wheel, gasping. Her vision went until all she could see were wildly colored jagged shapes that cut through her head and stole her breath with excruciating agony. Her skin turned to ice even as beads of sweat rolled between her breasts.

A scream tore through her brain. A scream not her own.

Amid the tearing color she caught glimpses of a scene. An unknown woman's face contorted in terror. A body lying on a pitted and stained linoleum floor.

The visions and colors flew at her, clawing at her

mind until the pain ran in bright red rivulets that slowly turned to black.

"Hey, lady!"

Delaney blinked, a god-awful noise blaring in her ears as she awoke with a jolt. She straightened, releasing the steering wheel. The noise abated at once.

The horn. She'd been leaning on the horn.

The fog of confusion dissipated through the ache that still filled her head. She'd had another vision. Or maybe just one hell of a migraine. A migraine with dead people.

The tapping resumed on her window, and she turned to find the garage attendant staring at her through the glass. She reached for the keys, remembered they'd fallen, and leaned down to search for them with shaking fingers. Finally, she managed to snag them, start the car, and lower the window.

"Are you okay?" he asked worriedly. "Did you pass out or something?"

"I fell asleep. I'm fine." With that, she backed out of the parking space and left the garage to join the heavy flow of traffic. Phil had told her she looked half-dead. She was beginning to think he might have been closer to the truth than she wanted to believe. Maybe she was coming down with the flu. The visions were just fever-induced hallucinations.

And maybe the man who'd attacked her had given her something in addition to the visions. Some kind of deadly disease.

She groaned. If she still felt so bad in the morning, she'd go to the doctor. Right now, all she wanted to do was to get home and sleep. Please God, *without* another vision, or she'd never make it home at all.

She white-knuckled it the entire trip to Fairlington, but made it without incident. As she fumbled with her keys in the lock of her condo, a cat leaped into her line of sight, startling her. Her keys fell from her nerveless fingers, but the pretty tabby barely seemed to notice, sliding instead around her ankle.

"Sorry about that, fella. Where'd you come from?" She stroked the animal's orange-striped fur as she bent down to retrieve her keys. "You're a pretty thing, but you don't want to stay near me tonight. If I'm getting sick, like I think I am, things are bound to get disgusting. Go home."

But he only purred and rubbed his face against her pant leg. Delaney gave his chin a scratch, then rose and managed to get the key in the lock. As she pushed open the door, the cat raced inside.

Blast it. She was so not up to chasing a cat. Unless he changed his mind fast, he was going to have to spend the night.

The animal turned and sat in the bedroom doorway, watching her as she set her briefcase on the large dining table that constituted the only real furniture in her living room. On the table sat her laptop and computer and a host of case files. Covering the walls of the room were maps, photos of the missing, and the crime-scene photos of the dead. Her office away from the office. Although Phil had made her promise not to come in to work any more than fifty hours a week, she never quit working, as the too-shrewd man knew all too well.

She met the cat's eerily sharp gaze. "Believe me, if you're looking for a home, this isn't it."

She swayed on her feet and grabbed the back of the nearest straight-backed chair wishing, for once, she'd bothered to buy a sofa. The only place she could relax was the bed. And that was where she needed to be.

The cat's soft, deep purr caressed her frayed nerves, as if he sensed how lousy she felt. It was kind of nice feeling like someone cared, even if he was really just asking for food. Maybe with her working more hours from home, she could take *having a pet* off that wish list reserved for the distant future. A future she hadn't thought she was going to see for a brief few minutes in the laundry room of the Potomac Side Apartments.

The cat moved out of her way as she went into the bedroom, then resumed his watchful pose as she pulled off her suit jacket and tossed it on the bed.

"I had a cat once," she told him. "I had a lot of things once, until a scumbag caught my mom on a deserted stretch of running trail." She shrugged. "Now I have a purpose."

As she divested herself of both weapons and kicked off her shoes, she felt like the cat was studying her. Something in his eyes almost seemed to be assessing her.

As if she hadn't gotten enough of that from Phil already.

She shook her head at him. "I don't have to justify myself to you, too. I didn't invite you in here, in case you've forgotten." She unfastened her pants and slid them down her hips, then turned her back on him as she reached into her closet for a hanger. "You're welcome to go anytime you want to, just don't look at me like I don't measure up."

"I'd say your measurements are just about perfect."

Delaney spun at the sound of the deep male voice. And froze. The D.C. Vampire stood in her doorway watching her as intently as the cat had moments before.

Son of a *bitch*.

Her headache and jitters disappeared in a rush of adrenaline and anger. This time, he was going down.

She whirled, reaching for her Glock. And never touched it. He slammed her back against the wall, wrenching her arms above her head, capturing her wrists in a single large hand even as he pressed his body against hers. Eye to eye with the buttons of his burgundy silk shirt, she fought for her life. Struggling to free her hands, she tried to ram her knee into his groin.

He stopped her cold, nailing her to the wall with his pelvis.

Her breath heaved. Fury swirled in her mind as his size and sheer strength overwhelmed her. Twice, he'd gotten her. *Twice*. It was inexcusable.

The blood pounded fast and hard through her veins as she stared up into his face, her own reflected in his dark wraparound sunglasses. God, she'd never seen anyone so ugly on the inside who was so incredibly good-looking on the outside. Was that how he got so close to his victims?

Her mind lurched with realization. "How did you get in here?"

"You wouldn't believe me if I told you." His voice was deep and rich, as pleasing as his looks even as he gripped her jaw, immobilizing her with an ease that terrified her. For years, she'd trained hard so this kind of thing wouldn't happen. So she wouldn't find herself the prey instead of the hunter.

So she wouldn't end up like her mother.

Yet, in the end, she had. The tightness of the killer's mouth, the determination in every line of his face let her know he intended to finish what he'd started yesterday. And her utter inability to move beneath his iron grip told her there was nothing she could do to stop him.

Blast it! If she thought begging would help, she might have tried to force the words past her pride. But not for a second did she believe he'd listen to her. The man had shown his other victims no mercy whatsoever. None. For God's sake, he'd killed two children.

He was utterly without a conscience.

Hatred flared hot and coarse, burning through her blood. "You're going to pay, you bastard, for all the lives you've stolen. Sooner or later, they'll catch you, and you're going to fry."

"Right," he muttered.

She tried again to jerk her face out of his hold, but he only tightened his grip.

"Hold still, or you're going to have bruises."

His words caught her so off guard, she laughed, a single, humorless release of sound. "*Bruises?* Are you kidding? I'm going to be dead."

"I'm not going to kill you." The words were terse. Frustrated. "Now will you look into my goddamn eyes?"

She stared at him. Was it possible she was dreaming this? Maybe having a fever-induced nightmare? Because the way this was going down made less than no sense. The killer, appearing out of nowhere, only wanted her to look into his eyes. *Right.*

But incomprehensible or not, she knew she wasn't dreaming. The bite of the man's fingers on her jaw was too clear. His scent too real. Too . . . luscious.

She groaned. "I've got to be dreaming."

"You are dreaming. Now look into my eyes!"

"I am!" she snapped back. "Or I'm trying to. It might be easier to do if you took off those ridiculous sunglasses. In case you hadn't noticed, it's nighttime."

He growled low, the sound almost that of a jungle animal. Oh yeah, she was moving from nightmare to delirium. Any minute now Phil the Easter Bunny was going to hop into the room. And she probably wouldn't even notice, so mesmerized was she by the killer's amazing mouth.

Definitely delirious.

Something brushed her mind, a softness, almost a warmth that eased the lingering pain of the vision.

"You won't remember my face," the man murmured softly in that deep, sexy voice.

"Of course not." Like she could ever forget *that* face.

He wasn't beautiful. Such a word implied a degree of softness, and there wasn't one soft thing about the man's features. Strong jaw, hard cheekbones, and a mouth that could have been sculpted by the finest artist. Not a single softness about him, yet his looks were utterly arresting.

"I'm dreaming, remember?"

The growl that rumbled in the man's throat sounded more pained than threatening, his mouth thinning with displeasure. The softness brushed her mind stronger than before, sending a shiver of pleasure rippling through her blood.

His scent teased her nostrils, increasing the pleasure playing with her senses. He smelled wonderful. Like the air after a thunderstorm, clean and fresh, and a little wild. The feel of his body pressing against hers sent heat coursing through her veins to pool damply between her legs.

Heaven help her, she was turning into one mentally disturbed puppy because this guy was actually turning her on.

The man sucked in a breath as if he could feel her body's traitorous response to him. The hand at her jaw gentled, his thumb brushing over her skin, melting her from the inside out.

Against her abdomen, the hard, thick length of him swelled. Her body quickened, her breasts turning tight and heavy.

This was sick. *Sick.* He was a killer!

"*Let go of me.*"

"Can't do that, brown eyes. Besides, it's a dream, remember?"

His voice slid through her like warm syrup.

She was losing it, absolutely losing it if she was getting turned on by the man who was preparing to kill her. *After* he raped her. Though, heaven help her, she wasn't sure it would *be* rape. The thought of him taking her, sliding that thick shaft deep inside her, made her body clench and weep.

"What are you doing to me?"

"*Rain and thunder,*" he growled. He released her face and reached for her hands, forcing them against her cheeks as his warm fingers brushed her skin. "We're going to try this again."

"Try what? What exactly are we trying to do?" If she knew, maybe she could help him. Or pretend to. If she got him to let his guard down, maybe she could find a way to escape.

He didn't answer her. Instead, he licked his lips, sending a shiver of longing shimmering through her. A need to feel her mouth against those lips. *Sick.*

He clenched his jaw and pressed his fingers firmly against her cheeks.

Like before, warmth brushed her mind, but this time it went deeper, flowing down into her body on a rush of pleasure so sharp she gasped. Desire swamped her, and she thrust her hips against his, rubbing herself on the hard length of his erection. Even as her body burned, her mind recoiled, horrified at her body's betrayal. She couldn't have played the part of the horny slut any better if she'd tried.

The thought brought her up short. What if she could use this ungodly attraction to her advantage? In war, anything was fair. And sexual desire had been wielded as a powerful weapon since the dawn of time.

All she needed was a moment to turn the tables on him, to outsmart him and seize control. A moment to take the bastard down.

Her mind spun. Rape wasn't his usual M.O. None of the other victims had been sexually assaulted. If she could get him to have sex with her, he might start thinking of her as something other than his next victim.

It would be the last mistake he ever made.

Chapter
Five

Tighe stifled a groan as the half-naked woman rubbed her lace-clad pelvis against the erection filling his pants. He'd never had this much trouble exerting a little mind control over a human.

What in the hell was happening? He could barely think through the flood of sensations assaulting his body. The sweet, exotic scent of her intoxicated him. The taste of her arousal danced on his tongue, making his body throb and ache. His hands shook with the need to free his erection, push aside the scrap of lace that covered her honey, and push himself deep inside her.

Get control! Yes, she was beautiful, and hotter than sin, but his life was at stake here. Sex was *not* on the agenda.

But, goddess, she was lovely. Her flawless skin was the light natural tan of the Mediterranean, her limbs long and slender, her body toned and strong, yet not without lush, perfect curves. Her hair, fire-lit mahogany, had come loose and fallen around her shoulders in soft waves. Her eyes were the same dark color, though while her hair sparkled with red-and-gold highlights, her eyes glittered with hatred.

The only thing, the *only thing* he should be thinking about was clouding her mind so he could climb inside and retrieve his visions. Maybe then, he'd finally be able to catch that good-for-nothing clone.

But getting control of her was proving to be damned difficult. Twice he'd tried to cloud her mind. Twice all he'd seemed to do was arouse her. Which was a disaster on so many levels.

Because he had to remain in control himself, and that was hard to do when one of the most beautiful women he'd ever touched was thrusting her hips against him, gasping with desire.

His gaze caressed her face, then moved to her eyes, staring into their dark depths as he once more pressed into her mind to control and cloud. But all she did was gasp, her passion thickening as she resisted his control as no human ever had before.

Hawke's words came back to him. *She's only 99.9 percent human now.*

And, apparently, immune to his control.

Maybe if he could calm her, he'd be able to breach her mind's unnatural defenses. He softened his hold on her jaw, his gaze drawn to the rich full-ness of her mouth. Heat swirled low in his body, his own mouth aching for a taste of her. "Don't be afraid of me. I'm not going to hurt you."

"It's not fear I'm feeling right now." Her voice was low and husky as she pressed that tiny scrap of lace against his raging erection. "You're a hand-some man. Sexy as hell."

Sweet nature, did she *realize* she was asking him to take her? He focused on the taste of her emotions. Desire was there, but barely discernible beneath the fear and the fury and the raw, hard-core determination.

He snorted with understanding. The lady Fed was playing him. Trying to use the attraction between them to distract him so she might escape.

Smart.

And damned annoying. Because he'd been attempting to play *her*. Clearly trying to calm her wasn't going to do an ounce of good because, at the moment, she had better control over her emotions than he did his.

So if calming her wasn't the way to get past her mental barriers, he needed to get her to lower her guard another way. Perhaps by earning her trust. And he knew just the way to go about it. With what was, amazingly, almost the truth.

"You don't have to be afraid of me, Delaney."

She tensed, her eyes flaring for only an instant. "You know my name."

"I had to find you. I'm not who you think I am." Hard eyes probed his face, the touch of her gaze

deceptively soft. "And who do I think you are?"
Her sultry voice felt like a stroke to his throbbing
cock.

Heaven help him.

"You think I'm the man who attacked you, the
man who's killed more than a dozen people in the
past few days. But I'm not him."

Sharp doubt ripped through her eyes, then disappeared behind a wary screen. "Who are you,
then?"

"His twin." He stroked her soft cheek with his
thumb, enchanted by the silky smoothness of her
skin. Would her skin taste as sweetly exotic as she
smelled? "That's why you're still alive, brown eyes.
My evil twin would never have let you live. I'm
not sure how you managed to escape him the first
time."

Her gaze searched his face as if looking for the
truth. "Someone shot him," she said slowly. "*I* shot
him." Her eyes narrowed. "Is he dead?"

"No. He's still very much alive. Which is why I'm
here." He opened his mouth to tell her he'd come to
protect her, then remembered who she was. *What*
she was. Delaney Randall was no damsel in distress.
She was a warrior. He needed to appeal to that in
her. "I want to stop him before he kills again, and I
know you do, too. If we work together, we can get
him, Delaney." He stroked her cheek, watching her
formidable brain debate his words.

"Work with me, brown eyes." He tasted her
doubt, her uncertainty, and pressed his advantage.
"Help me catch him before he kills again."

He tasted it, the small, secret lift of excitement amid her raging doubt. The opening of her mind, just a sliver.

It was enough.

Tighe pushed hard into her mind, pressing against the softened resistance. He had no choice but to force his way in. If he couldn't get control of her, he had to kill her.

No choice.

The woman's eyes widened, then fell heavily as she moaned, her body arching to rub against his arousal. Her passion surged, rising like a thick, exotic scent on her skin, ensnaring him, threatening to wrench him free of his own thinning control.

She groaned. "What are you trying to do to me?"

"*Not this.*"

Goddess help him. He *had* to get past the barrier in her mind. As he pushed harder, she flung her head back, gasping for air, looking for all the world like a woman about to . . .

She screamed as she came, her body rocking, shaking, shuddering with the force of her release.

Holy heavens and Earth. He was a heartbeat away from following her into that sweet oblivion, his own body hard as stone, dying for a taste of her, dying to be inside her. Never had he been in so much pain for a woman.

Her eyelids lifted slowly, heavy with passion above stunned eyes. "I want you inside me. *Now.*"

Heaven help him, that's all he wanted. *All* he wanted. And he couldn't take her. She was human, dammit. *Human*. And even if she weren't, his desire for her was nearly out of control. If he entered her, he feared he'd lose himself entirely. And if he went feral, he'd kill her.

That was something he was loath to do.

But he had to taste her.

His fingers released her wrists to slide into the softness of her hair as his mouth covered hers. She cried out, the sound halfway between a moan and a plea, as if she were drowning, and he was the only one who could save her. Or maybe he was just transferring his own feelings to her because that was exactly the way he felt. He'd die if he didn't taste her.

His tongue swept inside her welcoming mouth, reveling in the sweet, exotic lushness. She tasted just as he'd imagined she would, only a hundred times better. Like the nectar of a rare jungle orchid.

Like heaven.

His tongue stroked hers, then her teeth and the insides of her cheeks, exploring the damp depths of her, thrilled when she did the same, as if she couldn't get enough of him.

Heaven knew, he couldn't get enough of her.

Kissing wasn't enough. He unbuttoned her shirt with quick fingers and brushed aside the opening to cover her lace-covered breast with his palm, squeezing gently until she arched into his touch and moaned into his mouth. His fingers went to the tight little peak, pinching and rolling it between his finger and thumb until she was rocking against him in a half-crazed frenzy.

He pulled away from her mouth and tasted the sweet skin of her cheek and the salty tang of her brow.

His breaths were coming in short, shallow gasps, his own brow damp from the effort to retain some semblance of control. But why maintain control? Why not just take her? With his release, this crazed need would abate. He'd be able to get them both under control.

The logic almost made sense.

"Fuck me," the woman groaned, her freed hand sliding between them to clamp around his painfully hard erection. "I need you inside me."

Goddess. His hand slid to the button of his jeans, but as his fingers reached for the zipper tab, the bitter taste of hatred slid across his tongue. His hand stilled as he explored the taste and knew it was hers. A hatred of him, certainly, but also of herself. Self-hatred had a taste all its own.

She might have decided to play on their mutual attraction, but she was way past pretending, lost to passion's madness. And despite his assurance to the contrary, she still thought him a killer. She hated herself for wanting him.

Goddess knew, he didn't want this attraction any more than she did. He did not fuck humans.

It was all he could do to pull away from her, but he managed it. Barely. He gripped her shoulders and pushed her back to the wall. Her damp, swollen lips and slumberous eyes were nearly his undoing, until he saw the confusion in those eyes and the pain of betrayal, even if the betrayal was her own.

Once more he looked into those eyes and attempted to cloud her mind.

She shuddered. "Don't." The word was low, pained.

He was getting nowhere with her. Whatever had happened to thrust her in the way of his visions was making her immune to his control. And if he couldn't control her, he had to eliminate her as a problem. Kougar was right.

The Ferals never destroyed life without justification, but humans who threatened the Therian race or any of its members, in any capacity, were eliminated without hesitation. Always.

The woman watched him with fathomless eyes, her lips parted as she struggled to catch her breath. "What now?"

A hard knot formed in his gut. He'd promised he wouldn't hurt her. His hand reached for her, his thumb stroking her soft cheek.

From that first vision when he'd watched her face her death with a warrior's toughness and fury in her eyes, he'd known she was different. When she'd faced him tonight, thinking her attacker had found her again, he'd tasted her fear on his tongue, yet she'd never whimpered. Never begged. She'd fought him. Even while her pulse raced, her mind had remained clear, her words calm, laced with a bitter wryness that had tugged at him. She'd won his admiration, which was something no human had done in a very long time.

He met her gaze as his palm slid down the long column of her throat, and he saw the question in her eyes. She wasn't ready to die. He could feel her will to live rushing over him with a force like liquid steel. Yet she waited, watching him, with grace and courage.

As his palm stroked her throat, he knew he couldn't do it. Human and fragile as she might be, there was something peculiarly strong about her. Inexplicably rare.

Deep inside him, he felt something stir, as if the tiger within raised its head, scenting something on the wind.

He couldn't take her life.

But neither could he let her go. Sliding his finger to the hollow at the base of her ear, he pressed.

The woman collapsed, unconscious, and he swept her into his arms. Somehow, he was going to have to find another way to steal back his visions and get control over her.

Hawke and Kougar were going to think he was starting to lose his ability to reason.

And he wasn't entirely sure they'd be wrong. He didn't have to have premonitions to know Delaney Randall was going to be trouble.

Chapter
Six

Tighe pushed through the safe-house door Hawke held open for him, the unconscious woman in his arms.

Hawke lifted a single winged brow. "Any luck?"

"None." Frustration plucked at his fraying nerves. Nothing about this mission had gone right, with the possible exception of the ease with which he'd gotten into Delaney's apartment. From the moment he'd touched her, every plan had taken a nosedive.

Each time he'd tried to cloud her mind, she got more excited, as if someone had gotten inside her and changed all her wiring. And maybe someone had, if inadvertently. His clone. Goddess knew what had happened when that bastard attacked her.

It almost certainly explained Tighe's inability to catch her mind. It didn't explain how she'd gotten under his skin. The passion he drew in her was heady, certainly, but the fire that had burned in him when he'd pressed his body against hers, that burned in him still, was way more than a simple reaction to her own fire. There was something about the woman that sent his senses into a barrel roll.

"I couldn't cloud her mind," he informed his companions. "She reacts to my attempts, just not in any way that's the least bit useful."

"How?" Hawke's keen eyes gleamed with curiosity.

Tighe growled by way of answer. He glanced at the sofa, considered laying the woman down, then discarded the idea. Even though he knew she was fully out, some part of his brain, some instinct, made him certain she'd escape him the moment he released her. And he wasn't letting her go.

"The information might be useful, buddy," Hawke pressed.

Tighe scowled, then relented. "When I push into her mind, her body reacts."

"Reacts how?"

Damned nosy Feral. "Sexually, Hawke. She reacts sexually. I pushed hard enough that she came."

Hawke whistled, that eyebrow of his lifting again. "Interesting."

Tighe snorted. "Yeah. And bloody useless. I'm still no closer to clouding her mind."

"Did you try to seize control during her orgasm?"

Tighe stilled. "No. *Damn*." At the moment of

sexual release, the body and mind were most open. Open to bonding with a partner. And open to being captured by a mind capable of control. "It took me by surprise." Hell, he'd been fighting his own release so hard he hadn't given a single thought to taking advantage of hers. Not in *that* way. "I'll try it again."

If Jag had been there, he'd have demanded to watch, the asshole. Hawke just nodded.

"You should have killed her." Kougar stood in the doorway of one of the bedrooms, watching them, his arms crossed over his chest, his pale eyes emotionless.

Tighe's grip on the woman tightened. No one ever really knew what went on in that Feral's head. For as long as Tighe had lived at Feral House, rumors and speculation had swirled around Kougar. Of all of them, his past was the most deeply cloaked in mystery. They knew he was the oldest among them, but if anyone knew *how* old, he hadn't shared it.

Centuries ago, rumors had swirled that Kougar was half-Mage, that he'd been responsible for the deaths of *the seventeen*—seventeen Ferals killed in a mysterious cave, seventeen whose animals had never again risen to mark another. But Lyon trusted him. And that was enough for Tighe. In the six centuries Tighe himself had been a Feral, Kougar had never proven himself anything but loyal.

But he rarely spoke. Instead, he watched silently, waiting, until the time came to fight. Then he fought with a skill and ferocity worthy of any berserker.

He was a good man to have on your team as long as you weren't looking for anything approaching warmth or friendliness. Kougar didn't possess an ounce of either.

Tighe might trust him at his back, but he was a long way from trusting him not to eliminate the human woman the moment he got a chance. Particularly since they all thought Tighe was slowly losing his mind.

A warning growl rumbled deep in his throat as he met Kougar's pale gaze.

"Don't even think about it."

"Killing her might be a mistake," Hawke said.

"Why?" Not that Tighe didn't agree, but he was half-afraid his own reasons had more to do with fearless dark warrior's eyes than anything remotely logical.

Hawke shrugged. "There's no guarantee you'll get the full visions back if she's gone. Right now you're still getting snippets, right?"

"Sometimes. Hell, I don't know if I am or not. It's not consistent. At first I was seeing her as she got the visions, along with glimpses of the killing. Then just the glimpses. But I haven't seen anything in hours."

"What if she dies, and the visions die with her? We'll have lost a powerful weapon."

Tighe silently thanked his friend, his grip on his captive easing. Hawke was right. Maybe somewhere in the mess that was currently acting as his brain, he'd had the same thought.

"The next time she has a vision, buddy, try to

get into her head. Even if you can't steal it back, maybe you can share it. Enough, at least, to figure out where the attack is taking place."

He met Hawke's gaze. "I'll work on her. Both on clouding her mind and on accessing her next vision. But we don't need an audience. You're leaving." His gaze shifted to Kougar. "Both of you."

Kougar's expression didn't change, it never did, yet he sensed the warrior's disapproval.

"I don't think that's a good idea, Tighe." Hawke's brows drew down. "If you lose control, you could kill her."

Tighe's gaze swung to Kougar's. "Then problem solved." He looked back at Hawke. "It's a risk we're going to take, Wings. This woman may be human, but she's a fighter through and through. And FBI. She's already seen my face. She doesn't need to see yours, too. Not until I'm sure I can clean her memory. Besides, I've got to get her sexually aroused again, and I'm not having an audience for that."

An odd protectiveness had him tightening his grip on the woman in his arms. The thought of anyone else listening to her cries of passion, to her scream of release, filled him with a strange and jealous anger.

Calm, Tighe. Calm.

He took a deep breath and met Hawke's gaze. "Unless you want to see my claws, this discussion is over."

"Understood. We'll grab our things and take off, but we won't be far, buddy. We'll keep an eye on the house."

Five minutes later, as the two Ferals closed the door behind them, Tighe stood in the middle of the living room, looking down at Delaney Randall. His mind told him to lay her down, but his arms refused to let her go. Why? What was this strange need in him to hold her? A need that went beyond merely keeping her from escaping. It was a need that went against every ounce of logic in his head.

Was it merely the unruly attraction he had for her getting out of hand? Or was it the madness that was slowly disintegrating his ability to act logically? To act sanely.

A madness that could ultimately destroy them both.

Delaney eased out of sleep, a purr in her throat at the feel of warmth at her back. Warmth. *Man.*
The killer.

A cold wash of adrenaline cramped her stomach, sending her pulse careening into her ears as her mind snapped fully awake.

He'd knocked her unconscious. Which beat the hell out of killing her, for sure, but the arms of a killer was *not* where she wanted to be.

Slowly, she opened her eyes a slit in case the man at her back wasn't the only one in the room. But all that met her gaze were the shadowed furniture and walls of a dark, unfamiliar bedroom. A single, large window covered by sheer curtains glowed from the light of a streetlamp.

Not her apartment. He'd knocked her out *and*

kidnapped her. That could make escape infinitely more difficult since she had no idea where she was or who else might be around to stop her if she managed to escape him.

But that didn't mean she wasn't going to try.

In the distance, a truck downshifted, the sound merging with the low rumble of predawn traffic. City traffic. She doubted he'd taken her far.

And why had he kidnapped her at all? Why was she still alive?

Her senses took quick inventory as she shifted slightly. He was holding her, spoon style, his thickly muscled arm heavy across her waist. But she couldn't feel any bindings to indicate he'd tied her either to the bed or to himself.

She was still wearing the blouse she'd worn to work, the fabric soft but with little give. Her bra was tight against her rib cage. On her legs, if she wasn't mistaken, were the sweatpants she'd been planning to put on, the ones that had been lying across the foot of her bed.

The thought of his dressing her, of him sliding the pants up her bare legs and her hips, sent a cold chill rippling over her skin. Had he touched her? *Had he raped her?*

Her pulse pounded in her ears, but she forced herself to breathe. To think. She didn't feel sore down there. And she almost certainly would if he'd taken her when she was unconscious.

Besides, why would he bother raping her when she'd *begged* him to take her? When she'd been so hot for him, she'd come.

Her cheeks heated at the memory even as a familiar ache started up again between her legs. The man's scent brushed her senses, the scent of sleep-warmed male combined with the hint of wildness that had stirred her so thoroughly last night. And stirred her still.

God, what was the matter with her? Just lying beside him like this had her libido leaping all over again.

She gave a silent groan, forcing herself to tear her thoughts away from the man at her back and focus outward. If there were others in the place, the sooner she knew it, the better. But she heard nothing except the even breathing of her captor.

Apparently her plan to make him think she wanted him had worked well enough since she was still alive. Too bad it hadn't been an act.

He was a killer.

Or the twin of one. Could he possibly have been telling the truth when he told her he wasn't the man who'd attacked her? It was certainly a possibility. After all, she *was* still alive.

Then again, how did he know she'd been attacked if he wasn't the one who'd attacked her? How did he know who she was? Her involvement had never hit the news.

Whether or not he was the killer, he was clearly involved up to his sunglasses-covered eyeballs. And there was no denying he'd committed criminal acts. He'd broken into the apartment of a federal agent, overpowered her, and kidnapped her. For that alone, he was looking at jail time.

Either way, he had information they needed. Either way, he was going down.

She remembered how fast he'd moved last night and the lightning speed with which she'd been attacked in the laundry room. If she wanted to get him, she was going to have to move fast, without mercy. Because once he woke, her chance to take him down would be over.

Her gaze caught the gleam of the bedside lamp. Brass. Perfect. All she had to do was crack him over the skull with it and run for the nearest phone. Piece of cake. Assuming she managed to get out from under his arm without waking him. His warm breath stirred her hair on a soft rumble of a snore. He was definitely asleep. But would he stay that way?

Her pulse rose another notch as she prepared to find out.

Sending a quick prayer heavenward for luck, and keeping her body loose, as if she were still asleep, she rolled onto her stomach on the soft, cool cotton sheets, away from the man.

His arm slid away from her without protest.

Swallowing a surge of triumph, Delaney lay still as death, willing her heart's pounding to settle down as she waited for her captor's breathing to even out again. When she'd waited as long as she could stand, she eased the blanket off her, inch by inch, and swung her legs over the side, her bare toes settling on a soft, worn rug.

In a light, careful move, she rose from the bed and knelt by the bedside table to follow the lamp's cord to the outlet. When she found it, she gave a quick, silent tug and rose to her feet.

Her heart began to pound. This was it. If she hit him too hard, she'd kill him. At one point, before he'd planted the doubt in her mind that he was the man she sought, all she'd wanted was to kill him. Now she wasn't so sure.

Legally, she needed to *not* kill him. But if she didn't hit him hard enough, she was as good as dead. And she had a feeling it would take a direct hit by a cruise missile to incapacitate the guy.

She grabbed the lamp at its neck, her fingers closing around the cool metal as she took a deep breath. *Here goes nothing.* In a single move, she flipped the heavy lamp upside down and swung the base of it at the sleeping man's head as hard as she could.

The lamp collided not with skull, but with moving flesh as her captor's hand shot out, stopping the deadly arc cold. He wrenched the lamp from her hands and flung it across the room to crash against the wall.

Delaney's mouth dropped open. Her heart went to her throat, and she leaped back from the bed, her pulse pounding as she readied for hand-to-hand combat.

He was little more than a blur in the shadows as he grabbed her. The room spun as he flung her facedown on the bed. She dug her face out of the sheets, trying to flip over, but he pinned her with a jeans-clad knee in the small of her back. Her pulse thudded in her throat as she watched him over her shoulder, tensing for his retribution.

"You tried to kill me." His voice was flat as he loomed over her, staring down at her through those dark sunglasses she was beginning to suspect were permanently attached to his face. Who in their right mind slept in sunglasses?

She hated him for making her feel so blasted helpless. Fear slithered down her spine. With his strength, he could kill her with his bare hands without ever breaking a sweat.

Her breath caught, her body tensing, as she waited for him to do just that. But to her surprise, he climbed on top of her, straddling her hips.

She tried to push him off, tried to get to her knees, but she might as well have tried to lift a bus. He was playing with her. Toying with her.

"I'm not going to hurt you," he said softly, brushing the hair back from her ear. In her peripheral vision, she saw his face lower, felt his lips on her ear, his tongue tracing the cartilage, then delving into the cavern, drawing a shiver from her.

Her heart thudded as his hand slid beneath her until his fingers found her nipple through her shirt and squeezed just hard enough to send fire shooting straight to her loins.

His tongue stroked her ear, his lips grazed her cheek. Gently, so gently. Toying with her before he struck.

His fingers moved under her, tugging at her shirt, pulling at her bra until his fingers were against her bare flesh, his palm warm against her breast. Her breathing turned ragged.

She felt his hand move again, releasing her breast.

As the press of his thighs moved lower, to frame her own, he sat up and slipped his hand inside the waist of her sweatpants, his fingers sliding inside her panties to cup her butt cheek as he had her breast moments before. Then he leaned over her, his fingers kneading the flesh, his breath in her ear becoming as ragged as her own.

"You set me on fire." His voice was low, pained, as his fingers dug into her, letting her feel his need, sending hers into an upward spiral.

He was half over her, half beside her when his palm flattened, his finger sliding into the crease of her buttocks and down, to stroke her swelling lips. His teeth grazed her earlobe, sending a shaft of wet heat straight to her core. His finger slid inside her, meeting that rush of heat.

Delaney gasped, trying to arch into his touch, but with him still half-straddling her, she had nowhere to move, nowhere to go. He stroked her, playing with her until she was soft and hot and wild with need. Then he released her and rose, only to straddle her calves.

She tried to rise, her arms shaking, but he dug his fingers into her waistband and yanked downward, pulling her pants and panties down to her thighs in a single jerk of a move, baring her to the cool air. To his gaze. Stealing her last scrap of protection.

Heat turned to fear on the certainty that he meant to take his revenge upon her body. Panic flared, and she tried to roll away, but his palm fanned across the small of her back, slamming her to the mattress.

Her heart thudded. Her mouth went dry.

His free hand dug into her butt cheek. "I'm not going to hurt you." But the thread of anger in his voice did nothing to reassure her.

Tears burned the backs of her eyes. Fear knotted in her gut. If she was ready for him, it shouldn't hurt, but if he wanted to hurt her, there were other ways. She knew too well the cruelty men could visit on women before they killed them. *While* they killed them. She had the crime photos hanging all over the walls of her living room to prove it.

She already knew this guy had a sick mind. God knew what he might . . .

"Don't be afraid of me!"

She froze. "I'm not." Her words sounded calm, soothing, despite the tears closing her throat. Long ago, she'd learned to keep her emotions out of her voice and expression, and she desperately called on that trick now.

His hand squeezed her rear to the point of pain as the tension in the air thickened. Slowly, his hand relaxed, and she began to breathe again.

"I'm not going to hurt you."

But she didn't believe him for a minute. As she struggled against his impossible hold, his hand released her aching flesh to slide between her legs. She tried to clamp her thighs together, desperate to escape his touch, fear spiraling out of her control.

He was going to hurt her. He *wanted* to hurt her, to punish her for attacking him.

"Dammit!" In a sudden move, he released her and flung himself off the bed.

Delaney shot to her knees, yanking her pants up and straightening her shirt and bra, then turned to find him pacing the room like a caged animal, his tight, coiled tension filling the room.

Definitely bipolar. With violent tendencies.

Her heart raced in her chest as she edged toward the side of the bed closest to the door. But as she sat and swung her legs over the side, he whirled on her, his finger pointing directly at her face.

"Stay!"

Delaney froze, her mind scrabbling, fighting down the instinct to flee. He was too fast. She'd never get away.

Deep breaths. He hadn't attacked her. Other than squeezing her butt too hard, he hadn't hurt her at all.

She watched him pace, his hands clenching and unclenching at his sides like a man struggling to contain his temper. *He was trying to get control.* The realization slammed into her. The last thing she needed to do was make things worse by running again.

She forced herself to wait as she watched him warily. The streetlight filtering in through the sheer curtains played over his broad, bare chest, tripping in and out of the shadows created by the muscular definition. Scars, like claw marks, tore across his right nipple while a gold armband snaked around one thick upper arm. Even in the dim light, the man was a walking wet dream.

If she weren't so wary of him, she might have enjoyed watching him. With his long legs, trim waist, and sculpted upper body, he was truly a feast for the eyes.

Minutes passed as he paced, the tension slowly leaching from the air.

"Do you follow football?" he asked, at last.

Delaney blinked. "No."

"What's your favorite television show?"

Her brows puckered with disbelief. "Why?"

An animalistic growl rumbled deep in his throat. "Your fear sets me off, and I want your mind off it."

Delaney scowled. "I'm not afraid." She didn't show it. She *knew* she didn't show it.

Like a cat about to spring, he swung to face her, his body rigid. "Don't lie to me! I can taste it. No one else would know, but *I* know. You can't hide it from me."

He couldn't possibly *taste* her fear. That was ridiculous. But it was hardly a leap for him to guess that she was afraid. Any sane woman would be under the circumstances.

He returned to his pacing. "What's your favorite television show?"

Were they really going to play this game? "The news."

He scowled at her. "Lame."

His response inexplicably pricked her pride. "I don't have time to waste on mindless shows."

He stopped pacing and turned to her. "Your work is your life to the exclusion of everything else, isn't it? You don't even own a reading chair."

"Excuse me," she huffed. "What I do is important. I perform a valuable service to society by getting the monsters off the streets."

The man snorted. "You'll never get the monsters. You don't even know what they look like, little girl."

Delaney ground her teeth together, clamping her mouth shut before she said something she shouldn't. Something that would make him even madder, turning a bad situation so much worse.

The man stopped his pacing and started toward her. "You're pathetic, you know that? You got your life back, but you don't even know how to live it, do you?" There was an ugly taunting quality to his voice that infuriated her. "You're so hung up on your mother's death you aren't even living. Do you think this is what she'd want? You spending your entire life searching for her killer?"

She stared at him, shock vibrating through her body. It wasn't true. It wasn't true. Oh God, of course it was true. "How . . . ?"

"I heard you talking to the cat. It wasn't much of a leap. You're living an excuse for a life. You don't even own a sofa or a picture that isn't a crime-scene photo! Your life's a joke."

She felt as if her chest were caving in and at the same time exploding from the force of her fury. Damn him. *Damn him*.

She lunged to her feet and rounded on him. "You son of a bitch. How dare you judge me. How dare you?" She struck at his knee, a move that should have knocked even a man his size off his feet.

Yet faster than she could blink, she found herself flat on her back on the bed. Again. *Blast it*. She fought him, struggling with every ounce of strength she possessed. This was too much. Too much.

She reached for his sunglasses, intending to dig her fingers into his eyes and blind him, but he reared back out of her reach before she touched them. He grabbed her wrists and pulled them over her head, pinning them. Then he landed on the bed beside her, rolled onto his side, and pinned her legs to the mattress with one hard thigh.

"Let me go!"

"So you can claw my eyes out? I don't think so."

He grabbed her jaw with his free hand and kissed her.

She bit him. The taste of his blood ripped her back to her senses. *Stupid,* Delaney. Stupid, stupid move to risk setting him off again.

But to her amazement, he laughed, the sound rich and warm. Disturbingly nice. Then he bent his head and placed a kiss on her temple as gentle as a raindrop and lifted his head to look down at her, licking the blood from his lip.

She stared at him. "I don't understand you."

A half smile lifted his lips. "I'm not surprised. Fortunately, I *do* understand you."

She grunted with disdain. "Hardly."

"I know just how to make you mad, don't I? And anger is so much more pleasant than fear, isn't it, brown eyes?"

He leaned down to kiss her cheek as she stared at the darkened ceiling, speechless.

"You *meant* to make me mad?"

"It worked." She heard the shrug in his voice, then shivered as his tongue stroked her ear.

But her anger only spiked all over again. At him for saying the things that had cut her to the quick. And at herself for letting them bother her so much she'd lost control and tried to attack him again.

"I hate you."

"I'm aware of that." With the hand not holding her wrists, he pushed the lace cup of her bra down over her nipple, freeing her breast to his warm touch, then took the bare flesh into his mouth.

She gasped at the feel as desire sparked and flared, feeding her anger. She *hated* this control he had over her body. With his superior strength, all he had to do was lift an arm, and she was flat on her back. All he had to do was touch her, and she melted like butter in the sun. He made her *sick*. He made her want to . . .

She arched off the bed in pure pleasure as his tongue twirled slowly around her nipple.

"Oh, God, *don't stop*."

With a last, soft suckle, he released her breast and blew, chilling the wet peak before he turned to its mate, freed it, and pulled the aching, needy flesh into his mouth. She felt his fingers slide once more down the plane of her stomach and into her pants. Though her mind rebelled, her body wanted this. Desperately.

The weight of his thigh lifted, his leg curling around hers and giving a gentle tug, spreading her thighs for his seeking finger. She jerked as the pad of his finger stroked her clit, then gasped as it slid farther, deep into her heat. With a groan of pure need, she bucked, swallowing him deeper into the liquid fire he'd set ablaze inside her.

How could he do this to her? What was it about him that the simple feel of his mouth on her breasts nearly brought her to climax? Never had she gone so over the top with a man. Any man. She'd only had sex three times in her life, with two different partners, because it was so damned boring.

Even sex with this guy's *finger* was enough to turn her into a panting, raving, lunatic. If he ever pushed his cock inside her . . .

Just the thought of it nearly made her come.

"Look at me, brown eyes."

She opened her eyes, not remembering having closed them, and looked at the dark line of his sunglasses.

A rush of warmth flooded her mind, a hot wind on a roaring flame, turning her body into a superheated bonfire. Her hips rocked against his hand, desperate for more. She needed . . . she needed . . .

The orgasm broke over her in an explosion of light and pleasure so sharp it was like nothing she'd ever felt, hurtling her into a rainbow of colors and ecstasy. As she rode the explosion, her body bucked wildly, forcing that finger deeper, *deeper*.

Her eyes started to roll back in her head.

"Look at me, Delaney. Look at me!"

She did, somehow knowing she met his gaze through those sunglasses. Something happened. A hot pressure gripped her head, a sharp pain that was gone almost before it registered, disappearing in the clenching spasms of release.

Slowly, the pleasure eased, and her body floated downward. Her hips ceased their rocking, and she lay beside the man, trying to catch her breath even as his finger continued to play with her wetness.

As the roaring pleasure eased, she became aware of a strange sensation inside her head, like the soft brush of angel's wings against the inner walls of her skull whispering impressions into her mind. *He wasn't the killer. He didn't kill needlessly. He was honorable. Fine. And very, very dangerous.*

Honorable, the wings whispered. *Trust him.*

She looked up at him, exhausted and confused. "I don't even know your name."

"I'm Tighe."

"What have you done to me?"

"Nothing for you to be worried about. Now go to sleep, Delaney."

And just like that, she did.

Chapter Seven

"It's about damned time," Tighe muttered as he slowly withdrew his finger from the woman's hot depths. Sweet nature, what she did to him. He was shaking with the need to finish what he'd started with her, to push inside her with the part of his anatomy made for the purpose. A part of him that was more than up for the task.

But he was not a man who took advantage of women. At least not more than he absolutely had to.

Not even human women. Especially not human women.

He sucked the honey from his finger, groaning at the perfection of her taste. What was it about her that turned him inside out? Was it this odd connection they'd formed through his clone? Or was it the excitement of the unknown? An unknown he hadn't experienced in a good long while?

The only women he allowed himself to have sex with were Therians, and he'd known most of them for centuries. Delaney Randall was new to him. Young and exciting. And human, dammit. Completely and totally off-limits. He hadn't gotten involved with a human since Gretchen. And he never would again.

But, goddess, Delaney Randall was a beauty. He gazed down at her face, at her slender nose and full, ripe mouth as his thumb brushed the silken skin covering one high cheekbone. The longing to taste her again almost overpowered him.

What was she doing to him?

He needed to get her out of his life, fast, before he lost what little control he still possessed and pushed inside her, becoming a slave to this need for her until he destroyed them both.

Now that he'd finally, *finally*, captured control of her mind, it should only be a short while before he was through with her. He'd felt the catch, though not in the usual way. He hadn't been certain he really did have her mind until he'd ordered her to go to sleep, and she had. The connection lingered inside his head, like a pleasurable warmth fanning the insides of his skull. Odd. But nothing with this woman had been normal.

All that mattered was she was his, finally. He should be able to root around in her mind and figure out how to free her of those visions. Once he'd disconnected her from the clone, it should be a simple matter to steal her memories of him as well.

Meanwhile, the Delaney Randall who'd turned him inside out was gone. For the moment.

For him.

Ridiculous to feel regret at the thought.

No, this was the way it had to be. He'd keep her calm and semicomatose until one of them got another vision, then he'd take it from there.

But as he stroked her finely shaped brow with his thumb, he couldn't help the feeling of inexplicable loss. He was going to miss her fire and strength, her cunning and intelligence, and even the shadows in her eyes that spoke of loss and called to something deep inside him.

She would still be pretty to look at, but it was the fire that burned within her that made her truly beautiful. A fire gone cold, until he released her mind again. He was sorry for that. But there was neither reason nor time to delay the inevitable. With a sigh, he lifted a lock of her hair, the soft, dark wave sliding between his fingers.

"Wake up, Delaney."

Instantly, her dark lashes swept up, revealing eyes filled with confusion.

"You don't remember anything that happened after the cat ran into your apartment last night," he said softly.

Her head turned to him, her eyes narrowing. "O-kay."

His hand froze on her hair as he stared at her, blinking. Shit. *Shit.* He hadn't gotten control of her mind at all. Yet he *had* connected with it. Staring into her eyes he could almost see the gossamer thread, running between them, fanning the warmth in his head.

Outrage barreled through him. Every time he tried to control her, something else went wrong. He flung himself off the bed and strode to the wall, barely keeping himself from slamming his fist through the plasterboard. He not only had to seize control of her mind, but now he had to break this unholy connection.

He whirled to find her sitting up.

How could he not have her mind? She'd gone to sleep and wakened on cue. Unless . . .

"Lie down," he barked. And she did. Instantly. "Sit up." She jerked upright as if pulled by an unseen cord.

"Stop it!" she cried. "How are you doing this?"

He seemed to have gotten control of her body and not her mind. How in the hell had *that* happened? And what good did it do? He needed to keep her from remembering him!

"Lie down."

She fell back, mouth wide with disbelief, eyes filled with terror as she struggled to move, but he'd told her to lie down, and that was all she could do.

"*What have you done to me?*"

He smiled bitterly. "It seems I've got you under my control, Agent Randall. Just not the way I wanted, dammit."

He saw the realization in her eyes, the understanding of just how vulnerable she really was. Raw, icy fear rolled across his tongue, hurling him back to another time. In his mind, he saw Gretchen, his beloved Gretchen, her eyes wide with terror.

She should have known. She should have *known*.

At the hated taste on his tongue, fury ripped through him, tearing him loose from his control. He felt the burn of his claws unsheathing, the ache of his fangs getting ready to drop.

Not now. *Not now.*

He longed to hurt her, to punish her for her fear. For her betrayal. She'd destroyed him. Taken everything from him, everything that had ever mattered.

For a second, his mind cleared. He was staring at Delaney, not Gretchen. Delaney.

Desperately, he tried to wrench back control. But it was too late. Too late.

"Close your eyes and stay there!" He whirled away from her as the chaos swept him into that place of fury and violence, a place where he was neither man nor beast, yet utterly inhuman. As he lifted the chest of drawers and slammed it against the wall, shattering the mirror, the chaos swept him away.

The sound of shattering glass tore through Delaney's eardrums as she lay, stuck to the bed, unable to open her eyes. *Unable to move.*

This is not happening. It is not happening!

Pieces of furniture crashed against one another, wood splintering, glass shattering. *And she couldn't move to get out of the way.*

She struggled to sit up, grinding her elbows into the mattress as she pushed with all her strength, but it was as if an invisible hand held her down.

Her mouth went dry. Good God, she had to get out of there.

What has he done to me?

He had to be using some kind of mind-control drug on her. Twice now, he'd knocked her out. And just before he'd put her to sleep the second time, she'd had this strange urge to trust him. *Mind control.* With a sudden certainty, she knew he was no run-of-the-mill psychopath. There was more going on here. Much more.

But why experiment on a federal agent? Unless . . .

The answer, so obvious, chilled her to the marrow of her bones. She had access to information, to places, to *people,* most never would. He could turn her into the ultimate terrorists' weapon. Until her fellow agents killed her. Then he'd simply kidnap another.

The ramifications reverberated through her head. The lives that would be lost. The lives he'd force her to take.

I have to get out of here.

If she could escape before the drug fully wore off, while it was still in her blood, the lab might be able to identify it. They might be able to create an antidote. Or even find a way to duplicate it.

Except she couldn't escape. She couldn't even move!

He'd lost it. Completely. Even before he'd turned into Olaf the Berserker, she'd felt it, as if the storm swirling inside him were visible.

Had he, too, been experimenting with the drug? Was that to be her destiny?

A new sound burst into the room. "Tighe!" a man shouted as, closer by, strong arms lifted her.

"Let's get you out of here," a deeply masculine voice said.

"I'm all for that."

The man carried her from the destruction zone to lay her on what felt like a sofa in another room. "Are you injured?"

"No. He did something to me before he turned crazy. I can't move. I can't even open my eyes."

"Interesting. Stay here."

"That's what they all say," Delaney muttered, then lay there listening to the sound of fighting like nothing she'd ever heard. Thudding, snarling, slashing. Like they'd turned into animals or something. She wasn't sure if she was relieved or dismayed to learn there were more of them.

"Get off me." Tighe's deep growl carried to where she lay. "The woman?"

"Is on the sofa."

Delaney blinked. She froze as her eyes went wide. She could open her eyes again. *Halleluiah.* As her gaze took in the small, unoccupied living room, she tried to sit up. Grunting and straining against the invisible hand, she managed to prop her elbows under her. Elation swam through her as she panted with exertion.

The drug was wearing off.

"Is she sleeping? Or dead?" Tighe's voice carried from the bedroom.

"Unharmed as far as I can tell, but she can't move. What did you do to her?"

"I got control of her, just not her mind."

"Eliminate her," a third, hard voice chimed in.

Not the voice of the man who'd carried her to safety. Not the voice of anyone she wanted to come face-to-face with without her Glock.

Again, she struggled to sit up, and like magic, was free. The drug had worn off!

"No one's harming her." Tighe's voice. *Yeah, Tighe.* "Leave. I'll see to her."

"No," Delaney muttered under her breath as she swung off the sofa and crept to the door. "I'll leave. *I'll* see to her."

"We're staying," said the man who'd carried her out of the room.

"No you're not." Tighe's voice was too close. No longer in the bedroom. "*Hell.*"

He'd spotted her.

Pulse racing, blood pounding in her ears, Delaney lunged for the door. Her hand closed around the knob, twisted and jerked hard, but the door opened only a couple of inches before slamming shut again. Tighe's overwhelming presence loomed over her from behind.

She tried to whirl around, but he pressed her, face-first, against the door, his breath harsh in her ear.

"*Don't fear me.*"

"Let me go, Tighe. *Please.*"

"Can't do that." He eased back a fraction, not so much that she could turn around, but enough that he was no longer laying his full weight against her. "I'm not going to hurt you."

"Could have fooled me."

He grabbed her shoulders and turned her around, his expression grim as he appeared to stare down at her through the shades. "Where? Where did I hurt you?"

She gasped as she got a good look at him despite the shadows. He was a mess. Good grief. His face and body were streaked with blood, his shirt nearly shredded. Yet she couldn't make out any injuries. No open, bleeding flesh. Not even any scratches to account for the blood.

Did that mean it wasn't his? Yet how could he not be harmed with his clothing in tatters? The soft fluttering in her head intensified, as if the angel wings were agitated by the sight of him. The sensation echoed in her chest. As if she were worried about him. As if whatever he'd done to her made her think she cared.

His hands tightened on her shoulders. "Where are you hurt, Delaney?"

"I'm not, but I don't think I can say the same for you."

He glanced down at himself as if realizing for the first time what he looked like. "I'm fine. I didn't hurt you?"

"No. Your friend got me out of there before you chucked any furniture my way." She stared at him. "I *guess* he's your friend? Good grief, one of them nearly killed you."

Tighe grunted. "They look as bad as I do. And, yeah, they're my friends. They heard me destroying the place and came to offer a little well-timed intervention." He released her shoulder to stroke her hair. "Thank the goddess, I didn't hurt you."

She almost told him not to touch her hair, not to

stroke her, but couldn't bring herself to utter the words. His touch felt good. As if *he* cared. At least as if he cared that he hadn't hurt her.

"Was it the drugs that sent you . . . over the edge?" she asked carefully.

He stilled. "The drugs?"

She sighed. "Right. No drugs involved here. You just waved your magic wand and got control of me like that."

Oddly, the tension seemed to drain out of him. "Oh. That drug."

"Tighe, there's some nasty shit going on here," she said quietly, reaching for his face as if she meant to press her palm to his cheek. She snatched her hand back. Yet that fluttering in her head whispered that he needed her touch. *He needed her.*

She crossed her arms over her chest. "Why don't we both get out of here, Tighe? I can get you some help."

"You'd help me, would you, brown eyes?" His thumb rose to stroke her cheek as if he had fluttering angel voices of his own telling him she needed him, too.

She didn't. Of course she didn't. Yet, heaven help her, something soft and weak inside her wanted to lean into that gentle touch. She steeled herself against the urge, but didn't pull away. He was clearly a violent man she didn't want to antagonize. Not when she was unarmed. But the truth was, she didn't want to pull away. Angel voices aside, there was something about this man that drew her, something more than the flaming attraction.

There was a gentleness in his touch and a warmth in his voice that made her want to step inside the circle of his arms and lean against him, drawing strength and maybe just a little bit of comfort.

Was it more evidence of mind control, or was this her doing alone? Maybe she was starting to suffer from Stockholm Syndrome, that tendency of captives to identify with and care for their captors. She wasn't sure which was more disturbing.

Or perhaps it was neither. Perhaps she was genuinely beginning to glimpse facets of a man who was more than he seemed.

His hand lifted, his fingers sliding into her hair, sending a soft shiver through her body. "I'm glad I didn't hurt you."

And, heaven help her, she believed him.

His thumb traced over her bottom lip, sending shards of excitement spiking into her blood. Her breath caught. She could feel his gaze on her mouth.

"I want to kiss you, brown eyes, but I've forced you enough."

His words sent rich, warm desire pouring through her, turning her breasts heavy and her body aching to feel his mouth on hers again even as they lent more credence to her belief that he might be more than he seemed. A man who wasn't evil but had definitely gotten himself tangled up in some nasty stuff.

She knew rationalizing when she heard it, even in her own head. *She wanted him to kiss her.*

"Your friends . . ."

"Are busy. And not going to bother us."

She made a wry twist with her mouth. "And you don't care if they do."

He smiled, flashing a pair of sexy-as-hell dimples. "No."

Ripples of need raced through her body, and she gave herself up to the desire, captured his strong face between her hands and pulled his mouth down to hers.

Some small part of her brain shouted that this was all part of the plan to get him to let his guard down, but the shout was quickly drowned out by the roar of pure, unadulterated passion.

Tighe shuddered and sucked in air through his nose as if trying to inhale her. His arms went around her and he pulled her against his chest as he captured her mouth in return.

The kiss exploded inside her, filling her with equal parts sweetness and crazy desire. She opened her mouth as he did, her tongue sliding sensuously against his. He tasted like he smelled, like rain and thunderstorms and wildness. *Intoxicating.*

Why? Why do I have to be so attracted to him?

His hands slid over her back as he slanted his mouth over hers, deepening the kiss.

Pain exploded in her head.

With a gasp, she pulled back.

"What's the matter?" he asked sharply.

"My head. Headache. I need to lie down." Before she passed out again. This was the exact pain she'd suffered in the parking garage. Not now. *Not now.*

Tighe cupped her face with his hands. The light pressure of his palms seemed to ease the pain.

"That helps," she whispered.

"Lincoln Memorial," Tighe called. "I'll meet you over there."

She tried to open her eyes, to look at him in confusion. Had she blanked out after all? She seemed to have missed the other half of that conversation.

Through the haze of pain, she saw a pair of jeans and a shirt come sailing out the bedroom door.

"Change before you bring the cops down on yourself," a disembodied voice called. "And do something about the blood."

Tighe made a sound in his throat, that oddly animal-sounding growl, and released her. The pain in her head soared. She collapsed back against the door, pressing her hands to her cheeks, but her own hands didn't help.

She wasn't sure how long she'd stood there, fighting back the waves of pain, when she felt Tighe's hand close around her wrist.

"Come on, brown eyes. We're going for a drive."

"I don't think that's a good idea."

But he opened the door and ushered her into the night, and she didn't have the strength to argue. She let him steer her into the passenger seat of a car, in no shape to fight him. She tipped her head back and closed her eyes, her only concern to stay conscious and keep her head on her shoulders until the awful thing passed.

Finally, *finally*, the pain began to recede. The headache disappeared, leaving her feeling shaky and cold. What was happening to her? The head-ache had felt like the kind she got before she saw the murders, but just like in the car, she'd seen nothing this time. Which didn't please her in the least. If she had to suffer the pain, the least she could do was get a clue that might help her catch the killer.

Taking a deep breath, she opened her eyes to find Tighe pulling to an illegal stop near the Lincoln Memorial. He released her hand. She hadn't even remembered he was holding it.

"Get out, brown eyes."

"What are we doing here?"

"My twin's here."

Her jaw dropped as he pushed from the car. She joined him, her mind scrambling and coming up with nothing that made any sense.

"How do you know he's here?"

He grabbed her hand. "Come on."

She ran to keep up with him as he headed toward the steps of the memorial, but they were still ten yards away when Tighe emitted another of those jungle growls, released her hand, and pulled out two wicked-looking switchblades in a single, quick move.

Delaney leaped back, watching with disbelief as he began stabbing the air. He *was* crazy. Completely and certifiably mad.

But as she stared, cuts began to appear on his cheeks and tears in his clothing as if from invisible claws.

Goose bumps rose on her skin as her head shook back and forth. She wasn't seeing this. It wasn't real. It was the drugs. She *had* to be hallucinating.

A dark shape above had her looking up as a huge bird of prey, a hawk, dropped out of the sky. For a terrible moment, she thought Tighe was going to turn those deadly knives on the bird, but he barely glanced at him. Instead, the bird began clawing at the air with talons and beak as if he, too, were battling an invisible enemy.

A moment later, a huge cat, *a cougar*, joined the fight, and she *knew* she had to be caught in one giant hallucinogen-induced dream.

God. Delaney backed away. She had to get out of there. But Tighe's words came back to her. *My twin's here.* If there was a chance she hadn't dreamed that, too, she had to at least look for him.

She ran for the steps to the memorial and started up, as desperate to get away from the impossible battle as she was to find the murderer who'd nearly killed her.

With each step the question pounded in her brain.

What if I'm the only crazy one?

Tighe stabbed at the draden, tearing them off him as he tore out their hearts by the dozen.

Dammit, I've got to get behind cover and shift. Hawke's voice sounded in his head. Through the vicious swarm, Tighe could just make out the hawk, nearly covered in the ferocious little beasts.

My wings are being shredded faster than I can heal.

Since when do they attack animals? Kougar growled mentally. The draden were all over him, too, going for his eyes. Unlike Tighe, the cougar had no hands with which to stab and swat them away. *I'm going to have to shift, too, but it's too well lit here.*

The Lincoln Memorial was a glowing beacon on the D.C. nightscape, and even in the middle of the night, people were known to roam the National Mall.

Do it, Tighe said. *What in the hell's going on, Hawke? Care to take a guess?*

I think your clone's behind this. He was made from a draden. I'm guessing he can communicate with them.

Tighe groaned inwardly. *His own private army.*

Your human's on the run, Kougar said.

Tighe turned. Delaney was running, all right. Straight up the steps of the Lincoln Memorial. She finally had a shot at freedom, and she was throwing it away to try to catch a murderer. Exactly what he was coming to expect from her, but the reality made his blood run cold.

He took off after her, a swarm of draden at his back, fear stabbing through his chest like a twelve-inch blade.

If that draden spawn of a clone of his was still up there, she'd be dead before he ever reached her.

Chapter Eight

"Delaney, wait!" Tighe's voice echoed up from the base of the stairs.

Trust him, the angel wings whispered in her head.

Why she listened to either of them, she didn't know, but she was too rattled to fight the instinct to stop. Three-quarters of the way up the steps, Delaney doubled over to catch her breath as Tighe climbed to join her.

As he drew near, she saw he was a bloody mess again. Ghostly fingers crawled over her scalp as, deep in her head, the clanging bells of disbelief rang and rang and rang.

"Don't ever go after him alone, brown eyes. He's too dangerous, in case you didn't learn that the first time."

"You seemed a little . . . preoccupied." But, jeez, she wasn't even armed. Either the whole situation had her badly shaken, or she really *was* losing her mind.

Tighe took her hand and kept climbing, all the while stabbing the air with the knife in his free hand. That didn't bother her nearly as much as the blood that was beginning to trickle down his cheek and neck from wounds that shouldn't be there.

Don't look. Just don't look.

Sweat was rolling down her temples, her breathing labored by the time she reached the top step of the memorial. As her gaze scanned the area, out of habit her hand went for her gun and closed around nothing. Blast it.

Something caught her eye. A bare foot, facedown, poking out from behind one of the mammoth marble columns that framed the memorial.

"There," she told Tighe.

Together they ran, Delaney taking the path outside the pillars, Tighe running inside. They converged on another murder scene. She closed her eyes against the sight, then opened them again to study the bodies of a young couple, each partially undressed as if caught in the act of sex, now lying side by side, identical ovals of teeth marks on their necks.

Not far from them lay a female police officer. Had she heard the screams and come to investigate, only to meet with the same fate? It seemed probable. A wedding ring gleamed on her finger in the bright light of the memorial. She was married.

Probably with kids, who would never see their mother again. *Dammit.*

"Did you know her?"

She looked up to see Tighe watching her.

"No."

He nodded. "I'm going to try to find him."

As Tighe kept walking, Delaney bent over the cop and checked for a pulse. Nothing, but her skin was still damp with sweat. Her murder, at least, had only just happened. She grabbed the woman's gun and slipped it into her back waistband, careful to cover it with her shirt hem.

How had Tighe known the murderer had been here? Was he, too, getting the visions?

As she crossed to the kids, she saw Tighe again fighting something, *being injured by something*, which wasn't there.

Don't think about it.

She checked the young couple for pulses and again found none. The old fury welled up inside her at the waste of life. God, she wanted whoever had done this dead.

She saw Tighe turn and come back toward her, still stabbing the air, the blood running freely down his face now. He must be catching himself with those knives. That was the only explanation that made a bit of sense.

The gun weighed heavily against her back. If she wanted to shoot him, now was the time, when he was still far enough away that she stood a chance of getting the shot off before he stopped her. But the doubts had lodged too deeply in her head.

That *she* might actually be the one with the mental problem.

As sirens began to sound on the wind, coming nearer, she let him close the distance between them without pulling her weapon.

His expression was tight. "Those may be heading here."

Delaney nodded. "The cop has only been dead a matter of minutes. She probably called in the murders of the kids before he attacked her."

"Come on, we're getting out of here."

"Let me stay. Let me help the cops look for him."

"Not a chance." He took her hand and gave her no choice as he ushered her down the long set of steps and into the car. Then he dove in on the driver's side, slammed the door, and continued to stab wildly at his invisible foe. A foe who couldn't possibly be in the car with them. Not unless he was the size of a fairy.

The man was crazy. Whether or not he was in league with the murderer, he was nuts. And the cops were on their way. She reached cautiously for the door handle and never touched it. One of his knives whipped out to within an inch of her face.

"You open that door, and it'll be the last thing you do." His voice was low and deadly.

"Okay." Delaney slowly put her hand back in her lap, her breathing tight as she watched him slash at nothing. Her eyes widened as the gashes that appeared on his face out of thin air just as miraculously disappeared.

Okay, we're both *crazy, right?* No, they were both probably suffering from hallucinations, thanks to those drugs.

A couple of minutes later, Tighe stopped fighting and sank back against his seat, his breathing hard.

"Did you win?" she asked conversationally, pushing back the urge to close her eyes, cover her ears, and scream that *this was not happening.*

He turned his head toward her, his mouth opening as if he were about to reply, then closing again.

"Care to tell me who you were fighting?"

"Not who."

Well, that was a point in his favor, since clearly no real person had been doing battle with him in the car.

"Then *what*?"

"It's not your concern." He straightened, his breathing already back to normal, and lifted his shirt to wipe the blood off his face. "They won't bother you."

She stared at him, another thought breaking through the bafflement and disbelief that had become her mind. What if he really had been battling something? Something she couldn't see. Some kind of cloaked, supersecret weapon.

Had she accidentally stumbled into the middle of something far bigger than a psychopathic serial killer and his sexy, drugged-up twin?

Tighe turned to her as if he were reading her thoughts. "Don't try to figure it out, Delaney. Don't try to figure *me* out. You won't succeed. And if by some long shot you do, you'll only endanger yourself more."

Because then she really would know too much. A frisson of adrenaline pumped through her veins. She felt the gun at her back and wondered if she could bring herself to kill him. If she drew on him, she'd better be ready to shoot, because she'd only ever get one chance.

Her gaze studied his strong profile as he started the car and put it in gear.

No, she wasn't ready to kill him. If her theory was even partly right, that he was involved in something big and dangerous, she needed to know more. She needed all the information she could get if the Bureau was to have any chance of stopping it.

And, disturbingly, there was a part of her that wanted to believe the angel wings that continued to whisper, *Trust him*. There was a part of her that was genuinely drawn to him in ways beyond the sexual. His strength. His gentleness. He intrigued her mightily.

And yes, deep in her gut, she was starting to trust him.

As he drove, questions bombarded her brain. She tilted her head against the headrest behind her, watching him.

"How did you know your twin was here, Tighe?"

He glanced at her. "You told me."

She jerked upright. "*I* told you?"

"I saw him in your vision."

Her scalp began to tingle. "In *my* vision?" She'd never told him about her visions. She'd never told him *anything*. Was he reading her mind now? Could this night *get* any weirder? "I don't know what you're talking about."

"Don't you? I think you do, brown eyes." He glanced at her again. "I was the one having the visions until you came along."

She stared at him, the hair rising on the back of her neck. "What do you mean?"

He turned back to the road. "My twin and I have a psychic connection I don't entirely understand. When he first started killing, I was the one seeing the murders. I was the one watching those terrified faces as he went for their throats. Through his eyes, I saw the death of that blonde in the basement of the Potomac Side Apartments. A couple of minutes later, I saw him attack you. I thought he'd killed you as he had her."

No way. Her mind rebelled, yet she stared at him, her attention riveted.

He glanced at her and met her gaze. "But my next vision wasn't of death. It was of you staring at yourself in the bathroom mirror at work. You wondered out loud why you were being forced to watch him kill others. One of your coworkers found you leaning on the sink, white as a ghost, and called your name. That's how I knew who you were."

Her head rang like a gong struck too hard. Yet everything he said was true. Everything correlated exactly with the events as she knew them.

"You think I've come between you and your twin."

"I know you have, though I'm not sure how. Something must have happened when he attacked you and didn't kill you. You've disrupted our connection. Now when he murders, I sometimes see you watching the murder, and I sometimes get tiny glimpses of it myself. But so far, the only time I've seen the whole thing since you got involved is the one time I held on to you while you got the vision."

She blinked. "In your house just now. You saw it instead of me, didn't you? You *knew* he was in the Lincoln Memorial killing those people."

"Yes." Tighe released a harsh sigh. "But I didn't get there in time to catch him."

"Because something attacked you." She pressed her palms against the roof of the car. "Is this for real, Tighe? Is this all happening, or am I seriously losing my grip on my sanity?"

He reached over and gently squeezed her knee. "I'd like to tell you you're losing it. Or it's all a dream, or something equally inane. But you're not, brown eyes. You're perfectly sane. You've just gotten in the middle of things you shouldn't have." He nodded toward her window. "Keep your eyes peeled, Agent Randall. We may have missed him, but he could still be around here preparing to feed off someone else."

Delaney nodded, letting his words sink in. She wasn't insane, at least. Which was definitely something. Unfortunately, the deeper she got into this, the more convinced she became she was going to be lucky to get out of it alive.

She needed to trust her instincts and her instincts were screaming at her to trust him, to hold on to him and not let him go. Every instinct she possessed warned her that Tighe was her only chance of survival.

Tighe glanced at Delaney as he had every few minutes for the past couple of hours as they drove through the night streets of D.C. The woman drew him like a cat to cream, even in the dark where he could only glimpse her face in shadow. There was a depth to her that intrigued him. Alternating layers of strength and softness. Of fury and pain.

He was pretty sure he knew where the pain came from, but he wanted to know the whole story. He found himself wanting to know everything about her.

"Was your mother a cop, brown eyes?"

She turned toward him as the lights of a passing cab lit her face.

"No. Why?"

"I saw your expression when you saw the dead cop. I thought maybe you'd known her. Or that she reminded you of your mom."

Delaney sighed and tilted her head back against the seat as if exhaustion pulled at her. "I saw her wedding ring. I'd be willing to bet she had kids. My mom wasn't a cop, but I was eleven when I lost her. I hate the thought of any other kid going through that."

"Tell me what happened. I heard you tell the cat in your apartment that a scumbag caught her on a bike path." He wasn't sure she'd open up to him, but they'd been traveling together in a comfortable silence for a while now. He found he wanted to understand her better.

"He raped her. Murdered her, while I was at school. I don't know any more than that. They never found the killer."

"I'm sorry you lost her."

"It was a long time ago."

"Not so long. And you live with it every day of your life, don't you? It's why you became a federal agent. To catch the killers like the one who killed your mother. Maybe to catch *him*."

She turned back to him. Then slowly looked away. "Maybe I am a little obsessed," she said softly. "But, blast it, Tighe, people like that need to be stopped." She swung back to look at him. "How dare he steal her life? And not just hers. *Mine*. He took everything from me that day. Everything."

Tighe slid his hand over her shoulder and gave a squeeze. "Just don't devote so much of your life to revenge that you forget to live it."

"It's not revenge."

"What is it, brown eyes?"

"It's . . . a calling. I *hate* the killers. All of them." She groaned. "It is revenge, isn't it? Every time there's a murder, I wonder if it's the same guy. If maybe this time I'll get him."

She was silent for more than a minute, as if pondering that realization. Finally, she shrugged.

"Who cares why I do it? It's my job, and I'm good at it."

He squeezed her shoulder. "What happened after your mom died? Did your dad raise you?"

She gave a soft sound of disgust. "No."

That single word held a stunning wealth of emotion, emotions that trailed across his tongue. Anger. Hurt. And a deep, painful betrayal he knew the taste of all too well.

"My dad decided he couldn't handle being a single parent. Five days after I lost my mother, he ripped me away from everything I'd ever known— home, friends, school, my cat—and dumped me on my aunt's doorstep, more than two hours away. I guess in his messed-up logic it was the perfect solution. I needed a mother, and she needed help. She was single with four small children. Only I didn't get a mother. I got a full-time, unpaid job. I became her babysitter, cook, housekeeper, you name it."

"Cinderella," he murmured.

She made a sound. "Believe me, I thought that at least ten times a day. Which was ridiculous, of course. I wasn't abused, at least . . . Yeah, anyway."

Tighe looked over at her. Her abrupt silence was loaded. He reached over and stroked her hair. "I'd like to hear it all. Though I don't want to cause you more pain."

"It's not . . . I mean . . ." She took a deep breath and let it out slowly. "My aunt's boyfriend moved in with us when I was sixteen."

Ah, hell. He was afraid he knew what was coming.

"He managed to keep his hands off me for all of five months, but he watched me. I knew he watched me. He finally made a move two days after my seventeenth birthday."

His hand clenched the steering wheel, the strength of his anger catching him by surprise. "He hurt you."

She met his gaze, steel in her eyes. "No. He groped me and tried to kiss me. I ripped open his cheek with my fingernails, then slammed my fist in his eye." A glimmer of satisfaction arced through her expression.

Tighe grinned, a vicious smile. "Good girl." He tensed. "Did he retaliate?"

"Not directly. My aunt kicked me out that night and told me never to come back. I don't know what he told her."

"You went back to your dad."

"No. I hadn't seen him in years, not since I was thirteen. He came to see me a few times after he left me with my aunt, but I wouldn't talk to him. I was furious with him for deserting me." She groaned. "I was such a brat."

"No you weren't. Your anger toward him was deserved. If a man's blessed with a daughter, he protects her. No matter what." His grip on the wheel tightened as a sharp pain lanced his heart.

Yet he was no better than Delaney's father. How long had Amalie cried for him? How long had she hated him?

"Thanks," Delaney said softly. "I never forgave him. Maybe if I had, he'd have been there for me later."

He looked over at her. "What did you do? Seventeen is young to be on your own."

"I got a job waiting tables and rented a room from a lady down the street. After high school, I worked my way through college, my sights firmly on getting the man who'd ruined my life and all the others like him. Revenge." She yawned deeply. "As you said."

"You're exhausted." He patted his right thigh. "Lie down, brown eyes. Get some sleep." He was suddenly glad he'd grabbed the larger of the sedans, with its bench seat.

She glanced at him, a smile hovering at her mouth. "That sounds like a line if I ever heard one. And I'm too tired to care." Leaning sideways, she stretched out along the seat to lay her head firmly in his lap. "I don't know why I'm starting to trust you," she murmured sleepily. "I shouldn't."

He stroked her hair. "Thanks for not using that gun on me."

She groaned in disgust, drawing a chuckle out of him, but didn't move to reach for the weapon. Within seconds her breathing evened out, and he knew she was asleep.

He stroked her arm, feeling a warmth toward her, a protectiveness, he didn't understand. She was a human. Yet he didn't remember the last time he'd felt this close to another. Any other.

Human or not, she was a remarkable woman.

Determined and driven. Tough and courageous. But not without compassion. He'd seen her expression when they'd come upon the three bodies less than a dozen yards from the statue of Abraham Lincoln. She'd seen more than bodies. More than victims. She'd seen two lovers terrorized and destroyed. And a wife, possibly a mother, who would never go home to her family.

He'd tasted Delaney's fury over the wasteful destruction of life. Yes, she might have been driven to this job of hers out of revenge, but it was a deep compassion for life that kept her dedicated.

He'd have to remember to tell her that. He brushed back a lock of hair that was trying to fall across her cheek, then lifted it and ran the softness between his fingers.

Inexplicably, Delaney Randall had begun to matter to him. He wanted her safe and able to live her short, fragile life to its utmost. With all the things she'd missed, and still missed. A home. A family. A cat.

The thought made him smile, but his thoughts turned wistful. He sensed a large capacity for love in her, and he wished that for her. Children of her own and a man who would stand by her side no matter what, and love her as she deserved to be loved.

The tiger raised its head deep inside him, a growl rumbling in his throat.

Yeah, the thought of her in another man's arms didn't please him either. But he certainly didn't want her for himself. She was human.

And if she wasn't?

He shook off the weirdly disturbing thought and turned his attention once more to hunting for his clone.

Several hours later, as the sun rose behind overcast skies, Hawke called.

"Any luck?" the Feral asked.

"None. Not a sign of him. But no more visions. Which either means he hasn't fed yet, or Delaney doesn't get them in her sleep."

"We're back in the safe house, looking for a little sleep ourselves."

"I'm going to drive around a bit longer." He snapped the phone closed. As tired and hungry as he was, he couldn't bring himself to call it quits. Admittedly, he was loath to take Delaney back to the safe house with Kougar and Hawke there. And she was sleeping so soundly, he didn't want to wake her.

He stroked her hair as he had a hundred times over the past hours. But the real truth was, holding her like this, with her fragile head tucked against him, eased his battered soul the way nothing else had.

The tiger purred with satisfaction, a fact he might have found a tad disturbing if he weren't too tired to think about it. The tiger rarely paid any attention to the women he was with.

He glanced into the rearview mirror, lifting his sunglasses to look at his eyes. Yesterday, for the first time, he'd noticed a black streak across one of his irises, slicing through the green like the shadow from a lightning bolt. Today, there were several across each. He didn't know what it meant—Hawke hadn't either—but he had a sick feeling it wasn't good.

An hour later, when the rumbling of his stomach became so loud he was afraid he was going to wake half of D.C., he turned the car toward Capitol Hill and the safe house.

Minutes later, Delaney jerked in her sleep, then moaned with pain. "*Not again.*"

Tighe pressed a hand to her forehead as she lay on his lap. A vision roared into his head, knocking the breath from him as it punched him in the gut.

This bastard needed to die.

Chapter Nine

The scene flashed into Tighe's inner vision.

As before, it didn't steal his sight as the visions did when they were his alone. Instead, he continued to see the street before him clearly. He watched the two scenes as though through two separate pairs of eyes.

A young woman lay on the floor, her eyes filled with terror as she struggled to remove the gag from her mouth. Hands that weren't Tighe's held her down.

"*Do you know who I am?*" the clone hissed in the woman's ear.

The woman shook her head frantically.

"*I'm the D.C. Vampire.*"

Tighe's stomach clenched. The bastard knew

exactly what was going on. He must be holed up somewhere watching the news between attacks, a hugely disturbing thought because the clone was definitely past the stage of being merely a feeding machine. He was thinking. Plotting. *Learning.* And that was *not* good news.

The woman's eyes went impossibly wide with terror. Precisely what his clone intended, Tighe realized. Why else had he told her what the news media was calling him? He wanted her afraid. He was feeding off her fear.

Definitely evolving. An unthinking animal would feed the simplest way possible. In this case, by stealing raw life force, draining his victim. Feeding from fear took more finesse. More cunning. Something his clone was clearly developing.

Not good. Not good at all.

Delaney's hand moved to cover his, holding it tight against her forehead. "Don't let go," she pleaded.

"I've got you."

"How does your touch help, Tighe? How do you ease the pain?"

"I'm not sure, but I suspect it's all part of your getting in the way of my connection with my twin. When I touch you, I'm able to access the vision your brain is trying to shut out, completing that connection. The pressure in your head eases."

"That makes sense," she murmured. "And yet no sense at all. People are not electrical circuits. None of this should be happening."

If she only knew. She'd only glimpsed the tip of

what would appear to her human eyes to be a very large and terrifying iceberg. He prayed to the goddess she never saw the rest. The terror in her eyes would be more than he could stand. In his current state, he'd be flung into the chaos for good.

In that other place, the demon grabbed his captive's arms, breaking one, then the other as she screamed.

"Can you see this?" he asked Delaney.

"No."

He stilled as the clone's sights turned to a playpen filled with three wide-eyed toddlers. Rage tore through him as the monster closed the distance between them.

Behind the clone, Tighe could hear the injured woman's whimpers turn to outrage as the clone reached down and picked up one of the little ones, lifting her chubby neck to his mouth.

Tighe groaned. "*Sweet goddess.*"

"What's he doing?" Delaney asked, her voice tight with pain.

"He broke her arms. Now he's killing her babies. As she watches."

Delaney moaned, curling in on herself as if she'd taken a punch to the stomach. "We have to get him."

The devil who wore his face tossed the tiny, lifeless body aside with a thud and turned to pick up another as the woman's muffled and horrified cries rang in Tighe's ears.

"We don't know where he is. Wait." As the clone fed on the second child, his gaze turned toward the window. "Capitol Springs Apartments are across the street."

"Capitol Springs. I know that area." A thread of excitement laced her voice. "It's on East Capitol. Around 6th or 7th."

He released Delaney long enough to pull out his cell phone and give the address to Hawke. Second by second, he felt her body tensing as her pain burned across his tongue. He snapped the phone closed, tossed it onto the dash, and covered her forehead again with his palm.

Her pained sigh tore at him. Somehow he had to free her from these things. For her, now, more than himself.

"Are your friends going to meet us there?"

"Yes, but you won't see them." Hawke would probably shift and go by air. They'd both beat him there. He'd wandered far afield in his driving.

Hopefully, he wouldn't need to get in touch with Hawke. Once the Feral shifted, neither he nor Kougar would be able to communicate with him until they got closer. And out of the car. The magic shielding that kept the draden from penetrating the car windows kept the Ferals from communicating telepathically when one of them was in his animal form. Which was the only time they *could* communicate that way.

The woman's cries increased exponentially as the clone picked up the last child, a small boy. Tighe knew instinctively, the boy was the only one who was hers. Even through the gag, he recognized the unique sound of a parent's pain.

As he was forced to stop behind a line of traffic caught at the light, the clone tossed the third small body onto the floor and turned to the grief-stricken mother. *This* is why he had to get his soul back! Not only to stop this creature from killing, but to help find that Daemon blade so this scene didn't play out a thousand times a day. Every day. All over the world, as it would if the Daemons were ever freed again.

Thunder. He slammed his hand against the steering wheel. The Ferals didn't have the power to defeat the Daemons a second time. They'd sacrificed too much to imprison them the first time.

Delaney turned her head to look up at him, and he met her pained gaze, feeling his soul sink into her dark eyes and, for a moment, heal. "Is he still killing children?"

"No. They're dead. He's turning on the mother now."

Abruptly, the clone stopped.

"How far are we?" Delaney asked, still watching him.

"Ten minutes. Maybe less."

The clone turned away from the woman and moved to kneel beside the lifeless body of the last child. Tighe's stomach rolled as he realized what the clone was doing. With a lighter, he set fire to the boy's dinosaur tee shirt. Then with an even, purposeful stride, he walked to the apartment door and opened it.

"Three thirty-one. He was in apartment 331, but he's leaving. *Dammit.* I've got to tell Kougar."

Tighe reached for his phone, where he'd tossed it onto the dash, but couldn't get it without crushing Delaney against the steering wheel. "Brown eyes, I need my phone. Can you reach it for me?"

As she rose slowly, he kept his palm against her forehead. "Where? Oh, I see it." She pulled it off the dash.

Delaney held the phone in front of him, but to take it he had to release her.

"Speed dial five for me. When a man answers, tell him apartment three three one."

"Tighe says apartment three three one." A moment later she snapped, "Go to hell," and closed the phone.

Damn Kougar. "What did he say?"

"He said he told you to kill me."

Tighe sighed. "He figured it was the easiest way to free you from the visions."

The sound that came from her throat was half laugh, half moan. "If this keeps up much longer, I may ask for that cure."

"Hang on, brown eyes. No one's ending your life."

"That assurance would have made me happier before the little guys with the jackhammers set up the construction zone in my brain."

The vision faded.

Delaney sighed, the tension easing from her tightly strung body. "Is it over?"

"Apparently. At least for now. I have a feeling he set that fire for a reason."

"He set a fire?"

"Yes." He didn't see any need to burden her with where.

"We've got to call the fire department."

She pushed herself up and he released her, sorry to have to let her go. "Are you okay?"

"Yes. Thanks to you." She picked up his phone and pressed 911. "Is there a return policy on these visions I accidentally stole from you because I would *happily* give them back?"

"I may be able to free you of them. That's what I was trying to do when I inadvertently started to control you."

She threw him a wary look that said she didn't understand what he was talking about and wasn't sure she wanted to know.

But her sigh was one of exhaustion. "As soon as we get back to your place, you have my permission to muck around in my head all you want. Just get me free of these things."

"You got it."

As she called in the fire, he found the building and pulled up in front. Sure enough, smoke was already beginning to curl from one of the open windows.

Tighe tossed Delaney the car keys. "Wait for me."

"Yeah, right."

As he opened his door, she jumped out, pulling the gun he'd seen her take from the cop, as she ran for the building. *Hell.* Tighe raced after her. There was no way he was going to be able to talk her into staying outside. Any more than she'd talk him into it.

He pushed past the frightened residents rushing out the front door, following Delaney, who was threading her way through the crowd. He forced his way in and was heading for the stairs when he heard Hawke call, "Stripes!" The lean, dark-haired warrior crossed the foyer to his side.

"You catch him?" Tighe asked.

"No. No sign of him anywhere. Neither of us can sense him. Either he's fled the scene, or he's lost his draden smell."

"The latter. The son of a bitch set that fire just to create fear so he can feed off it. No way would he leave now. He's here somewhere, feasting on the terror.

Hawke nodded. "That explains it, then. Kougar found the apartment and said it was the source of the fire."

"What about the woman?"

"There was no one alive in there."

Crap. "Find Kougar and cover the exits. I'm going to try to flush him out. Delaney's with me."

Hawke lifted a brow but said nothing.

Tighe started up the open stairs, pushing past frantic residents. Children cried. People shouted, calling for one another. As he breached the throng on the landing and started up the second flight, he saw the woman from the vision and felt a quick, sharp empathy for her and relief that she, at least, had survived. Another woman had her arms around her hunched shoulders as she cradled both arms against her body.

Fury stirred at her unnecessary suffering.

The woman looked up, her eyes dazed until they landed on him. Stark terror flared in her eyes as a strangled scream wobbled from her throat.

The sight of terror directed at him from a woman's eyes slammed him with memory, igniting his fury. *Gretchen, you should have known.*

Deep inside him, the chaos leaped, wrenching him back to the present.

No. I can't go feral. Not here. Not now.

Tighe tore his gaze away from the woman's terrified face as he pushed as far to the right as he could. Keeping others between them, he ran past her and up the stairs. But he was losing the battle, that inner rage riding him, clamoring to be set free.

His fingers began to tingle. His teeth ached.

No! He wouldn't lose it. Not when he was so close to finding his clone. *Not with Delaney here.*

He pushed through the crowd in a growing panic as his claws slowly unsheathed. He couldn't lose it here. *He couldn't lose it here.*

At the top of the stairs, he saw an open doorway and dove through. With his last ounce of free will, he no longer fought the imminent change, but rode it through the feral, straight to the tiger as he shifted into his animal.

Only in his animal form could he call for help, unless one of his friends had already shifted.

With a surge of relief and joy, the change swept over him, and he raised his beast's head to the ceiling and let out one long, rumbling growl.

To his surprise, the storm inside him began to

abate. He apparently had better control in his tiger form than his human. Until a woman's scream had him swinging toward the open door. A woman stared at him in horror, as a man grabbed her shoulders and pushed her past.

Wildness clawed at his control all over again. Fury leaping to be set free.

They're running from a tiger, his logical mind roared. Any sane human would be terrified.

In his animal form, he managed what he hadn't been able to in his human form and slowly beat back the chaos. Before he shifted back to human, he took advantage of his tiger's ability to scent draden. But he smelled nothing but humans. And smoke.

He called to his friends. *Any sign of him?*

None. Hawke's voice. *We've got the exits covered as best we can with only two of us.*

Good. Delaney's in here somewhere. I'm going to try to send her out. Keep an eye on her. Do not let Kougar near her.

I'll do my best.

Tighe shifted back into his human form, then ran into the hall to search for Delaney. If she had to face that clone again, she was doing it with him at her side.

Chapter
Ten

Delaney stumbled down the hallway from apartment 331, her lungs sore and burning from coughing. Her nostrils fried from the stench of burning flesh. Her heart aching. Dear God, *he'd burned the children.*

In the hallway, the air was quickly filling with smoke. Even if Tighe's twin were here, she wasn't sure she'd see him.

A figure appeared at the top of the stairs. Her heart lurched at the familiar sight. Tighe or the killer? But the angel wings in her head fluttered with pleasure, and she knew it was Tighe. But at the sight of him, at the thought of what she'd just done, her stomach spasmed with guilt. She'd just gotten off the phone with Phil. FBI SWAT was on its way.

"Did you . . . find him?" she asked, coughing.

"No." He quickly closed the distance between them, his hands going to her shoulders. "Get outside, brown eyes. You need some fresh air."

"We've got to find him."

"We do. My men are watching the back of the apartment. I need you to cover the front while I flush him out."

She wasn't ready to leave, yet. SWAT or no SWAT, this was her investigation, dammit, but she was coughing badly. And Tighe was barely coughing at all. The smoke hardly seemed to be getting to him. Maybe she *should* leave him to root out his twin while she sought out fresh air. She'd heard and felt his reactions during this latest attack. There was no doubt in her mind he'd been as horrified by his twin's savageness as she was. God knew, he should be, but the certainty that he had been only confirmed those instincts of hers that kept insisting he was a good man. A good man who would almost certainly get caught and hauled in for questioning once SWAT arrived. Unless she warned him.

She coughed harder, her eyes and throat burning from the smoke. But warning him went against everything she believed in as an FBI agent.

Tighe gave her a gentle push toward the stairs. "Go watch the front, Delaney. Get out of here before I have to carry you out."

Coughing too hard even to answer him, she nodded and turned away. He needed to be taken in for questioning. Whatever else Tighe was, he was dangerous. And involved up to his well-muscled shoulders in this case, *her* case. At the very least, he'd kidnapped and drugged a federal agent. Honest, everyday citizens didn't do things like that. They didn't have access to weapons like mind-control drugs.

He *had* to be apprehended. She knew that. Yet there was a part of her that felt like she'd betrayed him.

Thank God she wasn't weak enough to listen.

Tighe systematically broke down one door after another on the floor where the fire started, searching for the clone and finding nothing. Not even any people. At least the humans were smart enough to flee. He was all too afraid his clone was way *too* smart now to wait for Tighe. Why fight when he could slip away unnoticed?

Frustration ate at Tighe's nerves, and he pushed it back. He couldn't afford to shift again. Not when the firefighters would be here any moment and he still hadn't found his quarry.

When he'd gone through every apartment on the third floor, he started down the stairs to search the second. A heavyset woman with a cane was struggling to climb up. Under her breath, she was crying, "My baby, my baby."

The smoke was already thick on the third floor. She had no business going up there. He told himself it wasn't his business. He told himself he didn't care.

"Ma'am, you need to go downstairs. The fire's spreading and the firefighters are going to need to get through."

She turned a tear-streaked face to him, desperation in her eyes. "My baby's up there. I left her alone for just a few minutes. She can't get out the door. She's only three."

Three. He remembered Amalie at that age. So demanding and bossy for such a tiny thing, yet he'd gladly been her slave and lackey. He'd have done anything for the daughter he'd loved more than his own life. Anything.

The woman pushed herself onto the next highest step. "She's crying for her mama. I know she's crying. I've got to get her."

He told himself they were humans. *He didn't care.*

"Which apartment?"

"Four thirty-one."

Hell. She was directly above the fire. It might already be too late. "Go down. *Hurry.* I'll get her."

"Wait! The key."

She handed him her apartment key and Tighe palmed it, then turned and ran. Three years old.

Amalie. Her face swam in his mind's eye as he'd last seen her. Crying, her face streaked with tears as her small arms reached for him, clawing the arms that bound her in her desperation to get back to him.

And he'd turned away.

Ah, goddess. *Amalie.*

They were so tiny at that age. So fragile. How long could small, mortal lungs breathe such smoke? How long before the fire burned through the floor and sent this child tumbling into the flames?

She needed him.

How many times had Amalie needed him? How many times had she cried out for him, and he wasn't there to hear her?

How many times?

Delaney watched the chaos in helpless frustration. *What if Tighe doesn't give himself up when the FBI arrives? What if they shoot him?*

A bloodcurdling scream went up to her left, and she feared her worries were coming all too true as she quickly sought its source. Her gaze found the one screaming, a woman holding badly misshapen arms against her body. Delaney followed the woman's line of sight and froze.

The woman was staring at Tighe. Except . . . *he wasn't Tighe*. He was dressed in the same navy blue shirt and too-short khakis she'd seen him in when he attacked her in the laundry room. And he wasn't wearing shades. Even from this distance she could feel the coldness in him that brought back nightmarish memories of the attack. A cold that was not Tighe's.

Goose bumps lifted on her flesh. *There* were *two of them*. Just as Tighe had said. And she was staring at the murderer. Hatred curled in her gut as she pulled her weapon and started running. The killer looked up as she came toward him. He was near the corner of the apartment building, standing among more than a dozen agitated residents waiting for the fire trucks.

"FBI!" she choked out, coughing. "Freeze!"

He ducked behind the other residents, and she lost sight of him. *Blast it*.

The guy was *not* getting away this time. If she had to empty the chamber in his head to stop him, she'd do it.

But when she reached the group, he wasn't there. And there was no way a man his and Tighe's size could easily hide. She took off around the corner, but could see no sign of him, so she kept running. By the time she was three-quarters of the way around the apartment complex, her lungs felt like they'd been rubbed raw with gravel.

She doubled over, coughing, desperately trying to catch her breath. She'd lost him. How in the world had she lost a man who had to be over six-six? *Did he go back inside? Or was he long gone by now?*

Pushing herself to keep going, she rounded the corner to find the street clogging with fire trucks, police cars, and two SWAT vans.

The gang's all here.

Except Tighe's twin had almost certainly escaped. Tighe was the only one they'd get. But he had to be apprehended. They had to figure out who he was, who he worked for, and what he knew.

She knew that, accepted it. She was an FBI agent, first and foremost. Her loyalty was to the Bureau alone.

But she couldn't help feeling the sick guilt of betrayal.

Tighe raced down the smoky hallway, alive with the screech of smoke alarms, to apartment 431.

Inserting the key, he pushed open the door to the sound of a child's coughing and crying.

"Come, little one," he called softly in a voice he'd once reserved for Amalie alone. "I'll take you to your mother."

A small shape flew across the floor to him and he swept her into his arms. Not Amalie. Black hair, not blond. Dark skin, not pale. Not Amalie.

But as her small arms wrapped around his neck he was swamped by memories of sweetness and loss. Not in six hundred years had he held a child in his arms.

Cradling the small, coughing body against him, he ran for the stairs as pain that he'd thought long buried swept over him in a blinding torrent.

He barely noticed the stairwell flying past until he heard a woman's glad cry echoing from below.

"Jensie! Baby!"

The little girl stirred in his arms and began to cry. "Momma." Her cry dissolved into a fit of coughing.

"Oh, baby, I'm so sorry. So sorry." The woman had stopped halfway down the final flight of stairs.

"Get outside!" Tighe called to her. "We're right behind you."

Through the front windows of the apartment building, Tighe could see the flashing lights of fire trucks, yet the firefighters had yet to race into the building. What was taking them so damn long? What if there were others trapped like this child had been?

Thunder. Since when did he care what happened to humans?

The hobbling woman finally reached the lobby and made her way to the front door, Tighe and the child close behind her. The moment they were outside, the woman held out her arms. Tighe had to force himself to release the little girl, but he did, allowing her to dive into her mother's arms.

"Thank you." The woman's eyes shone with tears. "You're an angel."

Tighe nodded, uncomfortable with the praise and still reeling from the barrage of raw, painful memories.

Tighe. Look out!

Hawke's voice sounded in his head at the same instant his warrior's instincts caught the quick, furtive movements and the glint of metal.

"Freeze! FBI!"

The child had distracted him. He'd walked right into a trap. A trap set, no doubt, by a woman with dark fathomless eyes.

Six armed SWAT members ran at him from both sides.

"Hands in the air!"

Behind the men, he saw her. Delaney stood, watching him, her jaw set, a plea in her eyes. To what? Forgive her? Give up? *Like hell.*

The last thing he could afford to do was get trapped by human law enforcement. He turned and ran back into the smoky building as two shots rang out behind him. One hit him in the thigh. The other went straight through his heart.

Jesus. He'd survive it. If he could get to a healer . . . in time.

He stumbled down the hall and fell through the first open doorway, shifting into his tiger. No. He couldn't remain a tiger.

Hawke. I'm heart-shot.

Where are you?

First-floor apartment. Second or third on the right. Not sure. Fading fast, buddy.

We'll get you. Hang on.

Using what strength he could gather, he managed to change his form once more, to that of a house cat. He lay there, his feline eyes glazed, his chest on fire from the gunshot, yet aching in an entirely different way.

Amalie's tear-streaked face faded to be replaced by the face of another female, a woman with hard warrior's eyes. She'd slept in his lap and said she was beginning to trust him, yet clearly she never really had. He'd known it. He'd been a fool to turn his back on her.

She'd won this battle, but the war between them was far from over.

If he lived long enough to fight another day.

Delaney clutched her chest as she watched the blood bloom on Tighe's retreating back, right at the level of his heart.

Blast it. *Blast it.*

He shouldn't have run!

Blast it, Tighe.

"Was he the one?" Phil asked, coming to stand beside her.

"He wasn't the killer, but the brother. The killer may still be inside, though he's probably long gone."

"We've got the building surrounded. The fire will flush him soon enough if he's still in there. As soon as we haul the brother out, we're letting the fire department in, or they'll never get the blaze contained."

A tall dark-haired man with sharply arched brows pushed his way through the front doors, a dead cat in his arms. An orange-striped tabby that looked a lot like the one she'd been talking to in her apartment. Right before she realized Tighe was there.

Her teeth clenched beneath the force of her anger. Damn Tighe. He'd chosen death over inter-rogation. And just what did that say about his lack of innocence? Plenty.

Tears burned her eyes, and she blinked them back harshly. He'd kidnapped her. He'd drugged her. He was one of the bad guys. She was being ridiculous to care what happened to him.

But she did care. He was a complex man. With-out a doubt, he went beyond the law, but she didn't believe he was evil. Not evil.

He'd shown her more tenderness, more care, than anyone since her mom died. And the passion . . .

She turned, pretending to scrutinize the area as she swiped away a traitorous tear before her boss saw it.

Tighe shouldn't have died like this. But, dammit, it was his own fault. If he'd allowed himself to be taken in, this wouldn't have happened.

She fought back the emotions, struggling to pull her FBI persona around her like a sturdy, comfortable cloak. When she turned back to Phil, no tears glistened in her eyes. Despite her less than professional attire, she was Agent Randall through and through.

"I need a blood sample taken, Phil, ASAP."

Phil's brows drew together with worry. "What happened, Delaney? You're not here by accident."

"It's a long story."

Phil's expression turned grave. "Are you okay?"

"I think so." She ran not-quite-steady fingers through her tangled, smoky-smelling hair. "There's more going on here than a madman with a penchant for killing. I was kidnapped and drugged." It sounded so sinister, yet he'd never hurt her. Instead, he'd given her such pleasure. Delaney sighed. "The sooner we get a blood sample, the better the chance the lab can figure out what he used on me."

"I'll take you to the lab myself." His gaze went back to the building. "What in the hell is taking them so long? I saw the bullet pierce his chest. There's no way he's still walking."

As Phil ushered her toward his car, her stomach cramped, and she feared she was going to be sick. She shouldn't feel this awful, wrenching regret. It went against everything she believed in. Tighe had not been one of the good guys.

Yet the thing that had distracted him was the child in his arms. A child he'd clearly saved.

Her eyes burned. Remorse grew and thickened inside her until she could barely breathe around the pulsing grief. *He shouldn't have died.*

She blinked hard, clenching her teeth as she struggled to keep the unacceptable tears from falling. Her hand went to the gun still tucked into the back of her pants, the solid weight against her palm grounding her, easing her inner turmoil.

Long ago she'd sworn an oath to uphold the law. She would not feel guilty over doing just that. Tighe had given her no choice.

What she'd done was necessary. It was right. And if she had it to do over again, she'd do exactly the same.

Even if she feared Tighe's face would haunt her for the rest of her life.

In the nearby Virginia suburbs, Paenther snapped his cell phone closed and shoved it into the inside pocket of his leather duster as he and Foxx strode through the doors of the Tysons Corner Grand Peerage Hotel. Late-afternoon sunshine ribboned across the plush oriental-style carpeting. Crystal chandeliers hung at regular intervals, illuminating the business-suited guests mingling in small, professional gatherings.

"What did Lyon have to say?" Foxx asked, as they started across the lobby, heading for the dark-paneled Roosevelt's at the far end. The bar was one of a dozen watering holes the Ferals frequented in that part of the county. A favorite of Vhyper's. And Paenther was damned well going to find him.

"Lyon's called a meeting in the war room in two hours. This is going to have to be our last stop."

"How's Tighe?"

"They got the bullets out of him. He'll live." For now. If Tighe didn't find that clone of his soon, it was going to be another matter. His hands fisted at his sides as worry for his friends twisted and braided with the barely controlled rage that lived in his bones and had for centuries. He refused to lose two friends to that sadistic bitch, Zaphene. *Refused*.

Lyon and the others were helping Tighe. It was his job, his and Foxx's, to track down Vhyper. Maybe, *maybe*, they'd find Vhyper downing a scotch at the bar. Yeah, and what were the chances?

"Any word from that gut of yours, Cub?" Paenther's gaze pinned the youngest Feral, walking silent and morose beside him. Foxx had fancied himself in love with Zaphene, not realizing she was a witch who'd enchanted him and used him to breach the Ferals' stronghold.

But it was neither pity nor sympathy that spurred Paenther to bring him along on the search. No, for the past year or so, Foxx's Feral talents had been starting to come online. He'd been showing some impressive talent as an intuitive.

With any luck, that intuition would eventually guide them to Vhyper. And if that didn't work, he wasn't sure what he was going to do. Other than continue to haunt Vhyper's usual hot spots in hopes of eventually stumbling upon him.

The young Feral shook his shaggy head of red

hair. "Gut's saying nada. Actually, my gut's saying it wants a couple of beers, then some dinner."

"That's not helpful," Paenther muttered.

As they passed through the lobby, businessmen moved out of their way, eyeing them warily. One small pack of well-dressed women watched them with a level of interest bordering on hunger.

Paenther ignored them all. The men, humans all, were harmless. The women were of no interest. Like any man, he had needs, but he took care of them with a willing Therian female at one of the enclaves. He couldn't remember the last time a woman had actually turned his head. Lust rarely broke through the surface of the ever-present torment that filled his body thanks to another Mage witch who'd ensnared him centuries ago. Even if, by some miracle, he stumbled upon a woman who interested him, he'd ignore her. All that mattered was finding Vhyper.

As they walked through the bar's entrance, through a thin haze of cigarette smoke, Paenther did a quick, fruitless scan. No Vhyper. *Dammit.*

Dull sunlight filtered into the dimly lit room through bare-branched trees. Only a handful of patrons sat at the polished-wood tables, most apparently deep in business discussions. Behind the bar, the local news lit the television screen, a video of a raging apartment fire. The same fire that Tighe, Hawke, and Kougar had gotten involved with that morning? Maybe.

Tearing his gaze from the television, he glanced at the bartender, recognizing the thin, balding man who'd served him a few times before. The bartender was missing his usual friendliness, his eyes wary as he eyed their approach.

"Scotch and a Bud?" he asked, as they slid onto a pair of barstools. Clearly, he remembered them. Then again, few people forgot a long-haired six-foot-six Indian with clawlike scars across one eye and a thick tribal tattoo on his neck. Or his red-headed sidekick. "I'll need to see your IDs."

"I haven't gotten any younger since the last time I was in here," Foxx grumbled, but he pulled out the license that gave a fake name and address and handed it to the man.

The bartender kept it and opened an unsteady hand to Paenther. His gaze tried to rise to Paenther's face, but faltered somewhere around the tattoo on his neck. "Both of them," he said bravely.

Paenther lifted one disbelieving brow. *Humans.* He supposed he admired the man's courage for insisting, especially when Paenther towered over him by close to a foot. He pulled out his own fake ID and handed it to him.

"Be right back. Got to get my glasses."

As the bartender moved off, Paenther watched the door, praying Vhyper would walk in. Everything pointed to Vhyper's joining forces with the Mage, but goddess, it couldn't be true.

The rage bubbled under his skin, burning his nostrils. The Vhyper he knew would *never* help the Mage. *Never.*

And that was the problem, the thing that scared Paenther the most. The possibility that the Vhyper he knew was gone.

A muscle began to twitch under his eye, his jaw clenched iron-tight as he breathed through his nose. He would save him. Just as Vhyper had saved *him* from a Mage captivity that had nearly destroyed him, body, mind, and soul, two and a half centuries ago.

But he had to find him first.

"Ease up on the Dirty Harry look, dude," Foxx said, his voice vaguely amused. "You're clearing the place again." Foxx nudged him with his elbow and nodded at the television. "Look." The volume had been muted, but damn if that wasn't Tighe's face plastered across the screen, right above the words, *D.C. Vampire.*

Shit.

His gaze snapped to the bartender only to find him hurriedly writing something down, his cell phone tucked between his shoulder and his ear, one of their IDs tight in his hand.

"Dammit to hell," he growled. He rose from the barstool and strode menacingly toward the traitor.

Walking behind the bar, he grabbed the cell phone off the man's shoulder, dropped it on the floor, and ground it beneath his heel.

"Hey!" the bartender cried.

Damned camera phones. The last thing they needed was two more pictures plastered across the television beside Tighe's. Paenther snatched up the two IDs, nodded to Foxx, and started for the lobby.

"I didn't get my beer," Foxx complained.

"Tough shit." As they started across the lobby, a flashing light outside caught his attention. His jaw set. "Walk calmly and follow me."

"Why?"

"There's a cop cruiser pulling up in front." He turned down a side corridor. "We'll shift if we have to, but I'd like to avoid it."

As they ducked out the back, Paenther knew their chances of stumbling upon Vhyper had just taken a nosedive into the toilet. Because Vhyper was going to have the same problem they were. He'd be instantly recognized as a friend of Tighe's in any of the many places they'd frequented together.

A friend of the D.C. Vampire's. A person of interest. Guilt by association.

Finding him now was going to be next to impossible. Unless Foxx's intuition started kicking in, Vhyper might be well and truly lost.

Chapter
Twelve

Lyon extended his arm to Tighe. "You're looking better."

Tighe smiled. "I'm alive." Hawke and Kougar had taken him to the healer, Esmeria, in the Georgetown enclave, where she'd taken the bullets from his flesh and healed his injuries. They'd then brought him back to Feral House, where Kara had filled him with radiance over and over through the day, healing and strengthening him until he almost felt normal again.

Normal was an illusion, of course.

His clone still lived. And as long as his clone lived, as long as his soul was split, he could never be right.

Hell, he wasn't sure he'd be right again even if

his soul *were* returned to him. Not until he found a way to get Delaney Randall out of his head.

From the moment he'd regained consciousness beneath the healer's care, he'd thought of her, worried about her. What if she got another of those visions without him there to help deflect the pain? And she would get another vision unless his clone had somehow, miraculously, died on his own, which he was certain hadn't happened. The other Ferals had reported feeling a sudden shift, almost a lightness inside, when their own clones had been destroyed. Tighe felt no lightness, nothing but tension. Frustration. And concern.

For Delaney.

Lyon slapped him on the shoulder. "Come. We're meeting in the war room.

Tighe followed Lyon into the wood-paneled room at the back of the house. A large oval conference table sat in the center of the room. Along the walls, Hawke had rigged up four large computer screens. All were dark, the chairs empty, as the Ferals paced.

Paenther greeted him, clasping his arm hard and long. "Glad you pulled through."

"Yeah, thanks. I can't tell you how much I wish that damn clone had gone after the Therian enclaves instead of getting me mixed up in the human world." Then again, he'd never have met Delaney. Which would have been a good thing. Definitely a good thing.

"Your eyes," Paenther murmured.

"The streaks?" Tighe answered Paenther's unspoken question. "No clue what they mean."

"Let's get started." Lyon took the seat at the head of the table and motioned the rest of them to take their chairs. All did, except Paenther and Tighe. Tighe was too damned tense to sit. He prowled the room like an animal in a cage.

Paenther remained standing by the door, back straight, arms crossed, a fine tension radiating from him that rivaled Tighe's own, thanks to an inborn rage that had tormented the black-haired warrior for centuries.

After dealing with his own unnatural tension, Tighe's respect for his friend grew another three notches. How he kept his sanity, Tighe couldn't guess.

Lyon turned to Paenther. "Report, B.P."

Paenther scowled. "Nothing good. No sign of Vhyper in any of the places he would have gone, were he still himself. Which isn't surprising. Tighe's face is splashed all over the news. A bartender recognized us as friends of his and called the cops on us this afternoon." He shook his head. "He's not hanging out in bars, Roar."

Lyon nodded. "Where do you think he is?"

"With the Mage." Paenther nodded at Foxx. "We've been afraid so from the beginning, but the cub's gut started confirming it last night. We drove out to the Mage stronghold on the Eastern Shore to have a look around, but it's gone, Roar. The mansion's still there, but by the look of the place, the Mage have been gone for months."

"I thought we had Therians keeping watch on the place," Hawke said.

"Two Therians were there, hiding in the woods nearby. They swore up and down every room in the mansion was lit when in truth they were all dark. Glamour strong enough to fool Therians for weeks, maybe months, is damn strong magic, Roar."

"Sensing a theme here, Chief?" Jag drawled.

Lyon threw Jag a sharp look, then turned his gaze to encompass all the Ferals. "I want to know how the Mage got their ancient magic back and how much of it they actually have." A deep growl rumbled from Lyon's throat as his gaze returned to Paenther. "Find Vhyper and the blade, B.P. And that Mage stronghold, while you're at it. I want to know what in the hell is going on!"

Paenther dipped his head, his shoulder-length hair brushing his cheeks like twin black curtains.

Tighe glanced up as Kara entered the room. He expected her to go to Lyon, as she usually did, but though her hand trailed along Lyon's shoulder as she passed him, she came straight to *him*, meeting his glance with a gentle smile that warmed the half of his tattered soul he still possessed.

"Hi," she said softly, taking his hand.

"Hi, yourself." He tugged lightly on her blond ponytail, finding a smile for her beneath the weight of his worry. As he felt the first warm surge of power flow from her hand into his, he knew what she was about. Her skin began to glow with the iridescence of radiance. "Thanks, little one."

With another soft smile, she turned to stand beside him where she could watch her mate and the others. Keeping their hands joined, he lifted his arm over her head so that his arm was around her, and tucked her against his side as she acted as the conduit for him to the Earth's energy and strength.

Lyon barely batted an eye at the move, to Tighe's relief. Lyon was as jealous as any mated male, but Kara's closeness strengthened Tighe almost as much as the radiance, and Lyon knew it. Besides, she thought of Tighe as more of a big brother, which suited Tighe just fine. Theirs was a bond he was coming to treasure. He adored her.

But it was another woman's face that wouldn't leave his mind. Damn Delaney. He'd admired her warrior's spirit, so it shouldn't have surprised him that she'd turn on him the moment she got the chance.

As if she couldn't even feel that soft connection to him in her head. Or it meant nothing to her.

And what had it meant to him? It hadn't changed his own mission or her place in it. He could hardly expect it to have changed hers.

Delaney Randall might be a woman, but she was FBI through and through. And the truth was, that was one of the things he admired most about her. She never let her emotions get in the way of what she had to do.

"Better?" Kara asked, looking up at him, the glow of radiance leaving her face.

"Much." He leaned down and placed an affectionate kiss on her forehead. "Thanks."

She gave him a quick hug, then slipped out of

his hold to join Lyon, hooking her arm around his shoulder as he tugged her down to perch on the cushioned arm of his chair.

Lyon nodded to Hawke. "Show them what you showed me earlier."

Hawke reached for the laptop sitting open in front of him. A moment later, one of the flat-screens came to life, replaying the local news channel's morning report. The sound was muted, but no sound was needed.

Tighe watched his own likeness with dismay. An amateur photographer at the scene of the fire had caught Tighe leaving the apartment with the child in his arms.

"Is that you?" Lyon asked him. "Or the clone?"

"Me."

"Who was the girl?"

Tighe set his jaw and shrugged. "Just a kid trapped in the apartment above the fire."

Jag snorted. "Since when do you give a shit about humans?"

Tighe threw the warrior a glare, but had no decent answer. He'd been asking himself the same question.

"The better question," Lyon said, "is why is that clone so damned hard to catch?"

Tighe nodded. "I've been asking myself why this one's different. Why did this one escape the battle when the others stayed to the bitter end?"

"The witch's control on him must have been weaker," Hawke said. "But there's more to it than that. The clones were created for one purpose only.

To perform the Feral ritual to free the Daemons from the blade since we'd never do it."

Wulfe leaned forward in his chair. "But Tighe's clone developed a will to survive."

Hawke nodded. "Maybe more than that. Those clones should have been the same. They were made at the same time with the same magic by the same witch. The only differences were the souls used. And the draden."

"The draden," Lyon murmured. "What if she accidentally caught one of the old ones in her net?"

"That's what I'm thinking." Hawke's palms flattened on the table in front of him. "The oldest ones were once Daemons. Though the souls were stripped and imprisoned in the Daemon blade, it's conceivable a bit of the Daemon's consciousness survived in the draden all that time."

Tighe scowled. "And now that he's been reanimated, he possesses the drive of a Daemon. He's acting like one, that's for damned sure."

Lyon turned to Hawke. "Does that mean what I'm afraid it does?"

Hawke's jaw clenched as he nodded. "His ultimate goal is bound to be freeing Satanan. And with that bit of Daemon consciousness, he may know things, ways to accomplish that that even the Mage and Therians have never known. At the moment, he doesn't seem to be doing anything but feeding. And maybe that's all he is doing, but it's clear he's evolving. Survival comes first, and sooner or later he's going to realize, if he hasn't already, that his survival hinges on you, Tighe."

"He can't live if I die. At least that's what your clone told Kara."

"I believe that was right initially. Before the clones were fully evolved. But I'm not sure that's true any longer."

"So what exactly are you saying, Wings?" Tighe asked warily.

"I'm saying, watch your back, buddy. I don't think killing you is going to automatically give him your half of the soul, but there may be other ways. He was born of magic. A magic I've seen evidence he may still possess."

"Explain," Lyon said.

"Kougar and I had him cornered. He slipped into a group of humans and disappeared. We're not sure how, but when we combed the group for him, he was gone. And he should not have been able to get away."

"Could he have acquired Tighe's ability to shift?" Foxx asked.

Tighe frowned. "My animal can't be split like that."

Hawke shook his head. "We don't know what abilities he's acquired. They could be anything."

"How are we going to catch him?" Lyon demanded.

"Daemon traps." Kougar pulled at his goatee. "If we can unearth some of those old spells."

Hawke groaned, shaking his head. "They haven't been used in five millennia. What are the chances?"

"Get on it." Lyon turned to Tighe. "Have you had more visions?"

Tighe quit pacing and faced his chief. "The lady Fed is getting them now instead of me, but when I touch her as she's having one, I see them clearly. I know right where he is."

Lyon met his gaze, his amber eyes thoughtful. "Hawke told me what happened. That you weren't able to take her memories."

"Not yet. I'm working on it."

"Where is she now?"

Tighe shook his head. "I don't know. I'll find her."

Lyon's hands fisted on the table in front of him. "I don't like that you don't have control of her mind."

Tighe's teeth ground together, his temper sparking. "I said, I'm working on it."

"I don't have to tell you how dangerous it is to have an FBI agent searching for us, knowing what we are."

"She doesn't have a clue what we are."

"Maybe not, yet. But she's an investigator. And I have to believe she's already seen things that have her questioning who you are. *What* you are. Am I wrong?"

"No. You're not wrong."

"Contain this threat, Stripes. However you have to do it. If you can't, we will."

Tighe heard the promise in his chief's words. The threat. Because there was only one way anyone else *could* contain this.

By killing Delaney Randall.

Deep inside, the tiger raised its head and growled.

"Whatever we do, we have to do it fast," Hawke said. "I called the Shaman and talked to him about those streaks in your eyes, Tighe."

Tighe lifted a brow. "And?"

Hawke's jaw clenched, his expression grim. "Your soul's beginning to disintegrate. Once your eyes are fully black, there won't be anything left of you in either body. Until then, there's still hope we can put you back together again."

But his time was running out.

Delaney sat on the edge of the bed while the blood-pressure cuff contracted around her arm.

"How do you feel?" Dr. Jensen asked for the fiftieth time. The doctor was a short, round woman with a tight cap of salt-and-pepper hair and shrewd blue eyes.

"Fine." Like her heart had been ripped out of her chest.

"Good. All your vital signs are normal." The doctor removed the cuff. "We'll have the lab results back in the morning. I'd offer you something to help you sleep tonight, but until we know if they drugged you, I don't dare give you anything."

Delaney shook her head. "I don't need it." The last thing she wanted was to be in a deep, unnatural sleep if one of Tighe's men found a way to track her.

Just the thought of Tighe made her jaw tighten with anger. Her eyes began to grow hot, stinging with unshed tears. He shouldn't have run. He shouldn't have died.

God, what an idiot she was to care.

Dr. Jensen said good night and closed the bedroom door behind her, leaving Delaney alone in the master suite of the FBI safe house. Phil had arranged for her to stay under a doctor's supervision until they figured out if she had, indeed, been drugged. In addition to Dr. Jensen, there were two highly trained guards inside with her and another two outside in case Tighe's brother, or others in his organization, came after her.

Until they understood what she'd stumbled into, they weren't taking any chances.

The only one she knew wouldn't come for her was Tighe himself.

She pressed the heel of her hand tight against her chest, trying to ease the awful ache. The tears she'd held at bay all day finally got the better of her, and she sank onto the bed, letting them go. Her tears turned to sobs as she cried, grieving for a man she'd never understood and barely even known. She couldn't regret her own actions, because she'd done what she had to do, but she could . . . and did . . . regret the outcome. She hated that Tighe had been so involved in illegal activities that he'd sacrificed his life rather than be taken in for questioning.

Lying back, tears rolling, she ached with loss. In some inexplicable way, they'd connected. She'd sensed a goodness in him, seen it in the man who'd been so intent on rescuing a little girl, he'd stumbled into the FBI's trap. And he'd understood her, maybe better than she understood herself. He'd claimed she sought the killers out of revenge. And she did. She absolutely did. But it was more than that, she could see that now. Somewhere in the back of her head was a belief held from childhood that if she could just catch the man who'd killed her mom, she could make it all right again. She could get rid of the ache she'd lived with all these years once and for all.

But that ache was so much more than righteous retribution. It was loss and grief. Betrayal.

Loneliness.

Once the tears started, tears she hadn't shed in years, she couldn't stop them. She cried for Tighe, and for the mother she still missed, and for the children whose own mothers had been stolen from them by a man Delaney couldn't catch. But mostly she cried for herself, for the loneliness that pressed in harder every day. A loneliness she hadn't even known she felt until a handsome, mercurial, strangely gentle man made it disappear.

A man who would never touch her again.

She didn't realize she'd fallen asleep until pain tore through her head with the force of a sledgehammer, slamming her awake with a breath-stealing gasp. She needed to call for Dr. Jensen. But before she could utter a sound, the darkness rushed up to envelop her. As the dark fog of agony stole her away, a single name screamed through her mind.

Tighe!

As Tighe stood in the war room, Delaney's cry tore through his head. He froze.

"Stripes! What's happening? Another vision?"

"Yes." He grabbed for the wall as blackness stole his sight. He saw Delaney lying on a bed, still and silent, her cheeks streaked with tears. His heart clenched, that warmth in his mind that connected with her throbbed with pain. Terrible pain.

Tighe! He felt the fog circling her, swirls of black threatening her.

He reached out to her, but the suffocating darkness had her in its grasp, pulling her down.

Tighe!

Her voice was smaller, more distant. And filled with such fear. Such pain.

Delaney.

He reached for her through his mind, but she slipped through his grasp, disappearing into the dark, perilous fog.

And then she was gone.

"Tighe?" Kara's voice broke through the fog.

The vision dissipated. He shook his head, clearing his sight as he blinked, trying to understand what he'd just seen, even as desperation to find her leaped inside him, rising side by side with a terror not his own.

Delaney's.

What had happened? Someone was hurting her. Or some *thing*.

He stilled. It had almost felt as if the vision itself had turned on her.

Goddess, yes, that was exactly what had happened. The visions had been growing too much for her human mind. Too strong. She'd finally broken beneath the weight of this one and fallen into that dark for good.

Deep in his heart he feared she wouldn't break free of it on her own.

He started for the door.

"What happened?" Lyon demanded.

"Delaney needs me. I've got to find her." *How?* She wouldn't have gone home. He was certain of that. He lunged from the room and strode down the hall toward the front door.

He heard her calling to him. Felt the pull of her through that accidental connection he'd formed with her when he'd tried to cloud her mind, and prayed it would be enough to follow.

Behind him, he heard Lyon barking orders. "Hawke, Kougar, and Jag, go with him. Take two different sedans this time, in case the humans took note of the first ones."

Lyon's voice receded as Tighe ran out the door. What if he couldn't find her? What if he did, and he couldn't reach her mind?

I have to save her.

Desperation and determination wove and twined inside him, fueled and fired by a rage that was all too real. The clone already threatened Tighe's own life. He would not let him and these evil visions destroy Delaney, too.

If they hadn't already.

As Tighe ran for the nearest car, he feared it might be too late. Even if he managed to find her, would there be anything left of her mind to save?

Chapter
Thirteen

Darkness swallowed her, swallowed everything. Sight, sound, even her sense of touch. Delaney felt nothing but the distant echoes of pain.

She had a sense that she was standing. Perhaps even walking. But where? With her hand, she reached out and touched nothing. She lifted her hand to her head, and it wasn't there.

Panic welled up, and she shoved it down, forcing logic into the void. *Not real. This isn't real.*

Her body was still lying on the bed where Dr. Jensen had left her. It was only her mind that had taken off, swept away by a vision she hadn't seen, into a darkness she didn't know how to escape.

The last time she'd glimpsed this darkness, Tighe had snatched her back before it could suck her in. But Tighe was dead.

Grief mixed with the panic that welled again, clawing at her mind. She struggled to escape, to find her way out of the dark, but it was as if she were trying to run with her feet set in concrete.

Lost. So lost.

Tears fell through the silent darkness as loneliness grew to gigantic proportions, a suffocating cold stamping out every thought.

The terror reared up, swallowing her whole as a single word screamed through her head again, shattering the choking silence.

Tighe!

"Turn right."

"You sure?" Hawke asked.

Tighe growled, his fingernails clenched into the palms of his hands. "Do it!"

The car turned onto a residential street in an upscale Arlington neighborhood.

"Expensive digs for an FBI agent," Jag drawled.

"The house isn't hers," Tighe said. "Ten bucks says it's acting as an FBI safe house. She's being guarded."

"We'll shift and knock them out," Hawke said. "Jag, you stay with the car."

Jag muttered something under his breath. Tighe didn't need to hear it to know the warrior was railing against the fates for not giving him the ability to keep his clothes on when he shifted.

"Which house?" Hawke asked.

"I'll tell you when I know." Tighe's sense of Delaney had been growing steadily since they left Feral

House, drawing him to her with a solid pull. His heart pounded as her terror weaved through his brain. Over and over, he heard her calling for him with a desperation, a hopelessness, that tore at his battered soul. She thought he was dead, yet knew he was her only hope.

She thought she was well and truly trapped.

"Here!" Tighe wasn't certain how he knew she was in the single upstairs bedroom with the light still on, but he knew.

Hawke continued to drive by the house, the night's darkness hiding the features of the men inside the car. They'd left the second sedan two streets over. If the situation went south, they'd split up and meet again elsewhere.

When they'd turned the next corner, Hawke parked along the side of the road.

"Shift," Tighe ordered, then called to the animal who lived inside him, pushing past the tiger, straight to the smaller form of house cat. As a younger Feral, he'd had to go first to his full tiger form before he could downsize. A serious handicap he'd quickly learned to overcome.

Jag, remaining in human form, opened the car door for him, and he leaped out onto the grass, Kougar behind him, Hawke soaring into the air.

As Tighe and Kougar ran toward the house on four feet, Hawke reported back.

Two guards patrolling the grounds outside—one in back, one watching the front from the bushes in the right front corner of the house. The fence is high and looks to be solid. I'll get the one in back.

Tighe replied. *I'll cloud the mind of the one in front and get him to open the door. Kougar and I'll go in. Wings, you keep watch.*

Will do.

Tighe ran through the yard, then slipped between the legs of the watching guard.

"Beat it." The man picked him up with his foot and tossed him half a dozen yards.

Damned human. Tighe came around behind him noisily, ensuring that the guard knew the movement behind him was a cat. Then he shifted and grabbed the man's neck before he knew what was happening. The moment the guard hit the ground, Tighe took control of his thoughts.

"You need to use the bathroom. When I tell you to, go into the house. Two cats will try to come in with you. You *must* let them in. Don't allow anyone to stop them. Once inside the house, you'll go into the bathroom and close the door, pull down your pants, then curl up on the floor and go to sleep."

The bastard's career would be over when they caught him, literally, with his pants down. But he deserved it for kicking a cat.

Tighe? Hawke's voice broke into his thoughts. *My guard's out. I'm flying up to the roof to keep watch.*

Good. Meet me beside the front porch, Kougar. We're going in.

"Wake, human, and do as I told you." As the guard rose to his feet, Tighe changed back into his cat form and raced for the front door.

The guard pulled out his phone. "I've got to take a crap. Change places with me."

Tighe trotted beside the human, leaping onto the front porch as the guard knocked on the door with a quick, light rhythm. As planned, the door opened and the two cats slipped inside.

"Hey!" The inside guard tried to stop their entry, but the one under Tighe's control blocked the swing of his foot.

"Leave them alone. They're not bothering anything."

Get control of things down here, Tighe told Kougar. *I've got to find Delaney.*

The Feral didn't answer, but Tighe didn't expect him to. He dashed for the stairs and the source of the terror clawing at his brain. The closer he got to her, the stronger the darkness swirled at the edges of his consciousness. And the stronger he felt her desperation. She was fighting her fate, as was her nature, but without help she was lost in there. And she knew it.

Her door was closed, which meant he was going to have to shift to reach her. The prudent thing to do was search out the rest of the upstairs first, to make sure he wasn't surprised again. But his need to reach her was too strong.

Tighe shifted in the empty hallway, but as he reached for the doorknob, he heard the click of a gun.

"Freeze! Hands in the air." A small, round woman with graying hair appeared at the other end of the hall, aiming a gun at his head. "Intruder!" she shouted.

Shit. This is so not happening. He needed to get to Delaney and he needed to reach her *now*.

He heard a short scuffle on the lower floor, then silence as a cat ran up the stairs. Kougar.

The woman was already talking into a phone. "It's him." She paused. "Agreed."

Tighe lifted his hands into the air, holding perfectly still. He could take another bullet if he had to, but he'd just as soon not. Not when Delaney needed him.

"I thought they'd shot you," the woman said conversationally.

Tighe didn't bother to answer as Kougar scooted past her, then shifted. The woman seemed to sense the change, but she was too slow turning around. Kougar jammed his thumb into the hollow at the base of her ear, stripping her gun from her hand as she went down.

Tighe grabbed for the door that separated him from Delaney. He found her exactly as he'd seen her in his vision, still and silent, her cheeks stained with tears.

"Delaney." He fell onto the bed beside her and reached for her hand. Like ice. "D, I'm coming for you. I'm not going to leave you in there. But you have to trust me this time. *Trust me*."

Raw terror pressed in around her, squeezing her mind until Delaney thought her brain would crumble beneath the weight. Her existence had narrowed down to this darkness, this place void of everything she'd ever known. This miserable pit of echoing pain and suffocating fear.

How long could she stay sane like this? Maybe it

was better if she didn't. Better to lose herself somewhere else. Anywhere else.

Delaney.

A voice whispered from the darkness. A deep voice she'd longed to hear so badly she'd started to create it for herself. Maybe that insanity would come quicker than she'd thought.

Delaney.

Tighe's voice. But Tighe was dead.

Trust me.

How many times had he asked her to do that? But she hadn't. Not fully. She couldn't. Not when she knew he was one of the bad guys.

Tighe?

Darkness swirled around her, a perfect void without sound, without sight, without feel except that persistent, distant pain. But the voice continued to speak in her head.

D, I'm coming for you. I'm not going to leave you in there, but you have to reach out to me. You have to trust me.

You're not real. You're dead. And yet there was something about his voice that brushed her mind with a familiar feel of warmth. Of strength.

I'm not dead, brown eyes. I'm right here with you. I'm trying to get you out. Can you feel my hands on your face?

No. I can't feel anything except the pain in my head, and even that isn't very strong.

Come to me, D. Follow the sound of my voice, then. Reach for me. Trust me.

I can't trust you. You ran from the Feds. The

words tore at her, sending a cascade of tears through her mind. *I can't trust you.*

Then at least trust me to get you out of here. You must reach for me.

Help me, Tighe.

Do you see the thread, D? The iridescent one?

I can't see anything!

Easy, sweetheart. Reach for me with your mind. Reach for me, D.

And suddenly she saw something gleaming, shining with a million colors. A tiny thread. As she reached for it, she felt the angel wings flutter inside her head, telling her she'd found it at last. No, not it. Tighe.

She felt his mind brush against hers, a soft thrill of pleasure in the feather-light touch, as she followed the thread. Little by little, it grew larger, brighter.

In a rush of warmth, he grabbed her mentally, his mind lifting her from the dark.

Sensation rushed back, overwhelmingly sweet, as she felt his strong arms go around her and pull her close against his warm body. She wrapped her arms around his neck and buried her face in his throat, clinging to him as joy squeezed her heart and rushed through her chest.

"You're alive." Tears streaked down her face as she felt his hand cradling the back of her head.

He pulled back, urging her to look at him. She did, her gaze searching the face of the man she'd thought she'd never see again.

His thumb traced her eyebrow. "You had me worried for a few minutes there, brown eyes. I wasn't sure I was going to be able to reach you."

"How are you alive?"

A shadow brushed past the open doorway.

"Tighe, we've got company. Lots of it by the looks of things. We're not going to be able to take her."

Tighe's expression tightened as he looked back down at her. "I'm going to have to leave you for now, but you need me, brown eyes. I'm the only one who can save you next time this happens." His mouth turned hard. "If you sic the Feds on me again, you're on your own. Don't turn on me again, Delaney. I mean it."

She forced herself to release him. "How do I find you?"

"Stand in the parking lot along the northeast side of the Tidal Basin at 5:30 A.M. In four hours. I'll drive through in a green Camry sedan and pick you up."

"How am I going to know it's green, let alone you, in the dark?"

"I'll have one halogen headlight and one normal one. You'll be able to tell."

"What if I can't get there that fast?"

"Do it. I want you with me before you get another vision."

"Tighe!" The man's voice shouted from the hallway. "We have to get out of here. Now!"

Tighe leaned down and kissed her hard, his hand sliding behind her neck, his thumb tracing her ear, then the hollow below it.

"Trust me, Delaney," he murmured against her lips, then pressed his thumb beneath her ear.

Darkness swallowed her again.

Delaney shoved her hands in the pockets of her blazer as she stood on the edge of the parking lot where Tighe had promised to pick her up. The sky was still dark, few cars on the road at this hour on a Sunday morning. Everything should go down exactly as planned.

As *she'd* planned, not Tighe.

Trust me, he'd begged her.

Her stomach felt like she'd swallowed nails. In some ways she did trust him. With her body. Oddly, she suspected, even with her life.

But she was an FBI agent. Sworn to uphold the law. She would not let her duty be derailed by feelings for a man she *knew* was involved in something hugely illegal. Feelings she didn't even understand.

When Tighe arrived to pick her up, he would be the one taken instead.

Her stomach clenched. The angel wings fluttered angrily. *He'd begged her to trust him.*

He had to be brought in for questioning. He was into something bad, and the Feds needed to know what it was.

He'd risked his life to come to her and free her from that dark prison. He hadn't even taken her with him, he'd just saved her.

Delaney pressed her fist against the aching lump sitting in her gut. *God, what had she done?*

Her job. She'd done her job. He was a criminal.

His brother a murderer. She had to catch them. She had no choice. He was a bad guy, blast it.

But he wasn't. Not completely. He had a good-ness in him, a gentleness. He'd rescued that little girl from the fire, hadn't he?

All her life she'd seen people as good or bad. Especially criminals. Yet Tighe didn't entirely fit either of those roles.

Delaney rubbed her fist against her churning stomach. Maybe he did. Maybe he wasn't one of the bad guys at all. All she knew for sure was that he was involved with something big and had refused to be taken by the Feds. All along her instincts had been telling her that he wasn't evil. What if her instincts were right? For all she knew, he could be part of some military special ops or other superse-cret team put together to battle terrorism and save the world.

Yes, he'd kidnapped her. And drugged her.

Good grief, was she really trying to convince herself he'd done all those things for the right rea-sons?

Yeah, maybe she was. He hadn't hurt her. He'd never hurt her. In fact, he'd gone to great lengths to keep her from being hurt. *He'd saved her.*

And she'd set him up *again* to be captured. What if he tried to escape and wasn't as lucky this time?

The knots in her stomach cramped.

She'd made Phil promise no one would shoot him, but even if they didn't intend to kill him, they abso-lutely meant to apprehend him. Too many people had died for them to let him get away.

She couldn't do this. She couldn't let them shoot him again. It was a mistake. A horrible mistake.

Delaney started running through the trees, toward the road. She had to keep Tighe from making that turn. She had to stop this.

But she'd barely gone ten yards when a car swung into the parking lot. A midsized sedan with one halogen headlight.

No.

A large bird of prey flew low over her head, but she barely noticed. She watched the car come to a slow stop not ten spaces into the lot, too far away for her to see Tighe's face. Immediately, half a dozen SWAT surrounded the car, weapons drawn. If he tried to get away this time, he was a dead man.

"Oh God, Tighe. What have I done?"

A large hand clamped around her mouth, as an iron arm pinned her against a hard chest.

"You did exactly what he expected you to," a deep, vaguely familiar voice said against her ear.

*Chapter
Fourteen*

Paenther turned at the sound of the blinkers to find Foxx preparing to pull the Mustang into a small, run-down convenience store set into the side of a steep, heavily wooded hill. An old sign hung above the single door. MARKET, it read. As if it were the only place to buy anything in this middle-of-nowhere deep in the mountains of western Virginia.

It probably was.

At the corner of the old brick building, a doe and a spotted fawn watched curiously until Foxx pulled into the nearly empty parking lot with a spray of gravel. The pair took off for the woods.

"Your gut telling you something?" Paenther eyed the redheaded Feral with a razor-sharp hope.

Foxx snorted. "Yeah. It's telling me I'm hungry."

With a thinly masked groan of disgust, Paenther tipped his head back against the headrest. Soon after the meeting at Feral House, Foxx announced that his gut was telling him they'd find Vhyper in the Blue Ridge Mountains, the narrow range that ran parallel to the East Coast from Georgia to Pennsylvania and met up with I–66 a little over an hour's drive west of D.C.

With nothing better to go on, he and Foxx had hightailed it out there and been driving aimlessly around this pastoral outback for the past seven plus hours. They'd covered nearly two hundred miles of country roads and so far found nothing.

Damned useless intuition. How was the cub supposed to read his gut when all it seemed to do was rumble with hunger?

The dust kicked up by Foxx's assault on the gravel covered the car in a light fog that wafted in the open window, making Paenther's nose twitch.

"Want anything?" Foxx swung his long, broad-shouldered frame out of the car.

Yeah, he wanted something. Several somethings. Vhyper, the Daemon blade, Tighe's clone. Not to mention the whereabouts of the Mage stronghold. None of which were likely to be found inside the Market.

With a growl of frustration, Paenther climbed out of the car and followed Foxx. For the moment, a hot dog and a Coke would have to do, but his always razor-thin patience was fraying fast. If that intuition of Foxx's didn't kick in soon,

Paenther was going to turn into some seriously bad company.

He strode across the narrow parking lot, his gaze constantly on the move. There were five cars scattered across the small parking lot, none of which looked like it was less than fifteen years old. None of which was Vhyper's. Across the rarely traveled two-lane was a small farmhouse set in the middle of a large pasture dotted with horses.

Not a mansion in sight. The Mage never lived in groups of fewer than thirty or forty, and there'd been no sign of any large residences around there. They were wasting their time.

Paenther pushed through the twin glass doors, spying Foxx in the middle of a narrow aisle, his hands already half-filled with junk food. How he could stand to eat that crap, Paenther didn't know. He grabbed the closing door as a harried-looking woman approached, pushing a crying baby in a stroller.

"Thanks," she said, smelling of stale milk and cigarettes as he held the door for her.

At the cash register, an elderly man bought a six-pack of beer. And at the magazine stand . . .

Paenther's gaze slowed, lingering with appreciation over the slender, feminine form of a young woman flipping through magazines. Her hair was very short and dark, her bone structure delicate. Ethereal.

Lovely.

As if she felt him watching, she turned her head and lifted sweeping, dark lashes to reveal eyes the bright blue of a summer sky. Their gazes caught, snapping together like two pieces of a puzzle. He felt the contact like a physical jolt. His pulse lifted. His blood began to run thick and hot, racing to the juncture of his thighs.

Goddess, when was the last time he'd reacted to a woman like that? Years ago. *Years* ago.

A soft gentle smile lifted her mouth, stealing his breath, causing his heart to do a slow tumble in his chest.

The beauty set down the magazine and walked back to the EMPLOYEES ONLY door a few yards away and disappeared.

"You ready, B.P.?" Foxx's voice called to him from the front of the store.

Slowly, Paenther turned to his companion, feeling as off-balance as a youth with his first crush. *Damn*. It was too bad he didn't have time to hang around there for a couple of hours. Or days.

He scowled at the foolish thought and grabbed a Coke from the cooler. The last thing he needed just then was his head turned by a woman. A human woman, no less.

The good news was, he knew he'd forget her as soon as they drove away. No woman held his interest for long these days.

Chapter Fifteen

Tighe paced the small bedroom in the basement apartment of the house in Dupont Circle as he waited for Delaney to wake. He hadn't dared take her back to Capitol Hill. Not when she'd probably been thoroughly debriefed by the FBI.

He crossed to the big bed, where she lay sleeping from Hawke's capture, once more clothed in that navy blue suit and white shirt that cried *Federal Agent*. Her dark hair was partially knotted at the nape of her neck, but tendrils had come loose to splay across the white satin pillowcase, framing her flawless olive-toned skin. Even in sleep, her expression was tense. Guarded. The shadows that darkened her soul refused to release her, even in sleep.

His body warmed at the sight of her, something

easing deep inside him. He hadn't been able to take a full breath, for worrying about her, until he had her back, safe in his keeping. Which he'd accomplished with relative ease. He'd known she'd set him up. From the moment he'd told her to meet him by the Tidal Basin, he'd planned for Hawke to grab her.

Tighe had ensnared the mind of a human male of his own approximate size and hair color and told him to drive the green Camry into the parking lot, stop the car, and fall asleep. Which he'd done. The FBI had been thoroughly put out, but the man hadn't been harmed.

And Delaney was back with him again.

No, this woman didn't trust. He knew that from what she'd told him of her past. And when he'd delved into her mind to pull her free of the darkness, he'd seen the scars of betrayal. Scars he himself had lived with for way too long.

While he'd been in her mind, he'd also seen the dark Daemon threads that formed her connection to the clone. The threads weren't strong ones, but they were tangled. He was going to have to find a way back into her head, then take some time to free her. Time he hadn't had at that moment.

The one thing he might have succeeded in doing was closing the door in her mind that had been dropping her into the darkness every time she got a vision. As he'd pulled her out, he'd tried to close it behind him, but he wouldn't know if he'd been successful until she had another vision. Even then, he couldn't be sure it wouldn't open and drag her down again.

A light rap on the door had Tighe crossing the

comfortable, expensively appointed room. Unlike the house on Capitol Hill, this one was lived in by a high-ranking Therian council member and his mate, Therians more than willing to accommodate the Ferals' request for the house. The town house had a setup far more conducive to their current needs, with a full apartment on the lowest level at the base of an open stair. Jag, Hawke, and Kougar would remain upstairs, taking turns keeping tabs on Tighe, while the others searched for the clone. With the separate levels, and a bit of luck, Delaney would never see them.

Tighe opened the door to Hawke, who handed him a tray laden with cold meat, hot stew, and a pitcher of cold water.

"Knock on the wall if you need anything." Hawke motioned toward Delaney with his head. "She should be coming out of it soon. I didn't press that hard."

Tighe nodded, then turned at a sound from the bed. Delaney was beginning to stir. Hawke closed the door as Tighe set the tray down on the dresser, then stood rooted, watching as the woman who consumed his thoughts slowly opened her eyes.

Her head turned, and she froze as her gaze zeroed in on him. She stared at him, a strong, enigmatic tide rising inside her, and he was suddenly glad he'd taken the time to take her weapons from her as she slept. Though that move might wind up saving his life, he'd done it to save hers. He'd have hated for one of those guns to have accidentally gone off as she slept. He'd never have forgiven himself if she'd died.

A fist clutched at his heart, possessiveness powering through him with a sudden, fierce anger. He paced in a tight, harsh path. It was all he could do not to lunge for her, to grab her by the shoulders and shake her.

"What would have happened if you'd had another of those visions, D? What if you got lost in there again?"

As he railed, she swung her long legs over the side of the bed and firmly closed the distance between them. He braced himself for her attack.

Until her lashes swept up, revealing eyes awash in tears.

"D?"

Her arms flew around his neck as her mouth reached for his kiss.

All thought flew from Tighe's head as he hauled her against him and kissed her, thrusting his tongue inside her warm and waiting mouth. Passion flared, a fire beyond anything he'd ever known. Sweet nature, but he needed her. He needed to touch her, hold her, bury himself deep inside her.

Delaney clung to him as her soft, warm body pressed against him, and her fingers slid into his hair. She kissed him as if she were starving, and he was the finest feast, filling his chest with a wondrous, powerful pressure. He drank of her kisses, sweeping his tongue across her own, over her teeth and lips, unable to get enough.

His tattered soul sang as her mouth left his to trail kisses along his cheek and jaw, traveling down his neck, setting his skin aflame, lighting a fire with every soft, damp touch of her mouth.

But he forced himself to pull away. "Delaney."

Her dark gaze swung to his. "I tried to stop you from driving into the trap. I couldn't do it, Tighe. I couldn't let them take you. But you knew I'd set you up. How?"

"I understand you."

Those dark eyes studied him, a contrast of hard and soft. "You're not angry?"

"That you endangered yourself, yes. But I understand why you did it. I *respect* why you did it. You're loyal to your job and to a greater cause, which you believe in. You owe me nothing, D. Not even your trust." He ran his palm over her soft hair. "But I can't tell you I'm not glad you'd changed your mind about letting them nail me."

Her palm lifted to lie warmly against his cheek, easing the tempest in his soul. "I shouldn't trust you. I'm not sure I *do* trust you. But I care what happens to you."

Tighe stroked her hair. "I've had the same thoughts, brown eyes. The exact same thoughts."

"It's as if . . . I need you." She looked so confused, so lost. Again, almost exactly the way he felt himself.

And needing her was the worst possible thing he could do. Because there were only two ways this could end for them. One, was death. The second, if they managed to catch his clone before his soul completely disintegrated, was apart. He'd take her memories of him and send her back to her life while he turned back to his own. Unlike her, though, he wouldn't forget. He'd never forget.

Goddess, but he didn't want to let her go.

Tighe swept her into his arms and carried her to the bed she'd just vacated, depositing her in the middle and following her down as her arms opened to embrace him. The expression on her face was one of soft welcome and rough need. His breath caught as lust and tenderness barreled through him.

He covered her mouth again, needing to taste her. When he felt her hands move to tug his shirt out of his pants, his heart stuttered. Did she know what she was doing? Did he?

Her hand slid lower, between them, a single, soft stroke to his cock through his pants. His eyes rolled back in his head at the exquisite pleasure and the desire that swamped him. When his body was capable of movement again, he lifted his hand and covered her breast, desperate to touch her. Without clothes. Goddess, he wanted her without clothes.

Somewhere in the back of his mind, his logical self warned him this wasn't a good idea. She was human. Unacceptable as lover or mate. Worse, he could be riding the edge of chaos again at any moment. What if during the act of sex, as he lost control to the lovemaking, he lost control of himself? What if it shattered his soul once and for all?

Deep inside, the tiger shook its head. Making love to her was all that would keep him together.

Tighe pushed himself onto his knees and straddled her as he unbuttoned his shirt and shrugged out of it. Then his fingers moved to her white blouse and quickly unbuttoned it, pushing aside the flaps to reveal a tan lace bra covering firm mounds, the dark nipples just peeking through.

Heat surged inside him, sending the blood pumping straight to his erection.

With a quick flick, he unlatched the front clasp of her lacey bra, unwrapping her soft, full breasts for his waiting eyes.

She was beautiful. *Beautiful*. He covered those perfect mounds with his hands, feeling the hard nubs graze his palms. His fingers pressed into the softness that molded to his shaking hands, drawing a low moan of desire from Delaney's throat. He squeezed her breasts, then pinched her nipples. Not too hard, but hard enough to elicit a gasp. He moved down on her, his head dipping to take one plump nipple into his mouth, stroking the hard nub with his tongue as his hand squeezed and kneaded the other.

"Tighe." His name on her lips was soft as a breath and filled with such need he thought he might lose it then and there. "I want you inside me."

With a last flick of his tongue over the hard bud, he lifted his face to peer down into hers. His breath caught at the need he saw in her face.

Her fingers rose to spread over his chest. A groan escaped his throat for one hot moment, before he dipped his head and took her other breast in his mouth.

Inside her. It was the only place he wanted to be, but he needed more. He needed everything. To touch every inch of her. To taste every part of her.

Now. He had to taste her now.

Tighe moved back and unfastened her belt and pants with shaking fingers, then yanked them off her, hooking his fingers into her panties and removing them at the same time, baring her long legs to his hungry gaze. Long legs tipped with dark socks and an ankle holster.

With a hungry grin, he removed the last articles of clothing, then sat back and stared at her.

Sweet thunder. His palms slid up those long legs, his palms rough against her satin flesh as he traced her trim calves, her knees. His thumbs brushed the insides of her thighs, eliciting a gasp from her, sending his pulse rate soaring.

Gripping her legs just above the knee, he opened her, lifting her knees and spreading her wide, like parting twin doors to reveal the treasure inside. His heart nearly stopped beating at the perfection revealed to his seeking gaze. Nestled between slender thighs, she was perfect. Swollen, open, and as dewy as a flower at dawn.

"Tighe." Her voice throbbed with desire.

He tore his gaze away from her body and met her eyes. The heat swirling in those dark, vibrant depths was nearly his undoing. He ached to enter her, but not yet. Not until neither of them could stand it a moment longer. Because he feared this might be the only time he ever would.

"Patience, brown eyes. I'm getting there. But I have to taste you."

Like a predator pouncing on prey, he knelt between her legs and went down on her, stroking his tongue along that long, perfect opening. She jerked, arching, her fingers clutching in his hair as a low moan vibrated through her entire body. Her pleasure weaved through his own, heightening his enjoyment and desire. He pressed his tongue deep within those open folds, tasting her sweet nectar, then found the hard knot between those folds and flicked it with his tongue.

Delaney cried out, her fingers digging into his scalp.

With a hard grin of satisfaction, he pleasured her until she was writhing beneath his mouth.

"Tighe. *Tighe.*"

She was nearly to climax, but he wasn't ready to take her there. Not until he was buried deep inside her. She would fly for him. For *him*.

With a last thrust of his tongue, Tighe moved up her body, kissing her stomach, then the cleft between her breasts.

Delaney cradled his head in her arms as he kissed first one breast, then the other, then lifted his face to her. She pulled him up and kissed him hard even as she rocked her hips against his painfully hard erection.

"Come inside me," she whispered against his lips. "Now, Tighe. I need you, now."

His hands cradled her face, then dove into her hair. "Not, yet, brown eyes. I'm not through loving your body. I may not be through for hours."

Her groan made him smile, and he thought he might just be telling the truth. He was going to love her so thoroughly, mark her so completely that even when he'd stolen her memories of him from her mind, she'd remember their lovemaking in her dreams. He wanted that. With a ferocity that made no sense, he wanted to live somewhere in her mind. Forever.

She tried to reach for his cock, and he grabbed her wrist.

"Easy, D. One stroke, and it might just be over. And neither of us wants that."

She made a sound that was half groan, half laughter. "Speak for yourself." She pushed at his chest. "But if that's the way you want it, lie down. It's my turn."

He didn't think it was possible, but he got even harder. "You touch me in any way, and it's going to be over."

A small knowing smile lifted her lips. "Then I won't touch you there."

Hesitating for only a moment, he moved off her and did as she demanded, watching, enrapt, as she stripped out of her jacket, shirt, and bra with a single move. She was glorious in her nakedness, her dark hair falling around her shoulders in soft waves. With a move that sent fire arcing through his veins, she lifted one leg and straddled him, her wet sheath nestled tight against his zipper.

From her perch, she watched him with a mixture of softness and power. On his tongue he tasted the sweetness of an emotion he couldn't quite put a name to, an emotion he could taste for the rest of his life and never tire of.

Delaney leaned forward, her fingers tracing the gold armband on his arm, then moving over the feral mark, the claw marks, above his left breast, exploring him. She bent her head until her lips brushed the feral marks, sending a shock of chills through his body.

She was kissing the very thing that had once destroyed everything he'd cared about, as if she understood. As if she accepted them. And him.

When nothing could be further from the truth.

Delaney Randall had no idea he'd been marked by the tiger. That he was immortal. That he was a shape-shifter. And if she ever figured out what he was, she'd turn and run. Just as Gretchen had.

No she wouldn't. Running wasn't her style. Delaney would get her gun and hunt him down like the monster he was.

She rose from kissing his chest, her eyes tight with question and soft with concern as she laid her hand over the scars on his chest.

"That bothered you. That I kissed you there."

Had his thoughts shown that clearly? He reached for her, stroking her cheek. "The scars bring back memories. Unpleasant ones. You didn't do anything wrong."

"I'm sorry for whatever hurt you, Tighe. Or whoever."

"It was a long time ago." But warmth filled his chest at the compassion in her eyes. Sweet nature, but he wouldn't allow anyone to hurt her. Ever. Even after he'd stolen her memories of him, he'd watch over her from a distance. Protect her in any way he could for the short years of her existence.

The thought of it, that she wouldn't be completely lost to him, eased the tight ache in his chest. She wouldn't be out of his life. His role in hers would just change.

But this would probably be the only time he'd ever make love to her.

*Chapter
Sixteen*

Delaney ran her hands over the hard planes of
Tighe's chest as she straddled his half-clothed
body, reveling in the beauty of the man. Sunshine
poured across his muscled contours, glinting off
the antique gold armband he wore, an armband,
she realized, with an attractive, stylized tiger's
head. Her gaze moved to the rippling muscles of
his arms as damp heat pooled deep in her body.
He was glorious, and she wanted him so badly, she
was shaking with it.

Bracing her hands on his chest, she rubbed herself
against the hard length of the erection between her
legs, an erection still fully covered by his pants. It was
a problem she was more than ready to dispose of.

"D." He gripped her hips, holding her still. "Not

yet." He looked up at her with an expression that seemed to be a mix of heat, pain, and tenderness. Seemed to be because she couldn't see his eyes behind those shades. He'd never once let her see his eyes, and she wanted to see them. Needed to see them.

She reached for his sunglasses, but he snatched her wrists. "No, brown eyes." He lifted his hips, pressing against her sensitive flesh, distracting her as he no doubt intended. "Undress me, Delaney."

For a moment longer, she looked at his face, always half-closed to her. He didn't fully trust her. And why should he, any more than she trusted him? They were on opposite sides of the law. From opposite worlds.

What was she even doing with him? She knew virtually nothing about him. She didn't even know his full name!

He rocked against her again, sending pleasure cascading through her body. Reminding her where she was. And what she wanted. At this moment, at least.

Theirs wasn't a relationship so much as an encounter. And it wouldn't last. It *couldn't* last. But for this short time, he was hers, and she intended to enjoy every moment of it.

She bent her head to trail her lips over the hard planes of his body, then reached for the zipper of his pants.

He groaned. "*D.*"

She pulled his pants off him as he had hers. Beneath the soft jeans she found green silk boxers and slid her palm against the ridge beneath.

Tighe sucked his breath in hard. "Take them off," he groaned. And she did, sliding the silky fabric down his hips, revealing the largest, thickest erection she'd ever seen. Not that she'd seen that many. All of two. Still, Tighe's was . . . extraordinary.

"You're huge," she breathed.

Even through his sunglasses, she could feel his gaze on her. His fingers slid between her legs. "That's why you're going to be ready, sweetheart. Wet and open and crying for me to take you before I enter you."

His words sent the heat inside her flaring as she groaned from his touch. "What makes you think I'm not already?" She pulled his boxers all the way off, but as she turned to toss them onto the floor, Tighe rose and grabbed her around the waist, turning her until she was on her hands and knees on the bed.

"Tighe."

He knelt beside her, one hand cupping her breast while the other traced her spine to her tailbone and lower, sliding into the crease of her buttocks. His finger found her wet, ready heat and slid inside.

Fire shot through her, and she arched, hissing with pleasure as his finger dove deep inside her. She pressed against his hand, wanting more. *Needing* more.

"Easy, brown eyes." He added a second finger, then a third. While his fingers probed her depths, his other hand played with her breast, twirling her nipple until she was gasping with desire.

"*Tighe.*"

By the time his fingers left her, her breathing was labored, her pulse thick, desire pounding through her body. She rose onto her knees and faced him, pushing at his shoulders. "I either want you inside me, or I want to taste you, as you tasted me. Your choice."

His mouth widened, not quite a smile, but definitely a satisfied look. Then he pulled her against him, chest to chest, and kissed her, sweeping his tongue inside her mouth.

Without warning, he fell back onto the pillow, pulling her down on top of him. "You can taste me. For as long as I can stand it. *Goddess*, but I want your lips on me."

He released her, and she smiled, pushing herself off his chest and turning, her gaze caressing that long thickness. With a single finger, she traced the throbbing vein running from the base of his shaft all the way to the head, delighting in the sharp intake of his breath.

Her fingers slid down the satin flesh, reveling in the feel of him. Clasping him gently, she bent and ran her tongue over the slit at the tip, tasting the drop of moisture clinging there. She twirled her tongue around the head and was just about to pull him fully into her mouth when his hands grabbed her hips.

"Lift your leg, D."

"I'm not through."

He moaned. "I hope not. But I want my mouth on you, too."

Her eyes widened, and she grabbed hold of his

thighs, bracing herself as he pulled her hips back and situated her knees on either side of his face.

Then . . . *oh God*. At the exact moment he thrust his shaft into her mouth, his tongue dove into her core. Sensations exploded throughout her body as she sucked on the flesh in her mouth, giving him pleasure even as she took it from him in return. His lovemaking was a heady mix of gentleness and aggression, his hands on her hips shaking, gripping her tightly, telling her clearly of his own barely restrained passion.

He began to suck on her sensitive nub until her hips were rocking of their own volition, desperate for the release that was almost there. Almost there. The closer she came to completion, the harder she sucked on him, until he suddenly pulled her away and flipped her onto her back.

Then he was over her, spreading her legs with his knee. "I have to be inside you, brown eyes." His voice was taut. Pained.

"*Yes.*"

"Look at me, Delaney. *Look at me.*"

But when she tried, all she saw was herself reflected in those damned sunglasses. Her spurt of annoyance disappeared as he pushed that thick head against her opening. She gasped as he pressed into her, stretching her. Her body was wet and ready, and the feel of him exquisite. Beyond pleasure. Beyond anything she'd ever dreamed she could feel.

"Okay?" he asked.

"Ah," she groaned, wrapping her arms around

his sweat-slicked back. "*Yes. Oh, yes.* Better than okay. Better than . . . *Oh, Tighe,*" she moaned, as he pushed all the way inside, pulled nearly out of her, then thrust back inside, faster than before. Her eyes rolled back, her eyelids dropping as incredible pleasure became her entire world.

"Delaney, *look at me.*"

She forced her eyes open as he thrust inside her again and again, his rhythm hard and demanding, at once rough and infinitely gentle.

Again, she stared at herself in the reflection of his sunglasses. *Blast it.* Here they were as intimate as they could possibly be, and she couldn't even see his eyes. On a spurt of annoyance, she reached up and grabbed the sunglasses, yanked them off his face, and tossed them onto the floor.

"D, *no.*" His eyes snapped closed before she could see so much as a hint of the green eyes she'd seen on his twin. "*Damn it.*"

"I want to see you."

Eyes closed, he thrust into her, his face a hard mask of concentration. "Your timing sucks, brown eyes." His mouth came down on hers, and he kissed her hard, almost punishingly, driving home just how little she knew him.

Just how many secrets lay between them.

A lump formed in her throat, mired in anger, even as her body rose, swept away by the desire that flared within her whenever he was close. When the orgasm finally swept over her, she gave herself to it, soaring briefly before crashing back to reality.

She'd given herself to a man in a mask. A man

who, even in lovemaking, kept a solid wall between them. What an idiot she was for thinking she could trust him. How could she forget she knew virtually *nothing* about him. Good grief, she didn't even know his full name.

She'd never even seen his eyes!

Tighe finished on a satisfied groan, then almost immediately pulled out of her and vaulted to the floor to fetch his sunglasses.

Angry with him and disgusted with herself, she rolled off the bed on the other side, gathered up her clothes, and strode to the bathroom visible on the other side of the room.

"D?"

She slammed the door and locked it behind her. Then she dropped her clothes on the cushioned stool and leaned back against the door.

Sex with a stranger. That's all it had been. A man she didn't even know. A man who wouldn't even look her in the eye. When she'd first woken up and seen him, she'd felt a rush of joy, a need to be in his arms, as if that were the only place she truly belonged. For a short while, she'd allowed herself to be swept away by the fantasy that he was a good man. A man who'd come after her because he cared about her. A fantasy that she was falling just a little bit in love with him.

Ludicrous.

For him she was only a means to an end. A way to catch his brother. And she was an FBI agent with the same mission. It was time she remembered that.

With a growl of frustration, she pushed away from the door to start the shower. He was her captor, plain and simple. Forgetting that small fact and deluding herself into thinking she was developing feelings for him could well get her killed.

Tighe stared at the closed bathroom door, Delaney's bitter unhappiness lingering on his tongue. He'd known there could never be anything real between them. There were too many lies. Too much she must never know.

And she was beginning to understand that he would never let her in. He'd hoped he could at least finish making love to her before the truth came crashing down on him, but even that wasn't meant to be.

He locked the bedroom door from the outside, then went upstairs to take a shower and change.

"No wonder you were so keen on getting your hands on this one again," Jag drawled as he walked through the upstairs living room. "I heard her screaming from here."

Tighe whirled on him. "Do you want to see my claws?" he bit out.

Jag lifted his hands, palms out. "Nope. Don't mind me."

Tighe took a quick shower and was back in the basement apartment, waiting for her, when Delaney came out of the bathroom.

Her gaze met his only briefly as she stepped into the bedroom, dressed once more in the white shirt and navy pants, her hair wet and slicked back from her face.

"Where are my guns?"

"Safe. And out of your reach."

She crossed her arms over her chest and lifted her chin in challenge. "You said once that if you could get rid of my memories of you, you'd let me go. Is that still true?"

Inside, the tiger shook its head in denial.

"Yes." He met that challenging gaze, his chest seizing. "If I can get into your mind, I can free you. Then I can absolutely let you go."

"I won't remember anything? I won't remember you?"

"No."

She nodded once with hard satisfaction. "Do it."

No. Not yet. He wasn't ready to send her back. Yet if he could get inside her head, he knew what had to be done to free her from those visions. Which meant he'd almost certainly succeed in stealing her memories, too. He'd succeed in wiping himself from her mind. And her life.

"Delaney."

That was what he wanted, wasn't it? Of course it was. No attachments, especially to a human. Her back in her own world. Him free to fight the battles he had to fight without worrying about her.

Without her calming touch.

Without those wide, dark eyes questioning his every move. Filling with heat whenever he touched her. Shining with courage and fire and life.

"*Now*, Tighe. I'm tired of being your captive. I

want my life back. I want you to get into my mind so I can be rid of you once and for all."

Her anger washed over him, a hot, biting rush that set off an ache deep in his chest. When he was through with her, she wouldn't remember him, not a thing about him. And he had a terrible feeling he would never forget *her*.

Tighe grabbed her face and kissed her hard, marking her, daring her to push him away. Daring her to prove she only wanted to be rid of him. Her resistance lasted all of five seconds, then she melted in his arms and kissed him back fiercely, her arms sliding around his neck, her tongue twisting and twining with his. Desire flared, and the next thing he knew, his hands were in her hair, and he was thinking of nothing but stripping her of the clothes she'd just put on and sliding into her all over again.

What am I doing?

He wasn't thinking. He couldn't think when she was close, let alone touching him, kissing him. Forcing himself to pull back, he stared down into her dazed eyes.

An odd mix of protectiveness and tenderness welled inside him, the ache in his chest intensifying as he raised his hand and stroked her cheek.

She was right. As much as he hated the prospect of wiping himself from her life, the sooner he did it the better. If he hadn't freed her by the time his soul splintered, her life was over. Lyon would see to it.

He traced her high cheekbone with his thumb.

"Are you going to do it?" she asked.

Tighe nodded slowly, pulling his scattered thoughts to the task at hand. Never before had he had any trouble clouding the thoughts of a human. But never before had he tried to breach the formidable barriers of Delaney Randall. And maybe that was the problem.

"Why don't you try helping me this time, D? When you feel me pressing against your mind, let me in. Don't fight me."

"I'm not fighting you."

"Yeah, you are, though maybe not consciously. This time, I want you to think about wanting me to come in. Do you remember when I pulled you out of the darkness?"

"Is this the same?"

"In a way, yes. But you weren't at the gates that night. You weren't there at all. I had to go deep to find you and pull you back."

"Could you have captured my mind then?"

"Probably. If I'd had time. Once I get in there, I have to disentangle you from the clone."

She watched him warily. "From the what?"

"From the . . . never mind. If it gets bad, tell me, and I'll quit. Are you ready?"

"Yes."

He pushed her damp hair back from her face with his fingers. "Think of that night, D, of how I came for you. Think of how you needed me. How you could need me again. Then let me in. Right now, right here. Let me in, Delaney."

His thumbs moved to her temples, and he rubbed

gently, staring deep into her eyes. "I won't hurt you, brown eyes. Let me in." He didn't push this time, but still, he tasted her desire on his tongue, rising more slowly, but rising all the same.

"You're going to make me come again, aren't you?" she whispered, but her voice was soft, with little inflection, as if she were at least partially mesmerized.

"That's not the plan, but it seems to happen every time I get too close to you, doesn't it? Relax, Delaney. Let me in."

Little by little, he felt her resistance give way. Excitement lifted his pulse. Dismay caught in his chest. It was going to work. He was going to be able to send her back.

He felt her mind catch with his and open. *He was in.*

"That's a girl. Just relax, D. Let's see what we've got here." With his mind he found again that twisted, tangled mass of dark Daemon threads and tried to follow it, to find the place where they attached. Damn, but they went deeper than he'd expected.

Beneath his hands, he felt her tensing. "Is this getting uncomfortable?"

"A little."

"Hang in there, sweetheart." Maybe it wasn't as bad as it looked. Maybe if he . . .

He gave a mental tug on one of the threads.

Delaney gasped.

"That hurt?"

"Yes."

Damn. Little by little, he eased deeper, feeling her stiffen. If he could just find the source.

Once more, he gave a gentle tug, but Delaney cried out, and he stopped. *Dammit.* There was no way he could hope to free her without damaging her. There was nothing he could do for either of them but kill that son of a bitch clone.

Deep in his own mind, the tiger raised his head and gave a soft roar of satisfaction, then leaped to his feet, eyeing the bright opening into Delaney's mind.

Tighe saw what was about to happen. His mind seized. He had no way to stop it.

The tiger, already intrigued by her, leaped through that opening, trying to claim her for his own.

Delaney screamed.

Tighe wrenched the tiger back, but it was too late.

Delaney reared back, her pulse rocketing upward, her eyes glazing with terror, triggering the ancient fury that lived inside him, the rage of Gretchen's betrayal, as fearful eyes always did.

But the fury was too much for his thinning control. He clawed to hang on, to keep from losing himself in a feral rage from which he might never escape. But it was too late.

End over end, his mind tumbled into the chaos, hurtling him headlong toward that black abyss.

Chapter
Seventeen

Delaney stared in horror as the frightening vision in her mind gave way to a far more terrifying one in front of her. As Tighe released her, claws sprouted from his fingertips. Fangs sprang from his gums.

She stumbled back, slamming into the wall, her pulse pounding in her throat.

"Tighe?"

As she stared at him, colored lights erupted beneath his skin. And suddenly he was gone.

A tiger . . . a tiger. . .

This. Is. Not. Happening.

She was *not* staring at a *huge* tiger. The very beast who'd leaped at her in her head!

Her blood went cold. Her head began to spin. *Not real. Not happening.*

She was crazy. *Crazy.*

The tiger turned to her, staring at her with the same hunger she'd seen in her mind. He started toward her. Panic ignited.

With a strangled scream, she whirled and lunged for the door before he attacked her. Before he tried to rip her limb from limb.

As she reached for the door, she looked back only to see the tiger disappear in the same wash of sparkling lights, returning to the creature that was neither man nor beast, but something horribly in between.

With a strangled cry, she grabbed the door, frantic to escape. *Too late.* Sharp knives plunged into her shoulders. She screamed from the pain, from the terror of knowing she was about to become tiger food.

The creature pulled the knives from her and whipped her around. Blood dripped from his claws. *Her blood.* He squeezed her shoulders, sinking those claws into her a second time.

Her mind went white with pain as she flung her head back. Unable to move. Unable to breathe. Blood ran down her chest and back and trickled down her arms.

"*Don't fear me!*" he growled between those terrifying teeth.

Tighe's voice. "*Tighe.*" The word came out on a hiss of pain as her vision started to darken around the edges.

Behind her, the door burst open, knocking her into the creature. Tighe. *Not Tighe.*

His grip on her tightened. She screamed.

Two large men hurtled into the room and pulled Tighe off her in a haze of blood and agony, attacking him. Tackling him to the ground, ripping at him with fangs and claws.

Not real. Not real.

One hard swipe ripped Tighe's face wide open. The flesh hung in bloody strips from the bones.

They were going to kill him.

She tried to lunge forward but was held back by a strong arm around her waist. "Let's get you out of here." That voice. The same one who'd rescued her from Tighe's violence. The one who'd knocked her out beside the Tidal Basin.

"They're going to kill him." She struggled against the heavy weakness and terrible pain, struggled to free herself. "I can't let them kill him!"

"He'll be fine, Delaney. You're the only one in danger here."

He half pushed her, half carried her out of the room, then swept her up as her legs gave way. The pain was too much. Tears slid down her cheeks.

The man lowered her onto a sofa. She collapsed against the soft back, then cried out at the pressure against her wounds.

The man took her hand and she gripped his hard, gasping to breathe against the pain.

"I'm sorry you had to get mixed up in this."

His long face swam in the narrowing circle of her vision. Her head was too heavy to hold up, and she had to let it fall back against the sofa, but she struggled to meet the man's dark gaze.

"Help him. *Please.*"

* * *

Dimly, voices penetrated the haze of violence.

"She's alive, but she won't stay that way for long unless we get her to a healer. She's bleeding like a sieve."

"Let her die. She's seen too much."

No! The denial rang through Tighe's head, but no human sound came from his mouth. Nothing but snarls and growls as he thrashed against the restraints, pinned beneath the weight of three men.

Hawke's face appeared in front of him. "Fight your way back, buddy. Delaney's going to die if you don't."

"Sounds to me like she's going to die either way," a third voice drawled.

Hawke scowled. "Shut up, Jag."

The faces bled together, merging with the colors that passed for his sight. Reds and yellows and oranges. Violence. Fury.

He growled, struggling to free himself. To attack.

"Can you hear me, Tighe? Fight your way out of there, buddy. You hurt Delaney. She's bleeding badly. She needs you."

"Why the fuck do you think he cares?" Jag drawled.

"He doesn't care," Kougar replied. "He's using her to reach the visions."

"He cares," Hawke said. "Don't you, buddy?" Hawke's face swam back into focus. "Do you know, she fought me when I tried to get her out of here? She was struggling to get to you. To save you. From *us*."

The words penetrated the feral rage to reach his mind. She was trying to save him. Save *him*.

"Brown eyes." The words were more growl than actual words, but he formed them.

"That's it, Tighe. Come back to us. *Fight your way back, buddy.*"

She needs me. Brown eyes needs me.

He fought the chaos, struggling against its hard grip until he was sweating and panting from exertion. Finally, *finally*, with a groan of exhausted triumph, he pulled out of its grasp and away from the fury, snapping back into his skin.

His fangs and claws retracted, and he collapsed against the floor.

"*Get off me.*"

"Let him go!" Hawke snapped.

Kougar and Jag released him, and Tighe struggled to his feet, exhausted and bloody. "*Where is she?*"

"The sofa."

Tighe stumbled through the door, his strength returning with every step. But he pulled up short when he saw her. Ice washed through his veins. She was sitting up, but barely, sunk deep into the sofa cushions, drenched in blood. *Her blood. Which he'd drawn.*

Sweet thunder. *What have I done?*

He sank onto the sofa beside her and stared at her too-pale face. "Delaney."

Her lashes swept slowly upward, her dark eyes glazed. "Tighe?"

His knuckles brushed her cheek. Unblemished. Thank the goddess he hadn't tried to hold her face. "I'm sorry, brown eyes. I never meant to hurt you. I'm going to get you help." He turned to find Hawke standing in the doorway watching him.

"Call Esmeria. Tell her we're on our way."

But Hawke didn't move. Kougar stepped into the doorway behind him. "It's forbidden to take a human to the enclave. You know that."

"I don't give a fuck what's forbidden. She's going to die!"

He grabbed his cell phone and speed dialed Lyon and began talking the second Lyon answered. "I went feral and attacked the Fed. She needs a healer. Either I take her to a human hospital or to Esmeria. Your call, but you're making it *now*. She's out of time."

"Have you taken her memories?"

"No."

"She saw you feral?"

"She's seen it all. Feral, tiger, shift, you name it. I lost control. I tried to shift to my tiger to regain it, but I couldn't stay there. I was too far gone."

"Tighe . . ."

"No!" He knew what he was going to say. "She lives, Roar. You have two choices, and that's it."

"She can't be near other humans with the knowledge she now possesses. Nor can you take her to other Therians when you can't wipe her mind."

Tighe began to growl low in his throat, the fury threatening to sweep him away all over again until Delaney's soft hand slid over the back of his, pulling him back into his skin.

"Tighe." Hawke's voice dragged his attention back into the room. "Put Lyon on speaker."

With only a moment's hesitation, Tighe pressed the button.

Lyon's deep voice echoed into the room. "Neither option is acceptable, Stripes. I'm sorry."

Hawke took a step toward the phone. "There's another option, Chief. If he binds her to him, she can't betray him. Or us."

Tighe's blood went cold. *Bind* her? *A human?* "No way. I'm not making her my mate."

Hawke shrugged. "Your choice."

He couldn't. *Couldn't.*

It wouldn't be for long. Sixty years. Maybe seventy. Not long. But she knew what he was now. Seventy years living with that look of fear, that loathing.

"I can't."

"Then she dies," Hawke said softly.

Marry her or let her die.

Your choice. But was it?

He looked down at Delaney and found her watching him, a glimmer of warrior's strength still visible in the dull pools of pain that had become her eyes.

A blade ripped through his chest at the thought of permanently quelling that bright, fierce spirit.

"Which do you choose, Delaney, knowing what I am? Death? Or me for the rest of your life? Your choice."

She didn't hesitate. "Don't . . . want to die."

He squeezed her hand. "Then you won't. You

won't die." *What am I doing?* He turned back to the phone. "I'm binding her." His gaze speared Hawke's. "Call Esmeria and tell her we'll pick her up in ten minutes. Bring whatever she needs to heal a human in the car. We're going to Feral House."

What am I doing?

But he knew. As he'd done six hundred years before, he was once again consigning himself to the hell of tying himself to a human.

Chapter Eighteen

Paenther's fist tapped with rhythmic frustration against the car's door handle as Foxx drove past yet another damned field full of cows. The hills of the Blue Ridge rose around them, keeping their secrets . . . if they held any.

He was seriously beginning to think Foxx's intuitive gift had flown. They'd found no sign of the Mage. No sign of Vhyper. Goddamn *nothing*.

Except a girl with eyes like a summer sky. A girl he couldn't get out of his head.

"Go back to that country store we stopped at yesterday. The one set into the hillside. The Market."

The words were out before he had time to think about them, but he didn't call them back. He flexed and fisted both hands, hating the uncharacteristic lack of control that had him needing to see her again.

Goddess help him, he was acting like a fifteen-year-old with a massive hard-on.

"Why?" Foxx threw him a questioning look. "I thought we were going to take this search systematically."

Paenther growled. "Just do it." He'd finally given up hope that Foxx would lead them to the exact location. Knowing the Mage would be in some kind of mansion, they'd downloaded satellite images of the mountains and had been traveling from estate to estate ever since. In his animal form, Foxx was able to run right up to the houses and have a look around. Paenther had to wait for nightfall to join him since he lacked the ability to downsize into a house cat. If they did stumble onto a Mage stronghold, his panther form would give him away in a heartbeat.

So far, they'd struck out.

Yet Foxx continued to insist they'd find Vhyper in the Blue Ridge.

For twenty-four hours they'd searched estate after estate. Paenther pressed his fists into his thighs. For twenty-four hours, he hadn't been able to quit wondering how the ethereal beauty with the sky blue eyes tasted. How she smelled. How she'd feel around his shaft as he buried himself deep inside her.

Foxx gave a put-upon sigh and turned the car around, heading back to the store.

She probably wouldn't be there. And even if she was, she was probably married, or taken, or completely uninterested.

No, not uninterested. Of that he was sure. She'd felt that heat, too.

If she wasn't there, he'd forget her. If she was there, and he didn't feel the same punch of lust, he'd walk away. And if she was there, and he felt the way he had yesterday?

He'd have to take it one step at a time.

A half hour later, they pulled into the parking lot in a spray of dust and gravel, just like before. The old brick store looked even more decrepit than he remembered, if such a thing were possible. Clean enough—no trash or broken-down cars littered the place—but the building was definitely in need of a little TLC.

Foxx's stomach rumbled as he threw the car into park. "I'm hungry."

"What else is new?"

Foxx pushed out of the car and headed for the store without a backward glance, not bothering to ask if Paenther wanted anything this time. It was clear he did, or he wouldn't have demanded they come back here. Fortunately, Foxx didn't seem to have a clue just what it was that his companion wanted.

Paenther climbed out of the car more slowly, feeling as off-balance as he had yesterday. After four hundred years, one would think a man would outgrow that peculiar awkwardness of first infatuation, yet here he was, palms damp, pulse racing.

The last thing he needed was the distraction of a woman. Her beauty had undoubtedly grown way out of proportion in his mind. That was the true reason he'd insisted on returning. Once he saw her again, saw that she was nothing out of the ordinary, he'd be able to forget about her and stay focused on the only things that mattered.

As he crossed the parking lot, the wind rattled in the trees, tugging at his hair and coat, the loamy scent of the woods mixing with the dust of the parking lot.

Hell, she probably isn't even here.

But as he reached for the front door, a movement out of the corner of his eye caught his attention. He turned . . . and froze. She stood outside, at the corner of the building, in a shapeless pale green dress that somehow only accentuated her delicate beauty. Watching him.

Damn, but she was even more lovely than he'd remembered.

She smiled. His heart rate soared, and he was closing the distance between them before he'd given any conscious thought to whether or not he should. As he neared, she backed up, one small step at a time, turning the corner into shade. And privacy.

Paenther followed her into the sharply cooler air of the shade, then stopped two arm lengths away, trapped between the invitation in her bright blue eyes and the disbelief of the warrior inside him. *What am I doing? Vhyper needs me.*

Squirrels chattered in the sun-drenched trees behind the building. Vhyper was nowhere to be found. And he just wanted a kiss. For the first time in as far back as he could remember, lust had risen, curling up through the burning wreckage the Mage had made of his soul. He wanted. *Needed*. And the feel of it was intoxicating.

He took a step toward her, then stopped again. The last thing he wanted to do was frighten her. Like all Ferals, he was bigger than most human males. And there was something innately fragile about her.

To his surprised relief, she took the pursuit out of his hands and closed the distance between them, gliding into his arms with lightness and grace. He instinctively cradled her against him like the most delicate flower even as she wrapped her arms around his neck and pressed her mouth to his.

Fire erupted in his chest, rushing out and down, heating his limbs and body and blood in a way that pleasured instead of pained. All thought of gentleness flew from his head as she swept her tongue into his mouth with a strength and certainty that had him suddenly wondering if her delicacy had more to do with a lack of age.

He pulled back from the kiss, keeping her tight against his body as he stared down into that exquisite face.

"How old are you, beauty?"

"Old enough." That smile played at her mouth, her eyes twinkling with a depth that reassured him she was no child.

He covered her mouth, sweeping his tongue into hers as he pulled her tight against him. She tasted like the raindrops of old, sweet and pure, and smelled like violets. And he wanted her with a need unlike anything he'd ever experienced. With each stroke of his tongue against hers, his body hardened until he was throbbing with the desire to be inside her.

Her arm slipped from around his neck and moved down to slide over that distended part of his anatomy. The air hissed into his mouth as he pulled back, his gaze driving into hers.

Blue eyes swam with passion and a need nearly as great as his own.

He pressed his lips to her temple as he slid his palm down her thigh, then up again, lifting the skirt of her dress until he found the hem. He reached beneath, his fingers skimming her warm thighs, his hand sliding between them, rising to the bare, damp core of her.

The woman wore no undergarments.

A smile pulled as his mouth as he kissed her hard and slid a single shaking finger deep inside her tight, wet sheath.

He needed to be inside her.

A movement in his peripheral vision had him pulling back, his head jerking to the corner of the building. Foxx stood there staring at him, one hand loaded with hot dogs, the other with a massive drink, his eyebrows shooting into his hairline.

"*Dude.*"

Paenther growled low in his throat, tempted to yank off the cub's ears.

With a small sound of dismay, the woman pulled out of his arms and fled.

Paenther curled his damp finger into his fist and let her go. His brilliant plan to get her out of his mind had failed. Spectacularly.

Chapter Nineteen

Delaney sat up slowly in the strange bed, logging her surroundings. Unfamiliar bedroom, daytime.

Tighe stood at the window, his back to her, in a pair of black leather pants and nothing else except the gold armband tight around his upper arm.

With a rush, she remembered what had happened. Or what her mind was trying to tell her had happened. Her pulse began to pound as she saw in her head again, the man turning into a tiger. Then morphing into a were-tiger or . . . *God*. He'd sunk his claws deep into her shoulders until she was soaked with blood.

She struggled to calm her racing pulse. It hadn't happened. It was just a nightmare . . . or an hallucination thanks to the drugs he'd pumped her full of.

Just to reassure herself, she shrugged and rolled her shoulders. No pain, just as she'd known there wouldn't be. But when she glanced down at herself, at the unfamiliar gray tee shirt dotted with bloodstains all over the shoulders, her eyes went wide. Cold washed over her scalp.

"Oh, *crap*." Her mind began to buzz with disbelief, even as goose bumps rose on her skin.

"You're safe, Delaney," Tighe said without turning around, his voice cool and sharp. "Calm down."

"Right. Like I didn't just step into the Twilight Zone." Her gaze slid around the large, well-appointed, and decidedly masculine room with its jungle green walls and heavy wood furniture. One wall held an assortment of framed photos of airplanes. The others, a vast assortment of knives and swords interspersed with paintings of tigers.

Tigers. She struggled to contain the fear trembling deep inside her, afraid what might happen if she didn't. How many times had he said, *Don't fear me?* And look what had happened when she had.

Dear God. "Where are we?"

"Feral House." Tighe turned around slowly, his hands clasped behind his back, his mouth tight. Sunglasses, as usual, covering his eyes.

A small bubble of hysteria tried to rise up her throat, but she swallowed it down, hard. Either she'd gone insane, or her world had. And if it was the latter?

Even as she shuddered, she squared her shoulders. One way or another, she had to deal with it.

She watched him warily. "Are you . . . did I really see you . . . ?"

"Turn into a tiger?" He bit out the words as if daring her to accept them. "Yeah. You did."

She sat up straighter, pressing back against the headboard. "How do you do that? Change . . . like that?"

"I think about shifting, and I shift."

Shift. From a man to a tiger. Her head rushed with cold. Ants crawled across her skin. "Have you . . . always been this way?"

Tighe scowled. "I'm not a science experiment. I'm a shape-shifter. I have been for more than six hundred years."

Her eyes widened. "Six *hundred?*"

No way. No way. No way.

"My people are not human, Delaney. We're immortals. We've roamed this earth since the dawn of time, but we stay under the human radar for survival purposes."

Shape-shifters. Immortals. The words banged around inside her head, finding no purchase. They weren't real. Men did not turn into tigers. They didn't live forever. They *didn't.*

No wonder he hadn't died when he'd been shot.

With sudden clarity she realized everything she'd believed about him was wrong. Everything he'd told her was a lie. She felt a pinch in that part of her heart that had softened toward him. A spreading ache.

Am I really believing any of this?

God, I need to get out of here.

Delaney dug her fingers in her hair, raking it back from her face as her heart raced and her mind spun.

"Do you eat people?"

His mouth tightened. "No. We don't kill unless someone needs to be killed."

"Your brother does."

"He's not my brother. He's a clone, an unnatural creation that's not even flesh and blood. He was made several weeks ago from half my soul, which is what's causing my anger-management issues. My soul's disintegrating. If I don't destroy him soon, I'm going to die."

She gripped her head in both hands, closing her eyes against the barrage of information her mind refused to process. *Six hundred years?*

How did he expect her to believe that? Yet how else could she possibly explain what she'd seen?

With perfect clarity, she understood why he was so determined to catch the scumbag. The *clone*. After more than six hundred years, his life was in serious jeopardy.

If she believed him.

Did she have a choice?

A thought occurred to her, a wicked irony. The serial killer she'd been pursuing, the one the press had semihumorously dubbed the D.C. Vampire, actually *wasn't* human.

What if the FBI found out about it? That non-humans actually existed? It would flip them on their ears.

And if the populace at large learned about them? Utter chaos.

Taking a deep, shuddering breath, she lowered her arms, opened her eyes, and met Tighe's gaze.

She'd never been one to bury her head in the sand. Clearly, she'd stumbled into something *way* outside her realm of experience. Her only real option was to figure out what was going on as best she could.

Then deal with it.

Another shudder tore through her. Easier said than done.

Delaney swallowed. "I kind of understand the physical shifting into a tiger. But how . . . how did you do it in my head? Is that going to happen again?"

"The tiger in your head wasn't precisely me."

She grimaced. "Someone else did that?"

"No." He dug a hand through his short, sun-bleached hair, mirroring her move of a few moments ago. "I share my body with an animal spirit. A tiger animal spirit. His being in me enables me to shift into the tiger, but he isn't the tiger. I am. I'm the tiger, I'm the man, and when I lose my temper, I'm even that thing that attacked you. Though, if my soul had been intact, I never would have lost control like that. I never would have hurt you."

His fingers ran across the scars on his chest. Scars that looked like an animal's claw marks, she realized. "I was twenty-four when the tiger chose me. Marked me. Before that I wasn't human, but neither was I a shape-shifter. He joined his spirit with mine."

"He controls you?"

"No, though on occasion he'll make his will known. Particularly when it comes to females." Tighe frowned. "He's taken a liking to you. When I entered your mind, he tried to follow."

"What was he going to do in there?"

"Nothing. He couldn't have done anything. If you want to know the truth, I think he was really just trying to say hello."

She laughed, though there was no humor in it. "*Hello?* He scared the shit out of me."

"Believe me, I'm aware of that."

"How am I not hooked up to a transfusion in the ICU? I know I lost a ton of blood." She glanced down at one shoulder, then met his gaze. "I can't even feel the wounds."

Delaney hooked her finger into the neck of the large tee shirt and pulled it open so she could get a peek. They were still there, all right, red and swollen dashes, dried blood caked around the edges. But the skin seemed to have already knit closed. Almost as if someone had cauterized the wounds.

"You'd seen too much to take you to a human hospital, so one of our healers helped you. There was only so much she could do with human flesh. You're not fully healed, but you're a lot further along than you would be on your own. Your own body will have to do the rest."

Delaney shook her head. She was trying to take it all in. Really trying, but . . . "This is unbelievable."

"Get used to it," he said coolly. "The mating ceremony will take place as soon as you're ready."

Mating ceremony. Her stomach clenched, his words coming back to her, hard and hurtful. *No way. I'm not making her my mate.*

"No." It was too much. She couldn't deal with this, too.

He studied her, his gaze enigmatic. "Either you bind yourself to me, or I kill you." His expression said he didn't much care which.

She looked away, blindsided by the swift, unexpected pain of that blow. A blow he probably hadn't even intended.

She meant nothing to him. Less than nothing. And she *hated* that it hurt.

Delaney swung her legs over the side of the bed. "I need my cell phone," she said tersely. "I have to call my boss and let him know I'm okay."

"No."

"Is the FBI looking for me? Did they see you kidnap me? Did they give chase?"

"It doesn't matter."

She gaped at him, lunging to her feet to face him. "Of course it matters."

"They'll never find you. You're dead to them now."

She stared at him, her jaw slowly dropping. "I have a job to do."

"Your only job now is whatever I say it is. You're not going back to the FBI."

"If you're trying to be an ass, you're succeeding brilliantly." She stalked toward him. "I heard you tell the guy on the phone that if I went through with this, I couldn't betray you. So I can go back."

"You're staying here."

Blast it. "Then I'm not doing this."

"You don't have a choice."

"I didn't know you were going to lock me up!"

He turned and picked up a royal blue silk nightgown and tossed it to her. "Put this on. Nothing underneath. Leave your hair down and your feet bare. It's your wedding dress."

She stared at the thing. "I'm not getting married in a nightgown."

"It's not a nightgown. It's a ritual gown."

The fabric was gorgeous, but there was nothing to it. No sleeves, no lining. Nothing underneath?

"What's the ritual? Sacrificing me to your tiger god?"

He didn't reply, just continued to watch her with that hard, cold expression.

"I'm not getting married without underwear. Or without my gun. Not with wild animals on the loose."

He took a step toward her, his mouth compressing dangerously. "You'll do whatever I tell you to do."

She threw the gown on the floor. "Go to hell."

He lunged for her, grabbed her arm, and hauled her roughly against him. "I don't like this any better than you do, but it's either bind yourself to me or die. I gave you the choice already. You chose this. You chose me."

"I was delirious."

His jaw went hard as he released her with one hand and flicked open a switchblade three inches from her face.

"It's not too late to change your mind." The tightness of his mouth spoke of barely leashed violence, but in the agitated flutter of those angel wings in her head she sensed an unhappiness as raw as her own. He was being forced to tie himself to a woman he didn't love.

No, not forced.

He could have let her die.

Her fury ebbed as her heart began to ache for him almost as much as herself. "Would you really kill me?" she asked quietly. She already knew the answer.

The anger drained out of him as he retracted the blade and shoved it back in his pocket.

"No." He released her along with a sigh that echoed with pain. "But if you won't go through with this, I'll have no choice but to step aside while someone else does. The survival of our race is too important." He shook his head. "Not just to us. If we die, there will be no one left to keep the Daemons from returning. Imagine thousands of creatures terrorizing the human population. Creatures worse than my twin. A dozen times worse."

She shuddered and stared at him, her mind struggling to accept round after round of evidence that the world was so much more complex than she'd thought. "So I really don't have a choice?"

His mouth turned rueful. "You really don't."

"But you do. A human death can't mean that much to you. Why bind yourself to me when you could have let me die? When you don't want me?"

His mouth turned up in a wry half smile. "Who says I don't want you?"

As she stared at him, he bent down and picked up the gown, then met her gaze again, his expression softening just a little. "Come on, D. Let's get this over with."

It wasn't quite the marriage proposal she'd

dreamed of, but there had been something in his expression, something in his words that eased the ache inside her. Not much, but maybe it was enough. Especially since she clearly didn't have a choice.

"I need to get cleaned up."

He handed her the gown and nodded toward a door in the corner. "Bathroom's in there. I'll see if I can find you a brush or something."

She nodded and took the gown from him. As he started to turn away, she stopped him. "Tighe?"

He turned back to her.

"Thank you," she said softly. "For not letting me die."

His gaze seemed to search hers for several moments, then he lifted his hand and traced her cheekbone with his thumb in a feather-light touch. "You're welcome." Then he turned away.

Delaney opened the shower curtain to find a host of items on the sink that hadn't been there when she climbed in. A toothbrush still in its wrapper, a comb and brush, a hair dryer. Beside them lay a small zipper pouch she discovered contained a small collection of makeup basics. Someone else's collection, by the looks of it.

Staring at them, she was reminded how little she knew the man she was supposedly marrying. Did he have a girlfriend? A dozen girlfriends? With looks like his, she'd be amazed if he didn't.

Was he in love with someone else? Was she doomed to have to watch him parading other women through her life?

The ache in her chest tightened, annoying her. The only way she was going to survive this was to stop caring. Hadn't she learned that lesson when she was eleven? The only way to survive, period, was to stop caring about anyone.

Which had always been easier said than done.

After she dried her hair, she put on a little makeup, then slipped the blue silk over her head. The sleeveless, scoop-necked gown slid sensuously down her body to midcalf, skimming her curves but not hugging them tightly. The color was gorgeous on her. A perfect nightgown. But she was far too busty ever to consider leaving the bedroom without a bra, especially in a gown like this. It would only highlight every bounce and jiggle.

Just the dress a man would pick.

With a sigh, she opened the door and stepped into the bedroom.

Tighe turned from the window to face her. "The dress looks good on you." His tone was still reserved, but there was a truth in his words that warmed her. Heated her.

"Thanks. It's a beautiful nightgown. Just how many people are going to see me in it?"

"Five, other than me. And it's not a nightgown. It's one of a collection of ceremonial gowns that have been passed down for thousands of years."

Delaney jerked. "This dress is *not* thousands of years old. It would have disintegrated eons ago."

"The fabric was woven with power and magic, as well as silk. That's why nothing else can touch your skin during the ritual."

Power and magic. She shivered. "Not even my gun?"

The corner of his mouth twitched. "Especially not your gun."

She glanced at his slacks. "Are those thousand-year-old Haggars?"

A grin lit his face for one brilliant moment, flashing his dimples and filling her chest with a terrible and wonderful pressure.

"They're not Haggars. And what I'm wearing doesn't matter."

"Why not?"

"This is the channel for my power." He tapped the golden armband with the tiger's head.

Oh.

Tighe held out his hand to her. "Come on, D. Let's get this ritual over with."

She took his hand, and he pulled her lightly into his arms and kissed her hair. "Trust me, brown eyes. It's all going to be okay."

To her dismay, tears threatened in her eyes, and she buried her face in the hollow of his throat, craving his touch, needing his strength.

His arms closed around her, and she clung to him, the pressure in her chest growing, expanding, cutting off her air even as it filled her with a terrible, anguished joy.

He said it was all going to be okay. But she wasn't sure of that. She wasn't sure at all.

Because, heaven help her, she was falling in love with him.

Chapter Twenty

Tighe led Delaney through what she could only describe as a gaudily decorated mansion and down a long, long stair into a basement that had to be a good twelve feet below the ground. No regular lightbulbs lit their way, only a couple of pairs of electric sconces made to look like candlelight.

With each step down, Delaney's uneasiness mounted, her hands fisting and clenching around air. If she'd ever needed to be armed, it was now.

The scent of fire teased her nostrils as curls of smoke lifted on the air. A bead of sweat rolled between her breasts. When she thought of weddings, her mind burst forth with pictures of sunshine and flowers, and yards and yards of white. Not dark stairs and smoke.

Wedding, my ass. Some kind of gang ritual, more like it. Or human sacrifice.

A shiver of fear snaked its way down her spine.

Of course, Tighe hadn't called it a wedding, had he? He'd called it a mating ceremony.

Mating ceremony? Like some ancient fertility rite? That included *sex*? He'd better not even think about it.

What did she really know about this man? Nothing. She knew nothing about him except that he seemed to be trying to keep her alive. Which was all well and fine as long as his friends agreed. But she'd heard them on the phone when she was trying to bleed out. They'd all been in favor of letting her die.

What if they overpowered him? Or what if he lost it and turned into Wolfman Tiger again? She couldn't protect them both. She was weaponless. Shoeless. *Panty*less.

Tighe reached back and took her hand, his warm fingers closing around her ice-cold ones. "Control your fear, Agent Randall. No one's going to hurt you unless I lose it again. And it's your fear that makes me lose control."

His use of her title had the desired effect, calling on years of training and control. Even as it reminded her that her career, everything she'd worked so hard for, might well be gone.

She knew Phil must be frantically searching for her whether or not they'd seen her captured. An FBI agent on the trail of a serial killer suddenly disappears. What was the Bureau going to think?

That she'd gotten too close to him again. Phil wouldn't be looking for *her,* she realized. He'd be looking for her remains. And when he didn't find them? It wouldn't much matter. He'd still think she was dead.

And in a way, maybe she was. Dead to her old life at least.

Goose bumps rose on her skin as she followed Tighe down the long stairs. She wasn't entirely convinced she wasn't about to die in truth.

When they reached the base of the stairs, Tighe led her through a dark, dimly lit hallway toward a wide archway flickering with firelight and curls of smoke. Low voices met her ears, too low to make out the words.

As Tighe led her through the doorway and into the room, Delaney stared around her warily, in no small amount of awe.

The room wasn't overly large, but the ceiling was higher than most and arched, giving the space the feel of a cave. A feeling heightened by the six small fires burning around the edges of the room, casting flickering shadows on the dark-paneled ceiling and walls. There was something intensely primitive about the atmosphere, a feeling only strengthened by the half-naked men.

Five men other than Tighe stood scattered around the room, each wearing nothing more than a pair of pants or jeans and an armband similar to Tighe's, though each armband seemed to have the head of a different animal on it. Maybe they weren't all tigers after all.

Never had she seen such a worrisome display of pure, undiluted male power. Not a one of them was under six-six, with a couple well over. Each possessed powerful shoulders and thick, dangerous muscles.

If they turned against her, she was dog meat.

A shudder tore through her as she remembered where she was. *What* these men were. And just how true that could turn out to be. Dog meat. Tiger meat.

Forget sacrifice. For all she knew, she was dinner.

Tighe squeezed her hand. "You're safe, brown eyes. Happy thoughts, hmm?"

"*Happy* thoughts?" she muttered. Right. Her *thoughts* were on the fact there were no windows. No possible chance of escape.

One of the men came toward them, a man with a mustache and goatee and cold, pale eyes. The eyes of a psychopath.

"Lyon says you don't want the altar?"

And the voice of the man who kept telling Tighe to kill her. *Great.*

Tighe shook his head. "I won't need it."

The psychopath's expression didn't change. He turned that pale gaze to her, flicking it over her dispassionately as if deciding between a thigh and a breast.

She squeezed Tighe's hand, desperate to control the shudder that threatened to tear her apart.

The psychopath turned away.

"Happy thoughts, D," Tighe murmured.

"I was just thinking about dinner."

"I can imagine what you were thinking, but you have nothing to fear. No one's going to touch you but me."

The men were all looking at her, most with a disinterest bordering on disdain. As if she wasn't worth their time. *Is that what they think of all humans?*

The last man her gaze landed on nodded to her with something almost approaching friendliness. A man with a long, aristocratic face and sharply arched brows.

Her eyes narrowed, and she nudged Tighe. "Have I met him?"

"Hawke? He was the one who grabbed you at the Tidal Basin."

And the same one who'd pulled her to safety both times Tighe went ballistic. Would he rescue her a third time if she needed it? Not likely. Not against this crew.

As her gaze peppered the room, she caught sight of a woman standing on the far side, against one wall, in a gown that appeared to be a pastel version of her own ceremonial nightgown. *Is the woman just another course on the menu, or does she belong here?*

As their gazes caught, the blonde gave her a small, sympathetic smile. Nice. A moment of rapport between one entrée and the other.

Tighe nudged her shoulder. "If those thoughts of yours are happy, I'd hate to taste your dark ones."

Her gaze jerked to his. "You really can taste my emotions?"

His mouth pursed, and he nodded. "Really can."

"Do I taste scared?"

"Not exactly. If I had to guess, I'd say you're thinking about what you'd do if you could get ahold of those knives in my room. Am I close?"

She lifted her brows on a rueful look. "No, but I like your idea better."

He nodded. "Always glad to help."

"I'm sure."

"Let's get started, Kougar." The man who spoke was one of the larger of the bunch, his hair down to his shoulders in thick dark blond waves. Everything from the tone of his voice to his body language proclaimed him the leader. Was this Lyon, then? The one on the phone who'd been so against saving her?

Tighe led her to a low pedestal in the middle of the floor. "Stand here."

"Alone?" She stepped onto the round platform that was about the size of a coffee table and turned to him, noting they now stood eye to eye. "Isn't it traditional for the bride and groom to stand together?"

"I'll join you in a moment. Our rituals involve magic, of which I have to be a part."

As she stood self-consciously, the men formed a loose, wide circle around her. She kept turning, hating the feel of any of these men at her back.

The psychopath—was this Kougar?—walked toward Tighe with a bowl that looked like . . . *Shit*. It was either the top of a human skull or a first-rate replica. She'd bet money it was no fake.

Tighe held out his hand for the bowl, then stood there as the freak with the pale eyes pulled out a knife and cut him! *Deep*. Right through the center of his palm.

Delaney gasped in outrage and leaped off the pedestal.

Tighe shook his head sharply, frowning at her. "Go back, D. This is supposed to happen."

She glared at Kougar, then slowly turned and climbed back onto the platform. What would she have done if Tighe hadn't stopped her? Would she really have gone after a hulk of a man with a six-inch blade in his hand?

Yeah. She would have. If she'd thought Tighe was being attacked, she would have. *She nearly had*.

As if she were trying to protect her mate.

Shit.

Her hands clenched and unclenched at her sides as she watched Tighe squeeze his injured hand into a fist, letting the blood run into the bowl. When Tighe lowered his hand, Kougar turned to the man beside Tighe, her aristocratic savior, and cut his palm just as he had Tighe's.

One by one, the men added their blood to the bowl in a ritual as barbaric as anything she'd ever seen. With the firelight flickering over the dark walls, the half-naked bodies and dripping blood, she could almost believe every step down to this place had taken her another thousand years into the past.

Chills rippled over her skin.

At last, Kougar handed the bowl to Lyon, cut his own palm, and added his blood to the mix. When he was done, he retrieved the bowl.

Tighe walked toward her, then stepped onto the pedestal in front of her. His expression was tight. Borderline angry.

Had she offended him by trying to come to his rescue? Undoubtedly. And in front of all his buddies. Big mistake.

"Sorry," she said softly. "Gut reaction."

He didn't say anything, just held his hands out to her. She started to lay her hands in his when she remembered he'd been cut. But as she looked at his palm, her eyes went wide. His flesh was blood-smeared, but whole.

Her gaze snapped to his.

"Fast healers," he murmured. "Take my hands, D."

Fast healers. *Immortals*. No wonder no one seemed the least bit bothered about all the blood.

A shiver ripped through her, but she placed her hands in his.

Kougar began to chant something in a language she couldn't even identify. As he chanted, he walked slowly around the circle, dribbling the collected blood onto the floor.

Three times, he circled them before throwing the remaining blood into one of the fires. The flame rose, spitting, then died back to the size of the others.

"It's time," Kougar said, his voice almost hushed.

Tighe released her hands. The chanting had done something, something she couldn't see but could feel. Like a tingling in her blood and a heaviness in the air.

Tighe lifted his hands to frame her face. "Listen to me, brown eyes, because this is important. I need you to look into my eyes and not look away."

"It would help if I could see your eyes."

"No. It wouldn't. It may feel like I'm trying to get into your mind again, but don't let me in this time, do you understand? You have to fight it."

His words were doing nothing to calm her. Fight it, why? Because if she didn't, the tiger would spring again? She was actually kind of curious about his tiger spirit; but his intensity told her this was nothing to mess with, whatever it was.

"Okay," she murmured.

"Look into my eyes, D."

As she stared into his sunglasses, the chanting started up around them, all the men joining in, a deep, low rumble entering her bloodstream like the pounding of ancient drums.

Tighe's warmth brushed across her mind as it had that night in her apartment when she'd first met him. Like that night, she felt the stroke deep and low inside her. *Oh, hell.*

Again, that warmth stroked her, making her catch her breath as the heat built between her legs. Over and over, that invisible touch brushed her, driving her until she was hot, and gasping.

"*Tighe.*" If he didn't stop, she was going to come. Right here. In front of everyone. "Tighe, stop."

"*Don't move.*"

Oh, God, it was too late. Her body was out of

control, the rocket launched. She was gasping, rocking against him, moaning.

Oh, *shit*.

Tighe held Delaney as she screamed her release, her face a mask of passion. She was beautiful. *Glorious*.

His.

But he wasn't hers.

He shook from the hard thread of control that kept him from freeing himself and burying himself deep inside her, joining her, binding himself to her as the magic bound her to him.

A thing he couldn't do. *Couldn't do*.

As her climax peaked, the power rushed out of him like a storm, and into her, making her cry out a second time with as much pleasure as the first.

She was his, now. Bound to him. Her loyalty and fidelity unbreakable.

His.

But the rush of pleasure, of power, went only one way, leaving a deep, hollow void inside him. An emptiness he hadn't anticipated.

He'd done the right thing. The only thing.

She clung to him with shaking hands as her body quaked from the force of the twin storms. Dark lashes swept up, revealing eyes shimmering with disbelief and bright with dismay. Slowly, she straightened, her cheeks staining with color even as her gaze hardened, raking the Ferals as if daring them to comment.

Her gaze swung back to him, the pleasure gone

from her eyes. The bitter taste of her embarrassment streaked across his tongue along with a healthy dose of anger.

"It's done," he told her quietly.

Her eyes narrowed. "You did that on purpose."

"Sexual release opens the body and mind."

"What about you?" Her gaze dipped to the front of his pants. "You didn't get off?"

"No."

Her expression turned brittle. "You didn't marry me, did you? I married you, but you didn't marry me."

She was too sharp, by half.

"I did what I had to do to keep you alive."

And to keep them from being stuck with one another for the rest of her life.

Deep inside him, the tiger howled with fury.

Damn him.

As Tighe stepped down from the pedestal, Delaney remembered the words someone had spoken as she'd lain on a sofa soaking in her own blood.

If he binds her to him, she can't betray him. Or us.

Binds her. Not *marries* her. Not *promises to love, honor, and cherish* her. But *binds* her. Like a slave. Was that it? Was that what she would be to him? A slave?

Or worse. What if she was nothing to him? A castoff. A useless, cast-off human.

Tighe held out his hand to her, to help her down, but she just stared at him, knowing she wasn't masking her anger nearly as well as she wanted to.

"*D*." The word pulsed with regret. With pity.

She turned away from him, hating that he knew she was so much more than mad. This sucked. It *sucked*. All she'd ever wanted was to do her job, and now she couldn't even do that. She was locked in a marriage that wasn't even a marriage.

A *binding*.

His hand cupped her shoulder. "Delaney."

Pain shot through her head, out of nowhere, arching her back as her jaw dropped open. Her sight disappeared as a screen rose in her head. A house. On fire.

She felt Tighe snatch back his hand with a groan. "I forgot about your injuries."

"Not . . . *Tighe*." Her hand shot out, reaching for him blindly. "*Vision*."

And then she was in his arms, cradled against his bare chest, his palm tight to her forehead. "Easy, sweetheart. Are you seeing it this time?"

"Yes."

"Good. I think. Better than the slide to nowhere, anyway."

The view was of the back of an old two-story house. Fire licked at the base from one end of the house to the other as if . . .

"He's poured gasoline around it again," Tighe said.

"Any identifiers?" one of the men asked. Hawke's voice, she was almost certain.

"Nothing so far. You don't recognize anything do you, D?"

"No. What do you mean . . . again?"

An old woman appeared in one of the upstairs windows, struggling to lift the window sash.

"This is the fourth time he's done this in the past twelve hours. We found two of the houses, but too late. He was long gone. But we know he's using flammables to trap his victims."

"I didn't have the visions."

His arm tightened around her, pulling her even closer against his chest as if he'd shield her from this horror. "Oh you had them, you were just unconscious at the time. I was holding you. I saw them for you."

The old woman was making no progress with the window. It appeared to be stuck. She disappeared only to appear at a different window. Delaney could feel her terror in the frantic way she beat at the window frame, and in the screams barely filtering through the window.

While the clone watched, feeding on her fear.

The men's conversation went on around her.

"He's not feeding as well this way."

"Maybe he's needing to feed more often to counteract the disintegration of his soul."

The fire was beginning to creep up the wood siding of the house. Delaney's arms slid around Tighe's waist as she buried her face in his chest. "I don't want to see this."

Tighe's hand caressed her head. "I can knock you out."

"No."

The woman finally threw a chair through the window, the glass shards sparkling like gold in the fire's glow. Her screams for help tore through Delaney's mind. She felt the strong arms around her tighten as if he, too, could barely stand to hear this.

"We've got it!" Another male voice. "Not that far from here. A Falls Church address."

Tighe brushed her hair with his hand. "I've got to go, brown eyes. I've got to try to stop him."

She nodded. "Help her."

"If I can." But they both knew by the time he got there, if no one else had come to her aid, it would be too late. "Let me knock you out."

"No. I can't leave her. Besides, maybe I'll see something."

She felt the press of his lips on her hair. "Lyon can knock you out as easily as I can. If you need help, ask him."

"I'll stay with her," said a woman's voice. The blonde, no doubt.

He helped her sit on the pedestal before he released her. The rush of pain had her cradling her head in her arms. Through the old woman's hoarse screams, she heard the sound of male feet pounding up the stairs. Then the soft brush of silk.

To her surprise, a gentle hand began to rub her back. A woman's hand.

"I'm sure this isn't helping at all, but it's what my mom always did when I needed any kind of comforting."

"It helps."

"Good. I'm Kara, by the way. Lyon's mate, as they put it. His wife."

The soft voice helped drown out the sound of the woman's coughing cries, as they helped ground Delaney in the real world.

"*As they put it?*" she asked, struggling to force her mind anywhere but that fire. "Aren't you one of them?"

"Technically. I thought I was human until about two weeks ago."

"Seriously?"

"Oh, yeah. Let me tell you, that was a shocker. I taught preschool in Spearsville, Missouri. I guess I should have known something was up when my cuts always healed within seconds, and I never got sick. But I was so average in every other way, I never suspected I was different. Who would? There's no such thing as immortals, right?"

"You're a shape-shifter?"

"No." Kara's hand rubbed soft, comforting circles over her back. "I'm just their power plug. Their Radiant. It's complicated. A lot more than you're up for right now."

"Are there many of them? The tigers, or whatever they are?"

"Only one tiger. One of each animal, nine in all. A lot more Therians, but only nine shifters."

"Hawke, Lyon, Kougar . . . ?" It finally dawned on her. "Their names . . . ?"

"Are the names of their animals, yes. Or close. Tighe is obviously the tiger." She continued to rub Delaney's back. "Is the woman still struggling?"

"She has the window open, but the fire's on the outside, so all the smoke's going in." Behind the woman, she saw a flicker of light. Had help finally arrived? The flicker rose higher. *Flame.*

"Why didn't she . . . ?"

"The fire's inside the house, too. She's trapped."

"Oh, no. *Poor thing.*"

As Delaney watched, the woman collapsed, falling out of her sight.

The vision ended.

"It's over," Delaney said softly, staying where she was until the pain began to ebb away.

"They didn't get there in time."

"No. No one did."

A very human growl sounded from the woman beside her. "I can't believe we let him get away. We killed the others. You knew there were others, right?"

"No."

"Eight in all. A clone of each of the Ferals except Vhyper. We had one heck of a battle here a week ago. We got them all but Tighe's."

Delaney slowly rose to a sitting position, lifting her head carefully. "Thank God there aren't eight of those things running around."

"I suppose. Look on the bright side, right? Things could always be worse."

Delaney snorted softly, thinking of all the people this thing had killed so far. "I'm beginning to wonder." Delaney turned to face her companion, a pretty blonde, in a wholesome girl-next-door kind of way. "Sorry. This hasn't been the greatest day for me."

"You and Tighe. Lyon said he bound you to him

because it was the only way you were going to survive."

Delaney nodded. "That pretty much sums it up. I'm alive. Beyond that, I don't know what I am. Apparently not married."

"Yes, I noticed that was only one way. Horrifyingly embarrassing, isn't it? I had to have sex in front of all of them when I married Lyon a few nights ago."

Delaney stared at her. "In front of them?"

"I made Lyon erect curtains around the altar. But they heard everything. Of course, Lyon and I had already done it in front of three of them, but that was in the heat of battle and didn't quite feel as strange." She shook her head. "*Shape-shifters.*" Kara's expression softened. "How's your head?"

"Better."

"You look . . . a little dazed."

Delaney sighed. "I guess I am. This is all happening a little too fast for me. I thought we were getting married. I understood that concept. Now I don't know what Tighe has in mind for me."

"If it helps, I don't think he does either. But I saw him when he brought you in, Delaney. You were white as a sheet from the blood loss. But he was just as pale. He cares more than you think." Kara patted her knee, then stood. "I suspect he cares more than he knows."

Delaney rose and followed her out of the room and up the long stairs. Could Kara be right? Did he care about her? And would it change anything if he did?

She sighed, deeply troubled and more than a little apprehensive. Because she didn't know what he wanted from her. Or what he meant to do with her. For heaven's sakes, she barely even knew the man, no matter what her heart thought.

The only thing she did know, the one immutable fact, was that she did not belong in this world. In *his* world.

And she never would.

Chapter
Twenty-one

Tighe opened his bedroom door quietly, not wanting to wake Delaney. But she sat up as he entered, a shadowed form rising in his bed.

He liked her waiting for him like that. Sweet nature, but he needed to touch her.

"I'm guessing you didn't catch him."

He sat on the edge of the bed and pulled off his boots. "No. He was long gone by the time we got there. The woman didn't make it. I'm sorry, D."

She pulled her knees up, wrapping her arms around them. She was dressed in soft blue pajamas—a loan, he assumed, from Kara. Her emotions tasted conflicted and were hard to identify. But he tasted no ripe anger, and for that he was grateful. His soul would splinter if he didn't touch her.

"I didn't know where to sleep," she said softly. "Kara thought I should stay here. She figured you'd move me if you didn't want me here."

Tighe stretched out on the bed and pulled her into his arms. "I want you here."

She didn't melt against him, but neither did she pull away, and it was enough. He drank in her scent, shuddering at the rightness of her being with him. All day, the chaos had been getting worse within him, building in strength and noise, like an approaching storm. But as he held Delaney, the storm abated. Not entirely, but enough that he felt like maybe, just maybe, he had enough time left to catch that damned clone before his soul was gone.

His fingers weaved through her hair as he pressed her head against his chest, tasting a drop of her unhappiness on his tongue.

"I'm sorry, D. I should have warned you about the ceremony. About what to expect."

"Why didn't you?" The question was simple. Without rancor. And he didn't have an answer.

"I'm not sure. All I can tell you is I did it for you."

"Not marrying me? You did *that* for me?"

He stroked her head, his gut churning. "Therian marriages aren't like human. A Therian is . . ." He sighed. "I guess I should start at the beginning."

"No need. Kara filled me in pretty thoroughly about the Therians, Daemons, Satanan—you name it. I'm not saying I'm ready for a quiz, but I think I've got the basics."

"Good." His hand stroked down her back and up again. "Anyway, the binding in an immortal marriage is real, not just talk as it is in a human marriage. There's no divorce. Once the pair are bound to one another, they're bound for life. That's why very few Therians ever mate."

Delaney pulled out of his embrace but didn't move away. Instead, she rolled onto her stomach and propped herself up to look at him.

"So what are you saying?" she asked, her voice calm, but strained.

He lifted his hand, as he looked up at her, and ran his knuckles lightly along her cheek. "By only binding one of us, the mating isn't permanent. If I'd bound myself to you, too, it would have been. The way it stands now, it can be broken. Once this is over, if I can take your memories, I can send you home. You'll get your life back, Agent Randall."

No joy leaped into her eyes. No relief. For a dozen seconds, she was silent. "So the bond was real, but not permanent. What's going to happen to me if I try to leave you?"

Tighe sighed. "Good question. I'm hoping I can break the bond when I steal your memories. Since you're human, I may be able to do it. Worst case, you'll probably feel this tug, this longing, for something you don't understand. It's not perfect, but few lives ever are."

"You really think I can go home?"

"I can't promise. I'm not the only one of the Ferals with the ability to steal the memories of humans, but my gift is the strongest. If my soul goes before the clone dies, one of the others will try to free you."

"What if it doesn't work?"

"You can't leave our world with the knowledge you currently have of us."

"I'll have to stay here?"

"Either here or in one of the Therian enclaves."

"Will your friends let me live?"

"Absolutely. I've talked to Hawke about it. He'll make sure you're taken care of."

"A prisoner."

"You'll have a life, D." He cupped her jaw and ran his thumb across her soft cheek. "I'm not planning on dying. I haven't figured out how, but I'm going to get that son of a bitch."

Something flared in her eyes. "Good."

Tighe slid his hand around the back of her neck and pulled her down until her mouth was firmly on his. The kiss filled him, strengthened him, and sent heat coursing through his veins. He pulled her on top of him until she covered him, then cupped her buttocks and pressed her against his growing arousal, pulling a moan of need from his throat.

Desire swam in his blood. "I want you, brown eyes."

Delaney pulled from his embrace and sat up, straddling him as she pulled the soft tee shirt up and off her body, revealing perfect breasts in the moonlight filtering into the room.

"You're so beautiful," he murmured, and reached up to cover the soft mounds with his hands.

She watched him with fathomless eyes. "Come inside me, Tighe."

He needed no encouragement. In seconds, he finished undressing them both, rolled her beneath him, and sank deep into her heat. His soul gave a shuddering sigh. If he could stay there, right there, he would. Forever.

After he'd driven them both to completion, he held her in his arms until she fell asleep. Would the desperate need to touch her, to hold her, leave him once his soul was complete again?

He had a bad feeling the answer was no. That the only way he'd ever truly feel whole was with Delaney by his side.

Delaney woke up alone the next morning, climbed out of bed and took a quick shower, then dressed in the jeans and one of the sweaters Kara had loaned her until she could get some clothes of her own.

Her body was loose and warm. Sated. When Tighe had come in last night, she'd tried to be cool. Tried to be mad at him for not marrying her and humiliating her in front of his friends like that. But she'd found she didn't have the anger in her. She was all too aware she wasn't in her own world, and the rules of this one were very different. And she was very much an outsider.

Then he'd pulled her into his arms, his body shaking, and held her like she was all that kept him together. She'd melted, overwhelmed by the depth of her feeling for the man and her desperate need to keep him safe.

The last of her pique had disappeared beneath the weight of her caring and the certainty that he needed her right now. Time was running out. His soul was disintegrating.

And, heaven help her, she was absolutely in love with him.

She reached for her boots, which had miraculously survived her bloodbath. The same boots she'd worn on the job nearly every day for six years. She stilled in the act of pulling on a sock and thought of Phil and her colleagues looking for her, thinking she was probably dead. She hated that they were expending needed time and resources looking for her, yet she was beginning to understand the Ferals' critical need for secrecy.

It didn't seem real that she'd gotten mixed up in a battle of inhuman forces, races no one else knew existed. It didn't seem possible she'd fallen in love with a man who wasn't human.

As she slipped on her sock, the door opened, and Tighe walked into the room. Her heart did a slow roll in her chest, setting off a fan of sparks.

He looked so damned good, dressed in jeans and a black silk shirt that hung loose around his trim waist. His short sun-bleached hair, curling slightly at the nape of his neck, was still damp from a shower he must have taken elsewhere. Sunglasses covered his eyes.

A slow smile spread across his face, flashing his dimples. "You found clothes."

"Kara loaned them to me."

He nodded. "Lyon tells me you've made a friend."

"I imagine anyone who enters Kara's orbit is going to become her friend. She's a good person."

"I agree. Lyon's a lucky man." He closed the distance between them and took her face in his hands. "I'm luckier."

His head dipped, and he kissed her, his mouth warm and inviting, with that intoxicating taste of thunderstorms and wildness. A wildness she was beginning to understand.

When her breath was ragged, and her body hot and pliant, he pulled slowly away, his hands returning to frame her face. "I'd take you to bed, brown eyes, but I've got a meeting in the war room in five minutes. And five minutes isn't nearly enough time to do what I want with you."

Damp heat flushed through her body. "I'm supposed to meet Kara in the foyer in a little while. She's going to show me around."

Tighe nodded, brushing his thumb across her cheek. "I've got a cell phone for you. It has GPS, but will only call two numbers. Hit any speed dial but two and you'll get me. Two will get you Lyon."

Two numbers. The word *prisoner* rang through her head all over again. The warmth from his touch slowly seeped out of her, and she pulled away. "Afraid I'll call the FBI to swarm this place?"

"No. You couldn't if you wanted to. You can't intentionally betray me now that you're bound to me."

Yeah, she was annoyed. "Right."

"It's for your safety as well as ours. Just because

you can't intentionally betray us doesn't mean you couldn't do it accidentally. I want you to have a way to reach me if you get another vision, and I'm not right here with you."

Tighe handed her the phone. "Take it, D. Please?"

Delaney did and slipped it into her pocket.

Tighe retraced his steps back to the door. "I'll find you as soon as I'm through with this meeting."

"Then what?"

His expression turned grim. "Kougar's working on something. Let's hope he's having some success. I'm running out of time." He left.

Delaney put on her boots, then did a quick search of the room to see if she could find her guns. Nothing. Her gaze scanned the knives on the walls. Heavy weaponry, to be sure, but not a thing suitable for day wear. She'd have to have a talk with Tighe about that. They were going to have to come to some kind of agreement about weapons.

Tighe had left the bedroom door partially open when he left. Since he hadn't locked her in, she assumed she was free to wander the house while she waited for Kara. And her curiosity about the place and these people was intense.

As she descended the wide, curved stair, the front door opened. Hawke and Kara walked in.

Hawke looked up and smiled as he met Delaney's gaze.

"Good morning."

"Good morning." At least there seemed to be one friendly face among the Ferals.

As Hawke strode down the hallway, Delaney turned her attention to Kara. No smile lit the other woman's eyes this morning. Delaney's trouble radar went up.

"Everything okay?" Delaney asked, descending the last of the stairs.

"I need to talk. Come take a walk with me."

Delaney nodded and followed the blonde out the door and into an overcast morning. She felt a little funny leaving, though Tighe hadn't told her she couldn't.

What was to keep her from running? That mating bond, apparently.

But even if she could, where would she run to? With the understanding of what he was, and what the clone was, everything had changed. No longer was she simply fighting for her own survival. There was so much more at stake. Tighe's life, for one. And almost seven billion other lives, if what he'd told her about the Daemons was true. Considering all she'd seen, she had no reason to doubt him.

No, of course she wouldn't run. Not when the battle was here. And when she possessed one of their only real weapons, her visions.

It pleased her that Tighe understood her well enough, *trusted* her enough to know that.

As they traversed the rocky woods, Delaney glanced at her silent companion. "What's up, Kara?"

"I need to show you something." She didn't elaborate.

"Okay." But they continued to walk until they'd once more left the woods and were walking along a residential street. Delaney's instincts began to crawl with unease. "Kara, tell me what's going on."

To her surprise, Kara pulled a set of car keys out of her pocket and pressed the button. The red minivan parked on the side of the road in front of them beeped in response.

Delaney shook her head. "Kara, I'm not going anywhere. Not without telling Tighe."

Kara held out her hand, a sly expression entering her eyes. "Give me your phone. I'll call him."

"No." The hair on her nape began to rise. This was not the woman she'd talked to for two hours last night.

And suddenly, in the blink of an eye, she wasn't.

The person standing beside her was no longer Kara but Tighe. No, not Tighe. *The clone*.

Delaney's heart skipped a beat and began racing with terror. Her head went cold. She whirled to run, reaching for the phone in her pocket. But like Tighe, the clone was too fast. He grabbed her hair and jerked her off her feet in a blast of tearing pain. As he swung her around to face him, she slammed her elbow into his solar plexus.

He slammed his fist into her jaw.

"I want that bastard found!" Lyon's hard growl echoed through the war room, giving voice to Tighe's own frustration. He turned his hard gaze to Kougar. "Anything on those Daemon traps?"

"I'm close. I've got three that may potentially work if I can finish piecing them together, but they have to be done at night."

"Tonight, then." When Kougar nodded, Lyon turned to Hawke. "What have you found out, Wings?"

Hawke folded his hands on the table in front of him. "The Shaman's been digging through old Daemon lore and believes the clone can indeed steal Tighe's half of the soul. He just isn't sure how he'll go about it. He's come up with a spell he can place on Tighe's soul so that if the clone tries to steal Tighe's half, both halves will be destroyed."

"What the fuck good is that?" Jag drawled.

Hawke's expression was grim. "It won't keep Tighe alive, but it will at least contain the further threat of the clone."

Lyon shook his head. "The only solution I want is one that destroys that clone and leaves Tighe alive."

"There's still only one of those. Kill the clone. Straightforward and simple."

"And damned impossible to do." Lyon's fist slammed into the table. "It shouldn't be this hard to catch him!"

Tighe looked up to see Kara standing in the doorway.

Lyon held his hand out to her, but she shook her head. "Sorry to interrupt. I was just wondering if Tighe's seen Delaney. I can't find her."

Tighe was on his feet in an instant.

So was Hawke. "She was with you."

Kara's brows drew down with confusion. "I haven't seen her. I just came downstairs a few minutes ago."

"I saw you," Hawke insisted. He blanched. "Or someone who looked just like you."

Tighe's blood went cold. "He's got the witch's glamour. He's taking on the form of other people."

"Anyone he's seen." Hawke's mouth tightened. "That's how he's been eluding us. It's how he got away when Kougar and I had him cornered."

Lyon pulled out his knife. "Palms. Pink! Join us please."

A fist of terror tightened in Tighe's stomach, every muscle raging to take flight, to find her. He drew out his own knife and sliced his palm, holding it up for his chief to see, then he pulled out his phone and called the phone he'd given Delaney just that morning. Maybe the clone was still pretending to be Kara. Maybe Delaney would answer. But as the phone rang and rang, he knew that son of a bitch had her. His skin felt as if it were tying to crawl off his bones.

That son of a bitch would kill her. No, not kill her. Not yet. His chest felt like someone were stabbing him through the heart with a hot poker. He'd make her suffer first. He'd feed off her pain and her terror, little by little, like the Daemons of old. Until her tears were spent, her mind was gone, and her body couldn't take any more.

He had to find her. *Now*. He turned to Hawke. "We can track her if she still has the phone."

Hawke ran for the door. "I'll get my laptop."

"Wulfe, follow her scent," Lyon barked.

"I'll grab Tighe's pillows for you," Kara said.

"No need." Wulfe stood. "Her scent is all over Tighe."

Within moments, they burst from the doors of Feral House. As Wulfe shifted into his animal and followed Delaney's scent, Tighe, Hawke, and Jag ran for Jag's Hummer.

"I've got the signal," Hawke said as Jag swung out of the circular drive. "It's fixed. Over on Oak Woods."

Tighe braced himself in the backseat, his senses going out to her. *Call for me, Brown Eyes.* When she'd been trapped, lost in that vision, he'd heard her calling for him. He'd been able to follow. *Call for me, Delaney.*

Was it possible she didn't yet realize she was in trouble? No. She'd have answered her phone.

Only one reason she wouldn't answer either call.

Goddess. Don't let her be dead. Not when I'm just starting to understand how much I need her.

Minutes later, Jag pulled onto Oak Woods.

"Here." Hawke snapped the laptop closed as Jag pulled the Hummer to a screeching halt. Tighe dove out the door, his senses open. She wasn't there.

But her phone was. He saw it gleaming in the light. As he picked it up, as he touched the metal that had been in her hands such a short time ago, he felt a piece of himself die.

Wulfe came bounding out of the woods, a monster of a gray wolf. He sniffed around the area where the phone had been, then lifted his head to Tighe.

The scent ends here. She must have gotten into a car.

Fury rose in a hot wash, burning through Tighe's blood. He had her. That son of a bitch had her.

A hand gripped his shoulder, and he turned to face Hawke.

"I'm sorry." Hawke shook his head, his expression grim. "I'd like to give you platitudes like *we'll find her*, but I'm out of ideas of how to catch him, buddy." His eyes narrowed. "How did you find her the last time? After she set you up?"

"I heard her. I think I inadvertently formed a mind connection with her when I was trying to steal her memories. I heard her crying out for me that night and followed. I can't explain how I knew where she was, but I knew." He met his friend's gaze. "She's not calling out for me, this time."

"She may be." Hawke frowned. "You just can't hear her anymore."

Tighe closed his eyes, listening. He had to be able to hear her. But, except for his own turbulent thoughts, his mind was silent. And he suddenly realized that the warmth that had brushed against the inside of his skull was gone. The connection was gone.

"What happened?" But like a fist to the gut, he knew. "The binding."

Hawke nodded, his expression bleak. "I'm afraid so. The accidental connection was probably severed when the new one between you and her was formed."

"Except it only went one way. If I'd bound myself to her, I'd be able to hear her like I did before."

"Yes. Probably more than before."

The knowledge pierced him like a dozen blades. He'd intentionally cut himself off from her. In not binding himself to her, in trying to protect her, he'd sealed her fate.

Inside him the tiger spirit shook his head and let out a furious roar.

Tighe squeezed his eyes closed, fighting the tiger's accusation. And losing.

Because he hadn't done it for her, as he'd told her. The pain of that realization shredded his heart. He hadn't been protecting her. He'd been protecting himself. Against a marriage he couldn't believe would turn out any better than his first one had.

He'd protected himself. And lost the only thing in his life that mattered.

Delaney.

Chapter Twenty-two

Delaney groaned, trying to rise out of the fog that encased her brain. *God, my jaw hurts.* An ice-cold vise clamped around her wrist and pulled, yanking her across . . .

Her hip plowed into something hard, jarring her fully awake. She was in a car. In a garage.

In a shock of an instant, everything came flooding back. *The clone. He'd caught her.*

She grabbed hold of the door handle as the man who looked just like Tighe tried to haul her across the center console and out the driver's side door. He'd kill her. If he got her out of the car, he'd kill her.

The clone reached in, hooking his arm around her shoulders and yanked her toward him, tearing her loose from the car door. *No.* She whirled toward him, jamming her finger deep into his eye socket.

A shudder of revulsion traveled from her hand all the way to the soles of her feet. His eye socket was perfectly dry. *Inhumanly* dry.

Her attack had no effect. He didn't scream as any normal man would have. He didn't even rear back. Instead, he jerked her harder, manhandling her out of the car and into the house as she kicked and fought for her life.

The moment he hauled her through the door, into a small laundry room, the smell hit. The hair rose on her arms. *Decomposing bodies.*

"You killed somebody here."

"Yes. This was my first stop after I escaped. My first feeding." Tighe's voice washed over her, at once wonderfully familiar and terrifyingly wrong. Because the man . . . *the thing* . . . speaking wasn't Tighe. "I'll show you." He said the last with a lilt of pride that had her stomach roiling.

"I've seen dead bodies before." She struggled to keep her voice calm and even. The creature fed off fear and pain. *Swallow your fear.* She tried, but her skin was turning clammy, her breaths coming in tight, uneven pulls.

Pinning her against him, the clone half pushed, half carried her into the kitchen.

Dear God, dear God, dear God.

In the middle of the floor, beside a cracker-strewn high chair, was a pile of rotting corpses covered with flies. *A pile.* As if the despicable creature had killed them and tossed them away one by one.

Delaney looked away, swallowing desperately against the rising bile, but the image was carved into her brain. Flies crawling across the face of a small boy, his head dangling over the curve of a man's shoulder, the rest of his body hidden by the bathrobe of a woman. A woman draped faceup over the pile, her arms spread as if even in death she tried to protect her family.

Delaney breathed through her mouth, panting between swallows. Her mind screamed at the wrongness, at the waste of life, even as hatred burned through her with the force of a wildfire.

"*You sick bastard.*" She stomped her heel hard onto his instep.

He jerked her around and slammed her against the wall, her head crashing into a picture frame and sending it clattering to the floor as pain crackled along her skull.

Pressing his body hard against hers, pinning her to the wall, the clone grabbed her face in his hand.

"Do you know what I'm going to do to you?" His green eyes had jagged black streaks running across them like cracks in two windshields. Streaks that hadn't been there the last time he attacked her. Would Tighe's look the same?

Oh, Tighe. Find me.

She spit in the clone's face. "Go to hell."

He didn't bother to remove the spittle. "You're going to scream, human. By the time I'm through with you, your vocal cords will be shredded from your screams."

His words twisted inside her, sending her pulse spinning like a tornado. He *wanted* her afraid. Fight it. Fight *him*.

The clone gripped her face, forcing her to look at him. Oddly, his expression softened, warmth flowing into his eyes. For a heartbeat, she saw Tighe in his face. Tighe as she'd never seen him, his sunglasses off, his eyes filled with soft emotion.

But this wasn't Tighe.

Any resemblance disappeared as cold rushed back into his eyes. His hand gripped her breast and squeezed until he brought tears to her own. His face took on an expression of deep pleasure.

He was feeding off her pain.

Maybe he should feed off his own. Catching him off guard, she slammed the heel of her hand into his nose. When he didn't so much as flinch, she raked her nails down his cheek. *He didn't bleed.*

The full understanding of his inhumanity hit her even as he jerked her away from the wall and threw her to the ground. She slid across the wood floor, stopping less than a foot from the bodies, sending the flies swarming into the air.

Oh God, Oh God.

Her body aching, her mind dazed, she tried to push to her feet, but he stomped her flat with his foot. How long before another body topped that pile of corpses?

Hers.

Tighe's chest burned as he climbed back into Jag's Hummer with muscles so tense they were cramping. Wulfe joined him through the opposite door.

Goddess, where is she? What is that piece of shit doing to her?

Is she even still alive?

"When I get my hands on him, he's not going to die fast," he snarled. "I'm cutting him up inch by inch until there's nothing left of him but his head and his heart. Then I'll shred those, strip by strip."

But what would it matter? How sweet would revenge taste when Delaney was dead? The blades in his chest twisted, slicing him anew until he felt the blood running in rivulets down the sides of his heart.

"Where to?" Jag asked, starting the engine. No one answered. Where did they go from here?

As he opened his mouth to reply, his vision went suddenly, totally black. As it had when he'd first had the visions. Before Delaney got in the way.

His hand grabbed hold of the door as he held on, knowing he was about to watch the demon feed, and praying, *praying*, he wasn't about to watch Delaney die.

Chapter
Twenty-three

"She's not a witch!" Paenther growled as Foxx pulled on his clothes after snooping on all fours around yet another mountain estate that had absolutely nothing to do with the Mage.

The clouds had rolled in, driven by a chilly wind, turning the afternoon hazy and gray.

Foxx finished tying his running shoes. "I'm just saying, you can't always tell anymore. Zaphene hid her Mage eyes so well, none of us knew she was a witch. She had me fooled but good," he added morosely. "I thought she was in love with me."

"*Foxx.*" Paenther sighed as they started walking back to the Mustang parked alongside the road. "*I* can tell." Which was an out-and-out lie. He hadn't known Zaphene was a witch any more than anyone else had. Still . . . "If she *were* a witch, she'd have enthralled me already, right? A touch of her hand, and I'd have been hers. She's not a witch. And it doesn't matter anyway, because I'm not going back there. I don't have time to get involved with a woman. *Any* woman. Especially one who lives hours from Feral House."

Foxx grunted. "If you're not interested in her, why do you keep talking about her?"

Paenther growled low in his throat, his hands fisting on his coat. "*I'm* not the one who just brought her up again!"

"Yeah, but you're the one who keeps growling. You're driving me crazy, B.P."

"The feeling is mutual, Cub," Paenther said, as they reached the car. "The feeling is mutual."

"I'm doing the best I can," Foxx snapped, guessing correctly Paenther had lost patience with the young Feral's worthless intuition. They climbed in and Foxx started the car, gunning it onto the empty road.

"I didn't say you're not, Foxx, but for two and a half days you've been certain Vhyper is in these mountains, and for two and a half days we've found shit. We might as well head home."

"*No.*"

Paenther looked at the younger man sharply.

Foxx met his gaze. "He's here. I know he's here. And I know we're going to find him. But not yet."

Paenther growled, his claws unsheathing for a frustrated instant. "*When?*"

"Later today."

Paenther stared at his companion. "You really think that?"

Foxx's gaze turned inward, but he nodded slowly.

"Yeah. You're going to be talking to him again soon."

"And just how are we going to find him?"

"He's going to find you. But later." Foxx turned the Mustang around in the middle of the road and headed back the way they'd come.

Paenther scowled. "Now where are you going?"

"Following another one of my intuitions. We're going back to the Market."

"You're going to hand me over to a witch?"

"I never said she was a witch. I was just making the point that you're not being very cautious for a guy who's lived long enough to know better."

Paenther growled, but damn, the cub was right. He'd been so blown away by the woman that he'd completely forgotten Zaphene had been able to hide her Mage eyes. Then again, he'd never known a Mage to be able to do that. And, honestly, the chances of his little beauty's being Mage were one in several million. Maybe a billion. Still, the thought probably should have crossed his mind.

But what he'd told Foxx was true. If, by some monumental coincidence, she'd been Mage and had wanted to enthrall him, she'd have done it already. She wasn't Mage. And damn yes, he wanted her.

As they pulled into the Market's parking lot twenty minutes later, she was standing at the corner of the building, her head tipped against the wall in a stance that was perhaps a little sad, perhaps weary, as if she'd been waiting for him for hours. Her shapeless dress was a pretty blue, the same summer sky shade as her eyes.

"Get her out of your system, B.P. I'm tired of all the growling. Besides, my gut's sure of this one. Hell if I know why, but you need to do this. She's going to be good for you."

Paenther climbed out of the Mustang and hesitated, a dozen reasons not to walk toward her bounding through his mind.

But then she straightened, and even across the parking lot he could sense the loneliness and longing in her eyes. A hunger less of the flesh than of the spirit. A need of the soul that spoke to something deep inside him, and he found himself unable to turn away.

The wind whipped, coating him with dust from the parking lot and flinging sharp, tiny raindrops against his cheeks and forehead. He barely noticed.

As he started toward her, her expression didn't change. No smile greeted him this time. But with each step, the air around him heated. As did the blue of her eyes.

His pulse began to pound in his veins, the blood rushing, thick and warm, hardening him in an instant. Her remembered taste danced on his tongue, her scent springing from his pores as if it had been moments and not more than twenty-four hours since he kissed her.

Goddess, but he needed to get her out of his system. There was only one way he was going to do it.

As he closed the distance between them, she held out her hand to him, watching him with deep, smoldering eyes. Her warm hand trembled as he curled his own around it. As the wind twirled leaves in the gravel, she turned and tugged on his hand, and he followed. She led him behind the building and up the steep, heavily wooded hill behind the store.

Surrounded by the rich loamy scents of the woods, all he could smell was violets. *Her.* The scent wrapped around him, sinking deep into his skin, further inflaming the heat already building.

He gripped her hand tighter, part reaction to his body's excitement, part possessiveness as they climbed together, far away from prying eyes.

He didn't even know her name.

He ducked under a low branch, pushing aside another for her. It didn't matter. All that mattered was sinking inside her and ridding himself of this obsession that had hounded him for two solid days.

She continued to try to lead him, but they were out of sight of the parking lot, and he couldn't wait any longer.

He pulled her to a stop. She turned, her expression enigmatic as she slid into his arms. He covered her mouth with his, and passion exploded inside him. Desire roared through his body, making him heavy and ready. Her taste was even sweeter than he'd remembered, her scent exhilarating.

As he pressed her back against the nearest tree, he was vaguely aware of a pair of deer wandering close, watching them curiously.

She kissed him frantically, as if she feared they didn't have much time. He kissed her back with the same intensity, desperate to taste her, to feel her, to know her in every way.

The feel of her hand on his zipper made his blood

pound. The touch of her fingers along the length of his bare flesh nearly stopped his heart.

Gentleness and care be damned, he needed her *now*. Shoving his hand beneath her dress, he found her as bare and ready as she'd been the day before. Hot, wet, and whimpering with desire as his finger probed her depths.

Without pretense, he yanked up her dress to her waist then lifted her, positioning her sheath to his height. As she wrapped her bare thighs around his waist, he pushed inside her, filling her in a single, perfect thrust.

Heaven. Nothing in his entire life had ever felt more right. He thrust into her, over and over, pressing her against the tree at her back until she was gasping and moaning with pleasure. Within moments, her release broke over her with a cry, her inner muscles contracting hard around him, driving him over the edge.

"Look at me," she cried on a husky groan.

As his seed pumped into her, his body and mind open as they only were during sexual release, he stared into her passion glazed eyes.

And froze.

"I'm sorry, warrior," she said softly, her eyes no longer the simple sky blue of a human's.

As darkness swallowed his vision from the outside in, he stared into blue eyes now rimmed in copper and knew his luck had followed his caution into oblivion.

For the second time in his life, he'd fallen into the trap of a Mage.

Chapter
Twenty-four

"She's alive."

Tighe felt the Hummer's upholstery at his back, but his mind was fully with Delaney as he watched her through the clone's eyes. But even as he rejoiced in her survival, he wondered how long it would last.

He felt Wulfe's big hand on his shoulder. "Any identifiers?"

"None. She's in a kitchen, I think." She was on her stomach on a polished wood floor lined with blue paint, in a room swarming with flies, a knee—the clone's knee—firmly planted in her back. While Tighe was forced to watch, hands that looked like his own stripped the sweater and bra from the body of the woman Tighe would right now give his life to protect.

The bastard flipped her onto her back. Delaney's eyes glittered with hatred, lanced through with pain. And fear.

Fury roared in Tighe's ears, melding with the sound of the chaos as his fingers began to burn.

"Stay in your skin!" Wulfe growled. "She won't stand a chance if you lose it."

Delaney. Goddess. Delaney.

He took deep breaths, fighting back the chaos. She needed him.

She tried to hit the clone, one feminine hand flying into his eyes only to be stopped and wrenched to the floor where a length of rope lay waiting. With Tighe's own nimble fingers, the clone tied the rope tight around her wrist.

Delaney tugged, but her hand went nowhere. Tighe saw why. The rope had been attached to an eyebolt screwed into the floor. As if the clone had planned everything.

"Of course he planned it," he muttered.

"Planned what?" Hawke asked.

"He's tying her to the floor. Already had the eyebolts and rope ready."

"Why? Why *her*?"

"Who knows. He must have seen us together. At the Lincoln Memorial. During that first apartment fire. He could have been anywhere. *Anyone.*"

The clone slammed his knee into the crevice beneath her rib cage, making her eyes bulge with pain as he yanked her other arm wide from her body and tied her second wrist.

Delaney grabbed the ropes, lifted her hips, and

kicked hard at her captor's face, but her strength and speed were no match for a Feral's, and the clone's were. He grabbed her heels and pulled off her boots and socks, one after another as tears glistened in furious brown eyes.

She was right there. *Right there.* Close enough to reach out and touch, *and he couldn't help her.*

He gripped the seat, his stomach cramping.

"Jesus! He's shredding the bleeding upholstery." Jag's voice. "Wulfe, do something!"

"How about I bang your head into the steering wheel?" Wulfe snarled. "Can't you see he has bigger concerns than your damn car? We *all* do!"

Tighe heard a low moan and realized it had come from his own throat. "*I can't help her. She's fighting him, and I can't help her!*"

With little effort, the clone stripped off her jeans and panties and tied first one ankle, then the other, to the last two eyebolts, spreading her wide.

"*Goddess.*"

Then he reached for her.

Tighe's roar of fury threatened to shatter the Hummer's windows.

"*Stay in your skin!*"

"He has her. He stripped her. *He's touching her.*" The sight of that demon's hands reaching between her legs . . .

His head pounded with the force of his fury. His fingers burned. The chaos swirled at the edges of his mind, black fingers of darkness curling toward him, ready to hook around him and pull him in. His claws began to unsheathe.

"Tighe! He's not going to rape her. He doesn't have any blood in that body, and a cock can't rise without blood. He's just trying to scare her. Whatever he does, she's alive, buddy. As long as she's alive, you can get her back. *But you've got to stay in your skin.*"

He fought the darkness, pushing away the fury. She needed him. *Needed* him.

Slowly, painfully, he pulled himself back from that edge, his thoughts clinging to Delaney. She had to be terrified. He knew she was strong. If any woman could survive this mentally, it was his brown eyes. But he had to reach her. He had to save her. *He had to stay in control.*

"You don't have enough fear in you," the clone said with a touch of disgust, at last pulling his hand away.

As he rose, Tighe's own sight of Delaney widened. The blue paint staining the floor suddenly took on an ominous significance.

"*Shit.*"

"What?" Hawke demanded.

"A pentagram. *She's lying in the middle of a Daemon's sacrificial pentagram.*"

"Stay in your skin!"

"I'm in it!" The vision ended. Tighe shook off Wulfe's massive hand, a deep, furious growl rumbling in his chest at the thought of Delaney in that bastard's clutches. His gaze flew to Hawke. "Why the pentagram? *Why does he have her in a sacrificial pentagram?*"

"Easy, buddy," Hawke said. "Daemons used

pentagrams for any number of purposes, most of which we don't know. At least we know he caught her for a purpose other than to feed from her. We just don't know what it is."

"Think, Tighe," Wulfe urged, his hand landing heavily on Tighe's shoulder. "What did you see in that vision? We need clues."

Tighe gripped his head, forcing himself to replay the scene though it tore strips from his soul. "Nothing but impressions. A big house. Lots of trees in the backyard. No houses easily visible."

"Could be around here," Hawke murmured.

"Could be anywhere in the Mid-Atlantic," Tighe snapped, then took a shuddering breath. "My gut says it was near here. He didn't take her far."

"What else?" Hawke prompted.

"He said . . . right before the vision ended he told her she didn't have enough fear in her."

"She wasn't feeding him. He may have gone to feed elsewhere."

Tighe closed his fingers around his hair until his scalp ached. "Or he killed her."

"You'd have seen it," Hawke said. "You're getting the visions again. At least when he feeds from Delaney."

Tighe lifted his head and speared his friend with his gaze. "*Why?*"

"Goddess knows. The three of you are connected, that's all I can tell you. If he were feeding from her, I think you'd be seeing it. But you may not see him feeding from anyone else. Delaney's probably still seeing those."

"The shitbag's probably setting another fire," Jag drawled.

"I agree. Pull over, Jag." Hawke turned to look at them all. "I think he has Delaney nearby, and he's going to set those fires the same. I'll take to the air. Wulfe, shift and try to pick up her scent. Jag, call Lyon, tell him what we know, get him or Kougar to get on the emergency bandwidths and listen for a fire to be called in, then drive through the neighborhoods looking yourselves. *And keep Tighe in his skin.*"

"Aye-aye, Admiral," Jag drawled.

Hawke opened the door, shifted, and flew out while Wulfe leaped from his own door on all fours.

"Get the doors, Stripes. Looks like it's just you and me, now, *Wigout*. Keep your eyes peeled for smoke."

Tighe pulled the two doors closed, then collapsed against the seat back as Jag called Feral House and filled them in. His body ached. *Delaney. What have I done? If only I'd bound myself to you. If only.*

I see the fires. Hawke's voice sounded in his head. *He's got three houses on Birch Terrace circled with flames.*

I'm on my way. Tighe opened the door of the moving car and leaped out, shifting into his tiger in midair. Behind him he could hear Jag's, "Shit!", but he never slowed. He could get there faster on foot than Jag could in the car, and all that mattered was finding Delaney.

* * *

Delaney lay alone and shivering on the hardwood floor, a grandfather clock somewhere in the deserted house chiming the quarter hour. Fifteen minutes, the clone had been gone. Maybe twenty. And she knew exactly what he'd been up to.

Three fires, three houses in a row, as if he wanted to get the biggest feed for his match. The pain of the vision was finally beginning to recede from her head.

"I'm not dead yet!" Her voice rang into the empty room as she jerked her head, jarring the stupid flies loose from her face. Her nostrils were so fried from the stench, she almost couldn't smell it any longer.

Is he just going to leave me here?

Cold sweat slicked her skin. Terror snaked in and out of her heart, slithering and gnawing as it went. *So cold.*

Tighe, please. Please find me. Use your superpowers. Find me.

A door clicked and opened. She lifted her head, for one desperate moment thinking Tighe had heard her. But the man who walked into the kitchen had eyes of pure evil.

Delaney shuddered, her shivers becoming violent as terror joined the cold. What would he do to her this time?

Despair nearly stole her will. How badly would he hurt her before he finally put his mouth to her neck again, as he had the first time, and took her life?

Tears burned in her eyes, but she fought them back. Tighe would come. He'd come for her. She had to believe that.

The clone stood over her, looking down at her body, his gaze crawling across her breasts.

"Did you feed?" she asked, struggling to keep her voice even. He could probably sense her emotions better than Tighe since he actually drank them. But not hearing the fear in her own voice helped her keep the rank hysteria at bay.

"I did." Squatting at her hip, he reached between her legs, his cold, awful touch stroking her, circling her opening.

Her eyes nearly rolled back in her head as she fought to scramble away mentally from the feel of that cold, inhuman finger.

"I feed on pain, but I think you know that. And I know a thousand ways to cause it. A thousand ways without killing you."

"You're only a few weeks old. How could you possibly know a thousand ways?"

"Daemon memories, thanks to my draden host. Ways to torture a human."

His finger slid across the tight, dry opening to her womb. "Imagine the steel hilt of a knife, heated over an open fire until it glows red, then shoved . . ."

He pressed his finger inside her. She gasped at the sharp tug of pain, her mind screaming against the invasion as much as the horror of his words.

"Can you imagine it?"

Oh, God. "Yes." Her heart thudded. She had to stop reacting. She had to get control of her fear. Get her mind on something else before he turned her into a trembling wreck.

"Why did you take me? What do you want with me other than my fear?"

His finger left her, his cold hand closing around her breast, stroking it with frightening gentleness. "I've never forgotten you. From the moment I first put my mouth on you, I've thought of you."

He swung his long leg over her and straddled her waist, bracing his arms on either side of her head as he stared into her eyes. Slowly, his eyes changed, the coldness pushed aside by a warmth, a depth of emotion that made her skin crawl.

"I love you."

Staring at him, she could almost believe he thought he did. "Then why do you want to hurt me? If you loved me, you'd let me go."

He grinned at her, flashing Tighe's dimples, intelligence gleaming in his eyes. "Nice try. But, no, I'm not going to let you go." He shrugged. "I may have feelings for you, but at heart I'm a Daemon. I need someone to help me get the other half of the soul I need to survive. And when I saw you with him, when I realized *he* was the one touching you, I decided to take you from him. You'll be the one to help me."

"I'll never help you."

He smiled, the coldness rushing back into his eyes. "Oh, but you will. Now, as a matter of fact."

He swung off her, then moved until he was kneeling at her head. Her heart thundered with terror as he gripped her face with both icy hands.

Cold flowed into her. *So cold*. Every time he touched her, her body temperature dropped another degree, until she feared she was at risk for hypothermia.

"What are you doing?" she demanded, unable to keep the quaver out of her voice.

For more than a minute, he didn't answer, just stroked her temples with gentle thumbs as he watched her upside down.

His fingers stopped their caressing and his grip tightened. "What am I doing? I'm making you mine, Delaney. I'm making you mine."

His fingers squeezed. Pain unlike anything she'd ever imagined poured into her head and began to pump through her veins like acid. Screams tore through her mind, raking her flesh.

Deep inside, she felt something unnatural, something *evil*, take root and grow.

Tighe tore through the woods, following his tiger's scent of smoke as surely as his own human sense of direction. The moment he reached the back of the burning houses, he knew Delaney wasn't in any of them. The lots were small, houses crowding too close in the back.

Sirens tore through the lightly falling rain, and he took off. The humans could take care of their own.

As he headed toward the more affluent area where a house might back onto nothing but woods, he caught a glimpse of Wulfe.

I may have picked up the clone's scent, Wulfe said. *It's not a smell, exactly, but I remember feeling something similar near where we found her phone.*

I'm right behind you, Tighe told him, and raced after him, his sleek tiger's body eating up the ground with ease. *"Wulfe's picked up a scent,"* he told Hawke.

I heard. I've got you spotted. I'm following.

Tighe recognized the trees behind a large brick-front Colonial a split second before he heard the scream.

"*I'll take the front,*" Wulfe said.

A large bay window framed kitchen cabinets. Without a single pause, Tighe flew over the high railing of the deck and crashed through the glass.

Delaney lay on the floor, staked in the center of the pentagram as he'd seen her in the vision. He could hear her heart beating. Unconscious, but alive. *Thank you, goddess.*

Hawke ran in from the front of the house. "Where is he?"

Tighe shifted back into a man. "He wasn't here. *Find him.*" He pulled out one of his switchblades and knelt at Delaney's feet, cutting her loose. He'd freed her feet and pushed her legs together, and was sawing at the third bond when Wulfe and Hawke ran into the room from the opposite door.

"Where is he?" Hawke demanded.

Déjà vu. Tighe froze and stared at his friend. Understanding crashed over him like falling ice. "He was here. He was *you.*" Tighe leaped to his feet. "Bleed! *Now.*"

Wulfe and Hawke each pulled a knife and cut himself, then held their palms up as the blood ran down their flesh.

Tighe sliced his own.

"Find him!"

Damn it. *Damn it!* He'd been so concerned with Delaney, he'd forgotten the clone could change shape at will. That error just might cost him his life.

But he'd found her. *He'd found her.*

At least he thought he had. He could take no more chances. Lifting her free hand, he pressed the tip of his knife into her finger, drawing a single droplet of blood. She flinched, jerking her hand, and stirred.

As he watched, her eyes fluttered open, her gaze going from him to the knife still smeared with his own blood. With devastating dismay he watched those brown eyes fill with hopelessness and fear.

Fear. *Of him.*

He hated her fear.

Inside his head, the chaos rushed at him in a deafening roar.

"No, D, no!" He growled, his jaw clenching, his fingertips burning. "You're safe."

But he wasn't.

The chaos broke over him like a tidal wave, the fury clawing through his limbs, into his heart and head, swirling inside him as he fought to battle it back.

But it was too strong. His defenses against it too badly cracked.

Too late. *Too late.*

His claws unsheathed. His fangs dropped.

His conscious mind disappeared in a bottomless well of darkness.

Chapter
Twenty-five

"Tighe?"

Delaney fought against the pain that encased her body, struggling to clear her mind as a battle raged around her. *He'd come for her.* For one horrible moment she'd thought he was the clone, but then she'd heard his voice. *He'd come for her.*

She forced her eyes open, then squeezed them shut as something sailed over her head. A battle. They'd caught him. But the sounds that reached her ears were oddly, frighteningly familiar. Growling. Snarling. The breaking of furniture, just like the two times Tighe had lost it.

Oh, no. Please, not that.

She tried to move and realized she was only tied by one wrist. *So cold.* Exhaustion tugged at her battered mind, and she curled onto her side.

Stay awake. Warn them.

Out of the corner of her eye, another Feral appeared. Jag, her mind suggested.

His gaze went to the pile of dead bodies, his face screwing up in disgust. "*Jesus.* Someone needs to teach that demon to clean up after himself when he's done eating. He's feeding the whole bloody fly population of Northern Virginia!"

"Bleed, Jag!" Wulfe roared.

Jag scowled, pulled out a knife, and cut himself. Blood rolled down his palm.

"Get Delaney. We've got to get Tighe locked up."

Locked up. Her chest squeezed. *Lost in the darkness.*

Jag bent over her, cutting the last of her bonds.

She tried to focus her eyes on him, but she was fast slipping away. "Not . . . Feral House. Did something to me. I'm . . . dangerous. And . . . get my boots!"

Delaney woke to the sound of the river and voices, and the feel of a cool wind in her face. She lay still, her battered mind trying to identify the voices as friend or foe. All male. No, a female voice.

She opened her eyes, finding a ceiling of stars high above her head, all but blotted out by a bright light just to her side. *Kara.* Her forehead wrinkled at the sight of the woman sitting with her legs crossed, glowing like a camp lantern.

"Hi there," Kara said softly, meeting her gaze. "You're safe, Delaney."

Delaney tried to shake her head, but nothing happened. "You're glowing."

"That's what I do," she said with a lilt in her voice. "Remember I told you I was the power plug? I wish I could use some of my power to help you, but they tell me only Ferals can handle it. But I'm keeping the light on and the rock warm for you. Are you still cold?"

"No. Warm." Surprisingly warm, despite the cool wind. She felt as if someone had wrapped her in blankets and laid her on a heated bed.

"Good."

"Where am I?" Her gaze moved to an oddly dressed teenager kneeling on her other side, his hand on her forehead, his eyes closed.

"The goddess stone," Kara told her. "The men called a Feral Circle, a mystic circle, to keep out draden and prying human eyes. The Shaman is trying to figure out what was done to you and whether you're really a danger."

"Tighe?"

Kara's brows knit unhappily. "He's at Feral House."

"In the prison?"

"I'm afraid so. He may still snap out of it." But her tone said she didn't believe it.

"I need to . . . see him."

The young man she assumed was the Shaman lifted his hand from her forehead. As she turned her gaze to him, he looked down at her with ancient eyes in his youthful face.

"Hello, Delaney."

"Hi."

He turned to face a distant point beyond Kara's light.

"He definitely left a mark on her, Lyon," he said. "Unlike anything I've ever seen. Not a dark charm. Nothing that concrete. More like shadows on her soul."

"Is she a danger to us?"

"I can't answer that for a certainty, but my instincts tell me those shadows are wounds, not magic. She needs to rest. To heal, both physically and mentally. It's too bad Tighe's not available to help the process."

Tighe. Tears formed in her eyes. But she felt the Shaman's hand on her forehead again, and slept before they had a chance to fall.

When Delaney woke again, she was in Tighe's bedroom. The room was dark, but light shone from beneath the closed door, and the rumble of voices carried from far below. It was probably still evening. She stretched, taking quick inventory, deciding nothing hurt, then shuddered as memories rushed into her mind. The clone. *Tighe.* Kara had said he'd lost it and was in the prison. She envisioned him trapped in a darkness as bleak and terrifying as the one he'd pulled her from.

If there was a way to free him from his own dark hell, she was going to find it.

She pushed off the covers and swung her feet over the side of the bed, noting that the pajamas Kara had loaned her were back on her again. For a brief moment, she considered trying to find something better to wear downstairs than Kara's p.j.s, and as quickly dismissed the concern. They certainly showed less of her than the ceremonial gown. And if she remembered that nightmare in the kitchen correctly, they'd seen her in less. Far less.

Flicking on the light, she did a quick search of the walls and pulled down a wicked-looking twelve-inch dagger. She was not going unarmed again. Barefoot, she flew from the room and down the richly curved stairs.

Kougar glanced up as he crossed the foyer, his pale gaze expressionless.

"Where's Tighe?"

He turned away. "He's lost to you."

"Like hell he is." She moved to cut him off. "I want to see him."

He towered over her, but stopped, eyeing her like he might an interesting little bug.

"Why?"

"I want to see if I can get him out of there."

"You can't." He started around her.

She lifted the blade, threatening him if he took another step. "Sometimes when I touch him, it helps calm him. I might be able to pull him back."

"He'll kill you."

"I'm willing to risk it."

He lifted his hand and stroked his goatee as he studied her. "You would've attacked me."

Delaney blinked, at first thinking he meant just then, when she'd raised the blade. Then she remembered the mating ceremony, when he'd cut Tighe. When she'd jumped off the pedestal, thinking they were in for a fight.

"His enemies are my enemies. At that moment, I

wasn't sure whether you fell into that category."

Without so much as an acknowledgment that she'd spoken, he turned and went back the way he'd come.

Delaney stared at his retreating back and released a frustrated sigh, then turned, figuring she'd have to find Tighe on her own.

But she'd barely taken two steps when Kougar spoke. "The human wants to see Tighe."

Delaney whirled back to find Kougar standing in a doorway partway around the corner.

"Like hell." Lyon's voice.

She strode to Kougar and walked past him into what had to be Lyon's office. The big man sat behind a desk with a computer, shelves full of books and binders on the wall behind him.

Lyon's brow lifted as he dropped his gaze to her weapon. "Is there a reason you're armed?"

"Tighe took my guns. And the last time I walked down those stairs, it didn't end so well." She lifted the blade, her eyes going hard. "I'm thinking maybe you should bleed for me."

A spark of respect lit his eyes. He pulled out his knife and drew blood from his palm, holding her gaze. "Kougar?"

She turned and watched as the pale-eyed Feral did the same, then before they could ask, she pricked her own finger on the tip of her blade. After showing Lyon the blood, she sucked it from her skin.

"I want you to take me to him."

"He wouldn't want you to see him as he is now."

"I've already seen him like that. The night he punched me full of holes. I need to touch him. I might be able to reach him."

"Impossible. You're only a human."

She moved forward and leaned on his desk. "We won't know whether or not I can help him until I try."

Something approaching sorrow warmed his amber eyes. "We've been trying to reach him for two days, Delaney. There's nothing to be done."

She stared at him, his words a painful shock. "*Two days?* He's been lost in there for *two days?*"

Lyon's eyes turned almost sympathetic. "I'm sorry."

But his revelation only made her more desperate to reach him. She turned to Kougar. "Show me where he is."

He gave an almost imperceptible nod and turned.

Behind her, Lyon leaped to his feet with a growl. "Delaney!"

She turned to face the chief of the Ferals, understanding why he was the leader as she felt the force within those amber eyes.

"He'll take your arm off if you reach in there. There's nothing in that cage but a vicious, wild animal."

She flinched.

He saw it. His expression tightened with a pain that might almost have matched her own. "There's nothing I can do for him except catch that clone."

Delaney shook her head. "I'm not leaving him in there another second if I can get him out." She looked at him forcefully. "I need you to hold him down."

"All it will take is a single slash of his claws, or one errant bite, and you're dead."

"It's a risk I'm willing to take. Twice he saved me when I needed him. Now he needs me."

Lyon stared at her for a long, heavy minute. "You're in love with him."

She nodded slowly with a wry purse of her lips. "I am."

On a huff of frustration, Lyon came around the desk. "If he kills you, he'll never forgive me."

"If I pull him out of there, you'll have another warrior at your side."

Lyon sighed. "True. Come on, then."

He led her back through the foyer and down the same stairs Tighe had taken her to be mated. They passed the cavelike room and entered a wide, open gym, a section of which contained surprisingly modern equipment, including weight benches, stationary bikes, and six of the biggest treadmills she'd ever seen. At the back of that room, Lyon opened yet another door hidden within a wall of mirrors onto a long, narrow, stone-lined passage. Rustic and a little bit spooky.

As she'd suspected, she never would have found Tighe on her own.

"The house doesn't look this big from upstairs," she murmured as she followed him. Kougar brought up the rear.

"It's not," Lyon said cryptically.

Sounds began to reach her ears, the grunts and

snarls of an animal. *Tighe*. She'd seen him feral before. A classic horror-show wolf man, only terribly, terribly real. Her fingernails dug into her palms as she prepared herself for that sight again.

The passage finally opened onto what was clearly a prison block with three thick-walled cells on either side, each with a heavily barred steel door. The floor was stone.

Gripping the bars of one door with fingers tipped by three-inch claws was Tighe.

Or rather the creature Tighe had become.

As before, his teeth were the wicked fangs of a tiger. His sunglasses were gone, his eyes those of an animal rather than a human—large, orange-gold pupils streaked with black. Not even a flicker of humanity lurked in their depths.

Tighe roared with fury, shaking the bars as if he wanted nothing more than to rip them out of their hinges and tear the limbs off anyone he could sink his claws into. With icy understanding, she knew that was exactly what he'd do if he got loose. She was not only risking her own life for what was almost certainly a waste of time, but she might even be risking the lives of the two men she'd dragged down there with her.

"Tighe?" Delaney stepped closer to the cage, but not so close he could reach through and catch her with those claws. "Tighe! Can you hear me?"

His growls only intensified.

"Tighe, it's me. Delaney. Tighe, I need you. Your men need you. You've got to fight your way back."

But the creature in front of her just snarled and shook the bars, his eyes at once wild and dead.

"I did warn you," Lyon said softly.

She turned and met his gaze. "I need to touch him. I may need to look into his eyes."

Lyon watched her for a long moment before he tossed her a key and nodded to the far cell. "Lock yourself in until we have him down. Don't come out until I tell you to."

With a nod, she went into the cell he'd indicated, pulled the metal door shut with a clang, then reached through the bars to lock it from outside. A shiver of claustrophobia had her curling her fingers tight around one cool steel bar. And Tighe had been caged like that for *two days*. Did he even know? Was he somewhat aware of where he was or, as she had been, was he floating around some dark void?

As she watched, Lyon and Wulfe shifted into the wolf-man feral state, their fangs and claws sprouting. Goose bumps rose on her arms. Unlike Tighe, though, they seemed to be in complete control. It wasn't the feral state itself that had sent Tighe into oblivion. It was his halved soul. The feral state was only the door into that place.

The moment Lyon unlocked Tighe's cage, all hell broke loose. Tighe sprang at them, slashing and ripping with his claws, going for Lyon's throat.

Delaney pressed her hand to her forehead. Kara was going to kill her if Lyon died because of this.

But Lyon had clearly been prepared for the attack. In a carefully coordinated move, the two thinking Ferals went at Tighe from both sides and, in a matter of minutes, had him pinned to the floor, facedown. While Wulfe sat on him, pulling his arms up his back nearly to his shoulder blades, Lyon crushed his face against the floor.

"Ready," Lyon said.

Delaney's heart threatened to pound right out of her chest. Her palms turned damp. Was she *really* going in there?

She remembered Tighe's voice when she'd been the one lost in the dark. The unbelievable relief.

Yes. She was really going in there.

Sticking her hand back between the bars, she unlocked the door and let herself out, then crossed the stone floor to enter Tighe's cage. She shivered at the sight of Lyon and Kougar watching her with animal eyes, fangs dripping from their mouths. Beneath them, Tighe thrashed and snarled, desperate to be free to annihilate them all.

And she was walking *into* his cage instead of running for her life as any sane person would do. Then again, running had never been her style.

Circling the edges of the cage, Delaney finally knelt near Tighe's head. He saw her. Oh yeah, he saw her. He snarled, his mouth dripping with saliva as he tried to snap at her with deadly teeth.

A wild, vicious animal Lyon had called him. And he was. On the outside. But the man she'd fallen in love with was in there somewhere. *Oh, Tighe. How much harder must this be for you?*

Shaking like a rookie on her first takedown, she reached for him, laying her hand on the bare flesh of one of the arms Kougar had pinned high up Tighe's back. His skin was warm and damp with exertion, but she knew that arm. How many times had it held her with gentle strength?

The thought grounded her.

"Tighe, I know you're in there. Come back to me. I need you to come back to me."

But her words didn't calm him, just as her touch was having no effect. If anything, he thrashed and struggled all the harder to free himself. As if dinner were within his reach and two fools were keeping him from it.

Despair pressed on her heart. Was she being totally foolish to think she could help him? She was human. Powerless. Tighe's thrashing body began to glisten through the tears filling her eyes.

"Do something, Delaney," Lyon growled. "We can't hold him forever."

With a bracing breath, she lowered herself to the floor until she lay beside Tighe, face-to-face. Until she was staring into those wild, golden orange tiger eyes with the jagged black lines.

"What's the matter with his eyes? The clone's had the same weird lines."

"The soul they share is disintegrating."

Disintegrating. *Oh, Tighe.* Fool or not, she wasn't giving up until she got him out of there.

"Tighe." As Lyon's big hand pinned Tighe's head, struggling to keep him from turning and biting off her fingers, Delaney gingerly reached for him, touching his stubbled jaw just below his upper fangs.

He growled low in his throat.

"Tighe, I know you're in there. Do you remember when I was trapped in the darkness? You came for me. You reached down deep in my mind and came for me. I don't know how you did that. I'm terrified it takes some kind of Feral gift that I don't possess."

Her voice caught as a tear escaped her eye to run over the bridge of her nose.

"I'm hoping you can follow my voice, Tighe. Follow my voice."

She stroked the rough stubble of his jaw, running her fingers gently over his warm skin, as she stared into those black and orange-gold tiger eyes that tracked her without recognition. Without humanity.

"You're not like him. Even feral like this, your skin's warm. Alive. Come back to me, Tighe." She couldn't stop the tears. "I need you to come back to me."

Keeping her gaze pinned on his, she thought of Tighe in there and tried to mimic the way he used to touch her mind when he was trying to get control over her. She'd been able to feel him like a warm presence in her head. If only she knew how to do that.

She kept talking, praying her voice might find its way down into whatever dark cellar he'd fallen into. "Tighe, I'm remembering how you brushed my mind when you were trying to steal my memories of you. How the touch of your mind against mine was warm and soft. And so much more. I'm remembering that touch of your mind, and I'm reaching for yours. In my mind, I'm reaching for you."

This was useless. Embarrassing. How could she ever think she could help him? A *human*.

With a suddenness that had her gasping, the face of a tiger leaped into her head as it had the other time, so clear, it almost felt real. A wild, beautiful sight. Like before she startled.

The tiger began to fade.

"No! No, come back to me, tiger." Her fingers dug into Tighe's jaw as she thought of the tiger this time, willing him to return.

He did. His ruffed, striped face rose in her mind until she could neither think of, nor see, anything else. And as it did, a warmth wrapped around her as strong and wonderful as Tighe's arms.

Her tears fell in earnest.

"Find him for me. I can't reach him, but you can. Find him. *Please* find him."

"She's connected with his animal." Kougar's voice fell on her ears as if from a distance.

"I'll be damned," Lyon replied.

D?

Tighe's voice sounded in her head, clear, but faint.

"I'm here, Tighe." She said the words out loud. "Can you hear me?"

Yes.

"Follow my voice."

Slowly, the hungry predatory eyes began to take on a glow of humanity. Even more slowly, his fangs began to recede, and the pupils of his eyes shrank until white showed around them again, and the color beneath the black shards turned to green.

"You're okay?" The words fell from his throat roughly, more growl than speech as his fangs disappeared altogether.

She lunged forward and pressed her cheek against his, drenching him with her tears. The next thing she knew, she was in his arms, crying with relief, battered by all that had happened since she last felt his arms around her. And scared by Lyon's words. That Tighe's soul was disintegrating.

Lyon cleared his throat behind her.

Tighe ran his hand down her hair. "Let's get up." She pushed off him and stood, brushing away the tears on her cheeks as he rose beside her. He reached for something in the corner and when he straightened those blasted sunglasses of his were back on his face, having miraculously survived the fight.

He reached for her, pulling her tight against his side as he faced the others.

"Welcome back." Lyon eyed him with a relief that glowed hotly in his amber eyes.

"What's the situation?" Tighe asked, as if he'd just woken from a quick nap. "Any news from Paenther?"

"Not today. I got a brief call from Foxx yesterday. They haven't found anything, yet."

"What about my clone?"

Lyon's mouth tensed. "In the two days you've been out, we've tried every Daemon-trapping spell

Kougar can come up with, but so far, no luck. Either the clone's not Daemon enough, or the rituals aren't right."

Tighe's arm tightened around her. "So I'm out of luck?"

"We're not giving up." But Lyon's tone held little hope.

Delaney pressed her cheek against Tighe's chest as fear twisted in her heart.

"How long do I have?" Tighe asked.

Lyon just shook his head.

Tighe stiffened. "Tell me, Roar."

The man, who was clearly Tighe's friend, cleared his throat, a suspicious glimmer entering his eyes. When he spoke, his voice was low and pained.

"Your soul . . . is almost gone. The Shaman thinks you may see another sunrise. But you won't see another sunset unless we get a miracle. I'm sorry, Tighe."

Delaney stiffened. "There has to be *something* you can do. You're *immortal*. Supermen."

Lyon shook his head slowly. "I'm sorry."

Tighe was silent. His body still. "What about D?" He asked finally. "Is she okay?"

"As far as we can tell. The Shaman's knowledge is of Mage magic, not Daemon. But she seems to be okay." Lyon's gaze swung to Delaney. To her surprise, he came to her, put his hands on her shoulders, and kissed her temple. He pulled back and met her gaze with eyes breaking with pain. "Thank you for giving him back to us."

His unspoken, *for now* hung in the air.

Delaney nodded, fighting back tears of her own. She wanted to rail at him for giving up, but she could see the pain in his eyes and knew he'd be doing something if he could.

"Is there anything I can do?" Tighe asked his chief.

Lyon shook his head slowly. "Kougar and Hawke are searching for any ancient spell they might have missed. The others are chasing fires in hopes of catching the clone that way. I'm afraid one more person isn't going to be of a lot of use."

Lyon put his hand on Tighe's shoulder. "If you want my advice, get something to eat and spend some time with your mate. Not necessarily in that order." His gaze swung to her, respect sharp in his eyes. "Human or not, she's a hell of a woman." He turned and started back down the tunnel.

Kougar came over to them and clasped Tighe's shoulder. "Never give up." His enigmatic gaze swung slowly to her. "Worthy," he murmured, with a single nod of the head, then turned and followed Lyon.

Tighe's hand squeezed her arm. "Was I hallucinating, or did Kougar just call you worthy?"

"You tell me."

She felt the stiffness enter his muscles a second before he released her, gripped her shoulders, and turned her to face him. His eyes took on a light she wasn't sure she liked. "*What did you do?*"

Delaney stared at him, her brows drawing together. "You know what I did. I led you out of the dark, just as you did me."

His hands tightened on her shoulders until his grip was almost painful. "*I could have killed you.*"

She stared at him, her temper flaring. "Well, you're *welcome.*"

"I mean it," he growled. "Don't *ever* do something like that again."

She kicked him in the shin with her bare toes. "*Twice* you risked everything to find me. *Twice.* Don't you dare get on my ass about helping you."

"I'm immortal. You're human!"

"As everyone keeps reminding me! I'm made of flesh and blood, not soap bubbles. I might not heal as fast as you do, but I do heal. Don't try to lock me away to protect me, Tighe. I won't have it."

She stilled, her words hanging in the air. She'd yelled at him about what not to do the next time, but it didn't look like there was going to be a next time.

"Oh, Tighe." Her eyes filled with tears.

With a growl, Tighe hauled her into his arms, burying his face in her hair with a shudder that shook the entirety of his big body. For long, long minutes he held her like that, shudders rocking him at regular intervals, while she clamped her arms around him and held him tight.

"I'm not mad at you, D. It's not you, though *goddess*, when I think of what I could have done to you like that . . ."

"I was so scared I wouldn't be able to reach you." Her voice broke. "I don't want to lose you."

The tears got away from her, and Tighe held her as she cried, stroking her back and running his hand over her hair.

"Don't cry, D. Kougar and Hawke will come up with something. We'll beat that bloodless sucker, yet."

But there was no real belief in his tone. Nothing but bleak despair.

When she got control, he pulled back until he could see her face, then cupped her cheek in his warm palm. "Are you really okay? I had a vision, D. I saw him stripping you, tying you down. *Touching you.*"

His words brought back that nightmare. Delaney shivered, the chills rippling over her skin.

Tighe pulled her against him, cradling her head. "I've never felt so helpless in my life. You were right there, and I couldn't help you. *I couldn't reach you.*"

"I'm okay. I knew you'd come for me."

"Always."

But *always* spoke of a future they didn't have.

How could this be it? How could this man, whom she'd just found, *whom she loved,* be dying? The weight of her grief was almost more than she could bear.

Chapter Twenty-six

Tighe held Delaney in his arms, deep in the bowels of Feral House, his heart filling with a pressure he wasn't sure he'd survive even if they did manage to kill his clone in time.

Was this love? He'd thought he'd been in love once before, but now he wondered.

Was this what real love felt like? This feeling that he couldn't breathe? The certainty that before he'd found her he'd *never* breathed? Never *lived*? And now he might only have hours.

Hours.

The knowledge echoed through his mind like the death knell it was. For the first time in his long, long life he faced true death. There had been threats to his life before, certainly. Mage battles.

Draden attacks that for short periods of time had gone south. But he'd always known he'd prevail. And he always had.

He was immortal.

Face-to-face, he'd be able to defeat the clone, he was sure of it. But his enemy fought from the shadows and behind the faces of the people he loved.

This time he might well lose.

The worst part was, for the first time since he was marked all those centuries ago, he had a strong reason to live. To watch over Delaney as she lived her life. To do whatever he could to make her short years safer, richer, even if she insisted on returning to her own world with no memory of him. He'd visit her in his cat form, then once she was asleep, he'd cloud her mind and hold her. She wouldn't be lonely. He'd make certain she was never lonely.

Slowly he pulled back, framing her face as he clung to her gaze, reassuring himself she was really in his arms, shaken anew by how scared he'd been that he'd never hold her like this again. Emotion caught in the back of his throat, burning a line all the way to his eyes.

"Goddess, D, when I realized you were missing, I nearly died." A shudder wracked his body. "When I finally figured out where you were, I heard you scream. I thought I was too late."

She brushed her cheek against his chest. "He touched my head with his hands. It felt like he poured acid in me. I really thought he'd planted something in me, but the Shaman couldn't find anything but shadows."

He slid his hands in her hair and pulled back to meet her gaze. "But you're all right?"

Her eyes filled with pain as she looked at him, but it was a pain not of the flesh. Grief, plain and simple.

He kissed her softly, reverently, drinking in the feel of her. The taste. Memorizing her sweet lips, so warm, so soft and precious. If all he had left was a few hours, he'd spend them like this. With her.

Tighe pulled away, then swung her into his arms, startling a quick gasp from her. "I need to make love to you, D."

Delaney hooked her arm around his neck and pressed her lips to his cheek. "I need to make love to you, too."

A pleased growl rumbled in his chest. "I need a shower first. I must stink like five-day-old garbage."

She shuddered. "I think my sense of smell has been permanently burned away."

Her words made his chest ache, and he remembered that kitchen, that smell, and could only guess what a horrifying experience that had been for her. His grip on her tightened, and he pressed his head gently to hers as he carried her, safe in his arms at last.

He took her back through the gym and into the open shower at the back, where he lowered her slowly to her feet. Kissing her briefly, he turned on one of the showers and began stripping.

Delaney did the same, lifting the soft pajama shirt to expose her beautiful breasts.

"Not here, sweetheart," Tighe said softly. "There's someplace else I want to make love to you. I'll only be a minute."

Delaney managed a sad smile. "I need a shower as badly as you do. Probably worse, considering where I've been."

He stared at her, understanding dawning slowly. "Is there a reason you didn't shower the past two days?"

She pulled off her pajama bottoms and tossed them on the bench. "I was out of it as long as you were, though not quite in the same way. The moment I woke up, I came for you, Tighe. The *moment*." Her gaze met his, her eyes filled with a silken strength and a tenderness that made him ache with love.

He pulled her into his arms and kissed her fiercely, tenderly, telling her silently what was in his heart. But the slide of her nakedness against his had his body revving, his eyes changing. If he didn't put distance between them soon, it would be over here and now. And this was not where he meant to make love to her.

"Quick shower, D." He forced himself to release her and turned on a second of the four shower-heads. He didn't dare try to stand that close to her right now.

As Delaney stood watching him, she cocked her head. "Are you really going to take a shower with your sunglasses on?"

"Yes."

"You've got to be kidding."

Her disbelief annoyed him. "There's a reason I wear them, D. It's important."

But as he watched her, an aching hurt entered her eyes. "All we've been through together, *knowing* we could almost be out of time, and you're still going to hide from me?"

A fist clenched inside his chest. "You don't understand."

"Then tell me."

He stared at her, feeling trapped. She didn't understand. She couldn't possibly understand. Yet everything she'd said was true. And, goddess, but he loved her. He could bare himself for her, couldn't he?

He lifted his hands and dropped them again. "It's because my eyes go feral whenever I'm attracted to a woman."

She gave him a look that said she clearly thought he was an idiot. "*So?*"

"*So*, they turn into tiger's eyes. They'd scare the shit out of you."

She fisted her hands on her bare, slender hips. "You're kidding, right? Have you forgotten I was the one who got you out of there? I stared into your tiger eyes for what seemed like *forever*, Tighe, and yes, I was scared. You were snarling and snapping, trying to bite my hand off, but the thing that scared me the most was that I wasn't going to be able to reach you."

With a growl, he stepped under the hot spray of the nearest shower and tipped his head back as that fist in his chest tightened. He heard her move, then felt her arms slide around him as she pressed her cheek against his chest.

"You don't scare me, Tighe."

"You *like* kissing monsters?"

"Take off the sunglasses, shape-shifter."

"Dammit. Can't you just leave it alone?"

"Nope."

In a fit of anger, he pulled off his shades and tossed them onto the floor. As much as he wanted to stare down at her with his animal eyes, he couldn't bring himself to do it. He couldn't stand to see her own eyes change, fear filling their depths.

Delaney's fingers curved around his jaw and with a feather-light touch, made him look at her. "Why did you use the word *monster*?"

He forced himself to meet her gaze, bracing for her reaction. But she just continued to look at him like she always did. "It's just a word, D. *Animal, Feral, monster.* It's just a word."

She shook her head even as she watched him with eyes warm and understanding, an understanding he wasn't sure he could handle.

Lifting her hand, she pressed her palm to his cheek. "I love your eyes, Tighe. Because when I look into them, I see you. Even when you were in that feral state, the moment you came back to me, I saw you. Your fierce strength and gentle protectiveness. Your courage and honor and determination. Whether your eyes look like a man's or a tiger's, I see *you.*"

He tore his gaze from hers and looked up at the ceiling. "Thanks."

She released a soft snort. "Thanks? Tighe, for heaven's sake, you're an amazing creation. Rare, powerful. *Beautiful.* In all your forms."

He heard her words, but the fist inside his chest only pinched harder. "You don't understand."

"Obviously not."

Her soft palm slid across his chest. "Tell me. Help me understand. If you give me just one last gift, make it this."

He groaned. "You don't fight fair."

"You can't always win with fair." Her soft mouth brushed his arm in a sweet kiss. "I want to understand you."

"Let me finish my shower, first." He needed space. Because she was getting too close. She was digging too deep.

Delaney sighed, her eyes frustrated and sad. "Okay." She moved to the other shower and picked up a bottle of flowery shampoo Kara must have left down there.

He washed thoroughly, scraping his skin raw, lost in feelings and thoughts he didn't know how to explain. Things he didn't *want* to explain even if he knew how. But Delaney's presence, the solidity of her acceptance, grabbed hold of him and wouldn't let him go.

He'd give her the sun and the moon if he could. He supposed he could try to explain what he didn't entirely understand himself. And if he was going to do it, it had to be tonight.

With a sigh, he turned off the water, wrapped a towel around his waist, and sat on one of the benches, tipping his head against the wall behind him as she finished her shower. His gaze fastened on the rocklike tile of the wall across from him as his mind looked inward.

"I love living here, D, fighting beside these men. And when I shift into my tiger, it's a rush unlike anything you can imagine. But I swear, I swear not a day goes by that I don't think about how I'd give it up . . ." He shook his head. "I'd give it up . . ."

The words burned in his throat.

Delaney joined him, wrapping a towel around her dripping body as she sat down beside him. Her fingers stroked his damp arm. "For what, Tighe?"

Pulling her against him, he struggled to find the words for a longing he'd never given voice to.

His voice shook. "To hold my daughter again."

Delaney started. He tasted her surprise. But all she did was press her head against his shoulder. "Tell me about her."

Where to begin? But as he clung to her, the words poured out.

"She was precious. Perfect. Her name was Amalie, and the last time I saw her she was five, with dimples like mine and a cloud of golden curls that she'd flick back from her face as she ran from one discovery to the next. She had a quick mind and an insatiable curiosity, and from the moment she learned to speak, all she did was ask questions. Why do the clouds move? Why don't all butterflies wear the same colored wings? Why did her cuts take days to heal and mine only seconds?"

"She was mortal."

"Yes. My wife, Gretchen, was human. The children of such unions can be either, but Amalie was mortal."

His eyes fogged, a lump forming in his throat. Goddess, but he missed her.

"Tell me about Gretchen."

Swallowing back the emotion, he forced himself to push past the anger that thoughts of her always brought and think about the girl she'd been. For the first time in centuries, he thought of the girl he'd fallen in love with all those years ago.

"I met her when I was fifteen. She was a year younger, but I knew I was going to marry her. From the first day I saw her, I loved her."

"Where did you meet her?"

"We both wound up with the same foster father. I grew up in a Therian village in Denmark. When I was nine, my mother had a premonition of a Mage attack. The Mage in that area, at that time, were trying to wipe out the Therians."

"*Why?*"

"A superiority thing we've suffered from the dawn of time. One of the women in our village had married a human a few years before, so my mother took me to her and asked her to let me stay there for a while. She promised she'd come back for me as soon as it was safe."

Delaney's soft hand stroked his chest. "She didn't come back, did she?"

"No. A few months later, the woman I was living with died of a mysterious illness. She was Therian, so of course it was no illness. It had to have been

Mage magic of some kind. I was too young to understand fully what was going on, but I had a feeling . . . I *knew* my mother would never come back for me. So I lived with the human, Anders, and his young son, helping with the farm."

"Did he know what you were? That you were immortal?"

"I was never really sure. In hindsight, no. He couldn't have known. When I was fifteen, his fourteen-year-old niece came to live with us. Gretchen. She was . . . incorrigible. Full of mischief and laughter, and I fell head over heels in love with her. Three years later, we married. Amalie was born a year after that."

A soft kiss brushed his shoulder. "What happened?"

He looked down at her dark head and lifted his hand to touch the cool sleekness of her hair. "Why are you so sure something happened?"

She lifted her head to meet his gaze, her heart in her eyes, and he knew she felt the pain in his chest. So he told her.

"I was marked by the goddess to be the next Feral Warrior."

Her eyes widened. "Literally?"

"Yes and no. By the goddess, I mean Nature. There's not a real woman or anything. But the marking is literal." He touched the four claw marks that scored his right nipple. "I woke up to these after a hell of a dream I can't remember. I kind of knew what they meant. I'd heard of the Feral Warriors and how they were marked, but I'd never seen one. That night, as we got ready for bed, I wanted to make love to my wife."

Delaney's breath sucked in audibly. "Your eyes changed."

Tighe nodded, the old pain driving a stake through his heart. "She screamed." He looked across the shower, his sight caught far in the past. "I thought she saw something behind me, something threatening my family. That emotional rush turned me completely feral. Not crazy, like you've seen me, but still feral. I was horrified as claws unsheathed from my fingers, and fangs grew in my mouth. She ran from me. She ran from our cottage screaming for help, yelling that there was a demon in her home. The villagers attacked me, hacking at me with knives and axes. If I'd been human, I'd have died. I managed to get back in my skin—back in my human form—and tried to explain, but they weren't listening. I had no choice but to run that night.

"The next morning, I snuck back into the village. I had to talk to Gretchen. I knew she loved me. If I could just explain, everything would be okay. But the moment she saw me, her eyes filled with such terror. Such terror, D."

Delaney looked up at him, and he met her gaze as she reached for his hand. "That's why my terror sets you off, isn't it? It's that memory."

"Probably. I was furious with her, but mostly . . . I hurt, D. She'd betrayed me. Betrayed everything we'd meant to one another. She started screaming again and ran from me, and I let her go. I understood it was never going to be okay. But as I left my house, *my home*, and started back through the garden, I heard Amalie. I turned around to find her running toward me. *Toward me*. She was crying for me. Gretchen's uncle snatched her up as the other villagers armed themselves, ready to drive me away a second time. All the while Amalie kicked and screamed, reaching for me, the tears streaming down her face." He covered his eyes against the burning that wouldn't stop. "I turned and walked away. I turned my back on her, D. I never saw her again."

"*Tighe*." He felt Delaney's strong arms go around his waist and her damp head press against his chest. "There was nothing else you could have done. *Nothing*. She knew you loved her," she added softly.

His arms went around her and held fast. "Did she? I never went back. A newly marked Feral starts to feel a pull, a need for radiance that will eventually lead him to Feral House, but it took me nearly a year and a half to find it, up in the Highlands of Scotland. Not long after I arrived, Lyon moved us to Ireland because of all the problems with the Mage. I immersed myself in my new life, shutting out the pain of the old. We were engaged in constant battle with the Mage, and after a time, we moved to Spain, and finally across the ocean to come here.

"The first time I considered trying to go back, we were discussing leaving for the New World. I needed to see Amalie again. Just one more time.

It seems ridiculous, maybe, but I still thought of her as five. In my mind, she'd stayed five all those years. When you never age, when no one around you ever ages, you tend to forget that others do. And it's all too easy to lose track of time. I finally stopped and did the math and realized nearly a hundred and twenty years had passed. My little Amalie was long gone. I don't know if she lived another year after I left her, or another hundred. When I pulled that child from the fire, all I could think, all I could wonder was how many times my own daughter had needed me that I wasn't there to protect her."

"I'm sorry, Tighe." Delaney held him, stroking his back, until the shudders left him, and the memories uncurled from his heart.

"It was a long time ago," he said, finally feeling like he could breathe again.

Delaney straightened and met his gaze. "I'm sorry for you, but I'm sorry for them, too. Poor Gretchen. She'd probably never heard of Therians, let alone Feral Warriors. All she knew was stories of demons and devils and bad things. Your changing like that would have scared the crap out of anyone."

She ran gentle fingers through his hair, holding him with her gaze. "Don't blame her, Tighe. It wasn't her fault." Leaning forward, she laid a feather-light kiss upon the corner of his mouth. "But it wasn't your fault either."

He sighed. "I tried to forget. I *had* to forget. But not a day goes by that my traitorous eyes don't remind me what I am."

A soft hand stroked his cheek. "I love what you are."

"I saw your eyes, D. When I went feral."

"Well, *yeah*. Under the circumstances, I had reason to be afraid. But, for heaven's sake, Tighe, it's your own fault you scare us humans. You guys are so damned secretive, no one knows you even exist. So of course we're shocked when you suddenly do something no human can do. But now that I know, *I'm not afraid*. Unless you go feral again. Then all bets are off."

He marveled at her courage. Even then, even when he'd been lost in that chaos, she'd pulled him out. She'd faced the worst he had to give and not run.

"Turn into a tiger for me, Tighe."

He stared at her. "*Now?*"

"*Right* now. I want to see you shift when I can pay attention. When I can touch you." Her expression changed, turning guarded. "Are you dangerous when you shift? When you're a tiger? I mean, to me?"

"No. It's still me in either form. Even in the feral form, I'd never hurt you if I weren't handicapped by half a soul."

"Then do it, Tighe. Shift for me. Please?"

"Delaney . . ." He shook his head. "You don't want this. Like you said, you're not used to this."

"Ah, but what I said was, I didn't understand it the first time. You looked damned dangerous and, as it turned out, you were. It's different now. I understand what you're doing. And I want to see it happen when I can really watch. I've never touched a tiger."

"If you get scared, there's no telling what will happen."

"Then don't do anything without warning me. No pretending to bite my head off or anything."

This was not a good idea. What if Delaney didn't handle his shift as well as she thought she would? If she got scared, he could lose it again. He could kill her this time.

Even if he didn't lose it, could she really accept an *animal* as her mate?

But in her eyes he saw such certainty. Such strength. And she wanted to see him shift. She *wanted* to. Wasn't that all he'd wanted from Gretchen? To be given a chance to explain?

He could give Delaney that. What she wanted. What they both wanted.

All he had to do was trust her to handle it.

Deep in his heart, he did.

Delaney's pulse raced with excitement as Tighe rose to his feet and led her into the gym.

"Stay here." Tighe backed into the middle of the room, giving himself room, and her space.

Then, as she watched, the man she loved disappeared in a breath-catching shimmer of colored lights. A second later a *huge*, *gorgeous* tiger stood in the place where he'd been. The very tiger she'd seen for such a brief moment before.

Delaney's heart pounded. Staring at the beautiful, deadly creature, adrenaline shot through her system, instincts bred over eons of human evolution warning her to *run*.

But she didn't. Because the dangerous animal wouldn't hurt her.

A tiny smile played around her mouth as her hand went to her chest. "My heart's racing, Tighe. But it's not from fear. Not much, anyway. This is so beyond incredible. Can you hear me?"

Of course. His voice sounded in her head. *Do you think tigers can't hear?*

Her eyes went wide. "Did you really just say that?"

D . . .

"Nod."

He bobbed his head. *I feel just like one of those damned dolls sitting in the back of a car window.*

"You didn't tell me you could talk in my head."

Telepathic communication is possible between shifted Ferals and whomever they choose. Very convenient when we're on the hunt.

"I'll bet." She took a step toward him, her pulse leaping. "You don't mind if I touch you, do you?"

There's nothing I'd enjoy more.

But she hesitated, her cavewoman instincts screeching that he'd tear her limb from limb. She took another step, caught her breath on a laugh, then walked slowly, cautiously to the amazing creature. But as she reached for him, as her fingers slid into his fur, a low growl rumbled from his throat.

Delaney snatched back her hand. "You said you didn't mind."

Sorry. I guess . . . I expected you to be a little more afraid. It's happened before.

To Tighe's surprise, she made a sound of disgust and, with no hesitation, wrapped her arms around his tiger's thick neck. "Gretchen would have accepted you, you know." She rubbed her cheek against his ruff. "If the situation had been different. If you'd been alone and able to discover your changes together."

Her words slid into him like warm syrup, filling the holes inside him, erasing the cold.

"I imagine the whole thing scared you nearly as much as it did her."

Yes. It probably did. I didn't actually shift until much later, after I reached Feral House, nor did I have a mirror to see myself. But I could see my claws and feel the fangs. I wasn't at all sure what was happening to me.

"It was a tragic set of circumstances all the way around, Tighe. But she loved you. Up until that day, you'd never doubted her, had you?"

Never. That's why her betrayal cut so deep.

"She didn't betray you. She didn't understand what was going on. Her uncle and the other villagers were simply trying to protect themselves and their families from a creature they couldn't comprehend. You'd have done the same, Tighe. With Amalie at your side, you wouldn't have taken any chances. You'd have attacked first and asked questions later."

With a deep mental sigh, he knew she was right.

Thanks, brown eyes. I'm seeing that day in a

*different light. A brighter light. I've been blaming
Gretchen, blaming humans all these years. For their
fears. For their close-mindedness. Perhaps unfairly.*

Delaney released him and rose to walk around
him, sliding her fingers through his fur from the
base of his neck to his tailbone. She moved behind
him and brushed her fingers along him as she
returned to his head. Then she knelt in front of
him, her fingers sliding through his ruff. Her eyes
sparkled with excitement even as they flowed with
a depth and clarity he'd rarely seen in any eyes,
human or Therian.

"Can you taste my emotions in this form?"

Not as well, but yes.

"Am I afraid?"

*I hear your heart pounding like it's about to take
flight.*

"But am I afraid?"

No.

"Right answer. I'm . . . awestruck, Tighe. Exhila-
rated. Completely enchanted. I have goose bumps
because I'm staring into the eyes of one of the most
beautiful, powerful, *dangerous* creatures on this
planet, and in his eyes I see the man I adore." Her
eyes gleamed with emotion. Softly, she added, "I
see the man I love."

Harsh joy barreled through him, taking down
his heart in a single blow.

Brown eyes. I need to hold you. Step back.

When she did, he shifted back into a man, then
stood and swept her into his arms. His mouth covered hers, and he kissed her, tasting the truth of her

words in the passion of her lips and the tenderness of her fingers in his hair. Hearing it in the beat of her heart. A heart beating in time with his own.

Goddess, but he loved her.

Finally, he pulled back to look down into her face. "You're really not put off by all this?"

Her eyes shone with love, her mouth forming the most beautiful smile he'd ever seen. His chest tightened until he thought it would burst.

She cupped his man's face as she had his tiger's. "*Put off* is about as far from what I'm feeling as you can get." Her thumb moved to trace his lip. He nipped her lightly with his human teeth, stroking her thumb with his tongue.

Then he kissed her again with all the tangled emotion trapped in his heart. Her words had soaked deep inside him, healing wounds he'd lived with for hundreds of years, shattering walls and defenses he hadn't even realized he'd built against a pain he didn't think he'd survive twice. A pain he finally understood and perhaps, at last, could relinquish.

In what might just turn out to be the last hours of his life.

With an aching heart, he pulled back from the kiss and stared into Delaney's precious face, into eyes he could drown in. Then he swept her into his arms and strode with her through the gym, out into the hall, and into the ritual room.

Delaney's eyes widened. "What are we doing?"

"What I should have done the first time."

Deep inside him, the tiger gave a savage roar.

Chapter
Twenty-seven

"You're not going to try to marry me, are you?" Delaney hooked one arm around Tighe's neck, holding tight to her towel with the other, as he carried her into the dark ritual room. With his elbow he flipped a switch and lit the pair of electric sconces that filled the room with a golden glow.

She didn't want this, did she? He wasn't thinking clearly.

"Tighe."

"Hush, D." He carried her to the wide, cushioned altar that stood on the far side of the room and deposited her in the middle.

"I don't think this is a good idea." She grabbed hold as he pushed the altar, with her on top, into the middle of the room.

Tighe yanked off his towel and tossed it aside as he strode to a small shelf on the wall and grabbed something. A lighter, she realized as he squatted and lit one of the ceremonial fires that had burned during their mating ceremony.

"Can we at least discuss this?"

"No."

With a huff of frustration, she climbed off the altar, pulled her towel tight, and followed him to the second fire.

"Tighe, you have nothing to gain from this and too much to lose."

He lit the fire, then moved to the third. "Take off your towel, D."

"Are you even listening to me? If they get the clone, you'll be bound to me when you know I can't stay."

He rose from lighting the third fire and turned to her, taking hold of her shoulders. His eyes were the golden orange of the tiger, yet within those golden depths swam a sea of emotion and a will of steel.

He squeezed her shoulders gently. "You asked me to bare myself to you, to show you my eyes and open my past as one last gift to you. Now I'm asking for one last gift *from* you. Don't fight me on this, D. It's too important to me."

"But why? What difference does it make?"

Releasing her, he lit the fourth and fifth fires before answering.

"The difference is, if I'd bound myself to you in the first place, I would have heard your cries in my head when he first captured you. I would have been able to find you immediately. You wouldn't have had to endure . . ."

Turning away, he lit the sixth and final fire, then turned off the sconces. Firelight danced on the walls, once more transforming the room into a cave of old and filling the room with whispers of magic.

Tighe ushered her back to the altar and tugged at her towel until she let go of it, then pulled it from her body. She grabbed hold of his shoulders as his hands spanned her waist, and he lifted her back onto the altar.

Stepping back, he began to chant the same odd sounds Kougar had during the mating ceremony. Three times, Tighe circled her, his powerful, naked body glowing in the firelight with strength and life, his armband gleaming.

Her gaze reveled in his raw, male beauty even as her heart clenched with the knowledge that he could be gone in a matter of hours. He could be dead. How would she live in a world without him? Any world?

Finally, he returned to her and came to stand before her. Taking her hands in his, he raised them to his mouth, one after the other, and kissed her knuckles.

"You asked why this is important to me." His eyes throbbed with emotion. "Because I love you, D."

Bittersweet happiness twisted through her misery. "*Tighe.*"

He lifted his hand and caressed her head. "I love you. It's not going to hurt me to bind myself to you. Because I'm bound, whether through ritual or the emotion in my heart, I'm yours. Always. No matter how long that is."

The tears started down her cheeks. "Tighe, I love you, too."

His expression tightened into something close to pain. Cupping her face in his hands, he kissed her, the kiss shattering in its anguished tenderness.

The saltiness of her tears mixed with the sweet wildness of his taste as she kissed him back, running her fingers along the back of his neck and into his hair, holding on. Holding on.

Tighe pulled away. "Lie down, brown eyes." Their gazes met, and for one awful instant, she saw the clone in his eyes. Her heart stuttered.

"What is it, D? You're scared."

"It's . . . I felt like he was here. Like he was watching me."

"He can't reach you here, sweetheart." But he swung away and went to retrieve a knife from the shelf where he'd found the lighter. With a quick swipe, he slit open his palm. Bright red blood ran down his hand.

Delaney held out her hand, ready to do the same. Or at least, the human version of it.

Tighe shook his head as he grabbed one of the towels and wiped the blood off his hand. "I would know the moment I looked in your eyes, D. I know you're not him."

Delaney frowned. "I should have known. I shouldn't have had that moment of doubt either."

His hands slid into her hair. "There's a difference, brown eyes. I look like him. Plus the fact, he terrorized you. It would be surprising if you didn't have moments like that." Stepping between her thighs, he pulled her against him and gently stroked her head. "Now, lie down."

As he stepped back, she did as he asked, positioning herself in the middle of the platform. Tighe pulled himself up from the end. She spread her legs, and he knelt between them. But the memory of the last time she was naked in front of a man stabbed at her, and she froze.

Tighe shook his head, his expression unhappy. "He's not here, D. Don't let him be here. Not now."

"I can't help it. I can't forget."

"I know, sweetheart. Maybe this is too soon." He sighed and moved as if to leave.

She reached for him. "Tighe, wait. I need you to help me forget. Touch me. With your warmth. With your love. Touch me everywhere and erase his cold touch. Please?"

A small smile flashed shallow dimples. "There's nothing I want more, brown eyes. Nothing." He grasped her ankles gently with his warm, strong hands, touching. Caressing. Slowly, he worked his way up her calves and her thighs, his touch warm and tender and so very different from that other touch. His hands slid over her hips, skimming her abdomen to tenderly cover her breasts. "Like this?"

She smiled for him. "Yes. Exactly like this."

He caressed her breasts, softly kneading and plucking until her breathing became slowly ragged. One hand left her breast to travel between her thighs.

But at the first stroke, she flinched. "I'm sorry."

"*D.* Look at me. Look into my eyes. He never looked at you with eyes like mine."

She stared into his golden tiger eyes and felt only warmth. Only love.

His warm fingers moved back to caress her inner thigh, sliding higher, one millimeter at a time, pulling her back to that place of heat and need.

"I'm going to touch you, sweetheart. I'm going to slide my finger into your honey. It's going to feel good, as it always does when I touch you. Because I love you."

His finger stroked her lightly, then pressed, warm and gentle, into her, so different from that last cold invasion.

She shuddered with revulsion at the memory, even as she lifted her hips, embracing the touch of the man she loved. He probed her slowly, with infinite gentleness, then quicker as she heated, as her body opened and wept for him. Over and over he slid his finger in and out until heat coursed through her, until desire raged through her veins, until she was rocking her hips, gasping with need.

Finally, he withdrew his finger and came to her, bracing himself on his arms, yet not entering her. Not yet.

His gaze held hers. He didn't have to tell her this time to watch him. His eyes were so tender, so full of love, she couldn't have looked away if she'd wanted to.

"I love you, Delaney Randall. I bind myself to you, heart and soul." As he began to chant, he slid deep inside her, stretching her, filling her, then out again, in rhythm with the ancient sounds coming from his throat. Her heart took up the beat until it pounded through her, lifting her in passion and excitement as if she were part of something beyond the body, beyond the earth, far beyond anything any human had ever known.

As he entered her over and over, she felt the warmth of a hundred angel wings brushing her mind. And saw the tiger lift his head to the skies with a roar of keen satisfaction.

A flicker of a smile lit Tighe's mouth as if he, too, felt the tiger watching. His eyes bored into her, holding her. Claiming her as he drove into her, driving her higher and higher, faster and faster, until the ritual pounded through her blood like ancient drums, lifting her, launching her . . .

As she stared into those beloved tiger eyes, she screamed with the roaring rush of pleasure, then gasped as Tighe's love rushed into her, embracing her like a tender warmth riding the wings of her soul, filling her with a fullness, a rightness, a *completeness* so perfect that chills raced over her skin and tears ran from her eyes.

She'd thought binding would enslave her. Instead, for the first time in her life, she felt whole.

Tighe watched her with moisture in his own eyes. He kissed her, and the sweetness, the passion, ex-

ploded inside her a hundred times more brilliant than
before as if she'd been living life in two dimensions,
two black-and-white dimensions, and through this
ritual, he'd lifted her into a stunning new existence.

She felt transformed. Reborn.

Tighe lifted his face and stared into her eyes with
infinite tenderness. Infinite sadness.

And the beauty of the moment shattered in bittersweet shards of truth.

Tighe was dying.

And even if, by some miracle, he survived, they
had no future together. They both knew it. She saw
the knowledge in the sadness in his eyes.

He gathered her into his arms, and they held one
another, clinging to a dream that couldn't last.

"You bound yourself to me," Delaney murmured,
finally, against his collarbone.

With slow, lazy brushes of his warm palm, Tighe
stroked her body. "I did."

"How? There was no blood."

"The previous ritual paired us. Opening myself
to you, in this place, was the only thing left to do."
His lips brushed her temple. "It was the most profound thing I've ever done, brown eyes. The most
perfect."

"I never dreamed it would be like that. That it
could be like that."

He brushed back her hair. "You're okay?"

She shivered as his question brought back thoughts
of the clone. "Yes. But, I swear, for a moment there I
felt like he was watching me. For an awful moment,
I felt like he was inside you, looking out."

Tighe stiffened. She felt the energy going through him like a lightning bolt.

"D, that's it! We see through his eyes, right? What if he's seeing through mine?"

Delaney froze. "Do you mean *visions*? Like he's seeing us? *Me?*"

"Why not?"

"*Now?*"

"I don't know. We see him when he feeds. I have a hard time believing he's seeing me when I eat. Don't get me wrong, I like to eat, but there's nothing powerful about it for me."

"He said he loved me. And, Tighe, he knew my name. Just before he grabbed my head, he said my name."

"He's getting the visions when I'm with you."

"*With* me?" Delaney croaked. "As in . . . ?"

Tighe squeezed her shoulder. "Think, D. Maybe this is why he stopped feeding on people directly and moved back to fires."

She gasped. "Of course. He realized we were getting visions of him when he killed. We were going to be able to trap him if he kept it up."

His hand clenched her shoulder harder. "I know when it happened. It was while we were driving around after the Lincoln Memorial murders. He was killing the babies. I stopped at the light and looked down at you and told you what he was doing. And where he was. He stopped midstep. *He heard me.*"

"But you weren't doing anything more profound than driving."

"Wrong, sweetheart. I was looking into your eyes. And there's nothing more profound to me."

He sat up, then hopped off the altar and started pacing, studiously *not* looking at her. His hands raked into his hair. "I was looking in your eyes the morning you told me you were going to meet Kara in the foyer. He showed up instead."

Delaney jumped off the altar and grabbed a towel. "Maybe that's why he told me he loved me. Because he sees my feelings for you in my eyes. He's reacting to that emotion."

"Exactly. I was looking into your eyes when I gave you the cell phone and told you it had a tracking system."

Delaney looked at him in astonishment even as he carefully kept his gaze averted. "How can you possibly remember all the times you looked into my eyes?"

He circled behind her, then pulled her tight against him, his arm warm and comforting across her rib cage. "Because every time I look into your eyes, I feel like I'm drowning. Like my feet are being swept out from under me. Looking into your eyes feeds my soul, D."

She covered his arms with her hands and held onto him as he held her. "Does that mean I can't look into your eyes anymore?"

"No." He squeezed her tight, and let out an excited whoop. "It means we may finally have a way to catch him."

Chapter Twenty-eight

Ten minutes later, Tighe paced the war room, adrenaline racing through his body on a riptide of hope. It might well knock his feet out from under him again, but for the moment, he had a chance at life, and that was all he could ask for.

Delaney sat at the big table, her back to him so they didn't accidentally make eye contact. At the table with her were Lyon, Kara, and Kougar. Jag and Wulfe were on their way and would be filled in later. Paenther and Foxx were still in the Blue Ridge. They only waited for Hawke.

As the warrior walked into the room, each man and woman pulled out a knife and cut his or her palm.

Lyon turned to Tighe, eyeing him with controlled excitement. "Tell them what you told me."

Tighe nodded and turned to the others, then explained how he and Delaney had figured out the clone was seeing through his eyes.

"So he's not seeing anything but Delaney?" Hawke took his seat and leaned forward, his eyes flashing. "But he's hearing whatever's said during that time."

"Right. Full sound visions, just as mine are." Tighe stopped and turned toward the table, his hands going to Delaney's shoulders, his gaze skipping from one Feral to the next. "We can use this to set him up. To set a trap."

Lyon's brows rose questioningly. "Do we know what he wants?"

"The other half of Tighe's soul," Delaney said. "He told me he was going to use me to get it."

"Did he say how?"

"Unfortunately, no."

Lyon's gaze swung to Hawke. "Any clue?"

"None. All we know is he had her lying in a pentagram and he possesses at least some of the knowledge of the Daemons. His plan could be anything, but everything points to its involving either Delaney, or Tighe."

"So we're going to make it easy for him to catch us." Tighe waited until all eyes were back on him. "We'll pretend to be planning to trap him again." He looked at Kougar. "One of your Daemon traps. Something that requires all the Ferals to leave Feral House. I'll tell D I'm staying here with her as long as I can, then tell her something went wrong, and I have to leave to help you. If I'm his target, he'll have access to me when I cross the woods alone. If D is the target, he'll have her virtually unprotected in the house."

Lyon grunted. "I'm not leaving Kara unprotected, but the clone doesn't have to know that. And the rest of them will be in their animals, hidden, watching you two."

"Exactly."

"He may not believe you'd leave Delaney alone," Lyon said.

Delaney gave a soft snort. "If there's one thing he doesn't understand, it's love."

"How would he get into the house?" Kara asked. "The doors are always locked."

"His life's on the line." Tighe kneaded Delaney's shoulders softly, gaining strength just from touching her. "A locked house wouldn't stop me if I needed in. It won't stop him. He'll try. We'll stop him before he breaks in."

Lyon's gaze met his. "It's a long shot."

"Maybe not, Roar," Hawke said. "The clone has to know he's dying, too. I'm willing to bet he's already planning some kind of move. If he senses how close his soul is to crumbling, he's planning it tonight. By giving him *our* plans, or our supposed plans, we'll be giving him exactly what he wants." He nodded to Tighe. "It might work brilliantly."

"If we can pull off the acting job," Delaney said softly.

He squeezed her shoulders. "We'll do it. Midnight?" he asked the others. When he received a round of nods he said, "Midnight it is." Then he took Delaney's hand, careful not to meet her gaze. "Let's go up to my room where we can concentrate."

A long shot, Lyon called it. And Tighe feared he was right. But it was the only shot they had. As he led Delaney from the room, his arm tight around her shoulders, apprehension knotted his gut. But it couldn't obliterate the hope that burned inside him.

Because he still had a chance to come through this alive. Not a great one, perhaps, but a chance.

If he did survive the night, the next task on his agenda was convincing Delaney to stay in his world instead of going back to her own.

He pulled her close and kissed her hair. One challenge at a time.

"You ready?"

Delaney shuddered, glad for Tighe's arms tight around her. They'd gone over what they needed to say and practiced it five times, now. But the thought of actually doing it was setting butterflies to flight in her stomach even as it covered her skin in goose bumps.

Because the goal was to let the clone see them. To let him see *her.* And the thought of bringing that evil presence into the room with them was making her ill.

"He won't be here, D. He'll just be watching."

"Have you started to read my mind now?"

His lips brushed her hair. "Not your mind. I can feel your emotions as if they were my own.

The nervousness. But also the aversion. And the fear."

"My fear doesn't bother you anymore?" But it didn't. She could feel his emotions, too.

His hand ran slowly up and down her arm. "All these years, fear has reminded me of that time with Gretchen. You stole its power over me today, D."

She tried to smile, but was too nervous to pull it off. "I'm glad."

"Me, too. But enough stalling. We need to issue this invitation, or he won't make it in time. Then we're really screwed."

She took a deep breath, trying to disperse the ants crawling over her skin. "Okay. Let's do it."

Slowly, he turned her around in his arms. She expected him to look into her eyes, to draw in the clone. But instead he kissed her, strengthening her even as he calmed her. Smart man, he pulled back before the kiss got out of control and stole all thoughts from her head. Including the ones she needed.

Running his palms over her cheeks, he stared into her eyes.

And she felt the clone.

Her heart started racing. Tighe's grip on her tightened.

"D," he said softly. "It's me, sweetheart. I know every time you look at me, you see him."

His words were a gentle reminder they were on camera. He'd told her just to think of it as a television camera. And she was going to blow the plan completely if she didn't play it right.

She gazed into his eyes, opening her heart, feeling Tighe's love engulf her, calm her. Yet looking into those green eyes, badly streaked with black, her heart clenched as she was reminded of just how little time they had left. Of just how critical it was that she pull this off.

With a determination born of desperation, she gathered her wits and her thoughts. And said her lines with all the raw emotion in her heart.

"What are we going to do, Tighe? How are we going to save you?"

"Kougar has a plan. He's figured out what went wrong with one of the Daemon traps he tried down by the river last night. He needs more Ferals, more power. Everyone's going at midnight tonight. Everyone but me."

She reached up, stroking his jaw. "Why not you?"

"We never leave Feral House unprotected if we can help it. And with my soul deteriorating, my energy's the lowest right now. If it doesn't work without me, they'll call me, and I'll have to go."

"Once they trap him, will they kill him?"

"They'll bring him to me to kill. We're not sure how far the soul can travel, but we're taking no chances."

It was done. They'd said all they had to say. But they hadn't discussed the last part, how to end the vision without simply turning away.

Tighe leaned in and kissed her, slowly at first,

then with increasing passion, stealing the fear that lurked in her mind, stealing all thought. He pulled away, and without looking at her, tucked her head against him.

"I love you," he murmured softly.

"And I you."

She wrapped her arms hard around him and prayed for a miracle. Prayed for Tighe's life to be spared so he could live another six hundred years, or another six thousand.

Even as she knew she could never be part of them. Even if she saved him, she'd lose him.

Because she could never stay there with nothing to do, no purpose in life, growing old and wrinkled, watching her perpetually virile, perpetually young husband's interest in her die. No, she wouldn't be able to bear it. It was better to go back to her life, to the place she belonged, even if it meant feeling a hole in her chest where her heart used to be.

His world could never be hers.

Tighe pulled Delaney onto the bed with him and peeled off her clothes, then his own, needing to make love to her one more time. Every move was slow, unhurried. He wished those moments could last an eternity.

While she kept her eyes closed, afraid, he knew, of engaging the clone, he touched her, loved her, with infinite care. First with his hands, then his mouth, and finally with his body as she spread her thighs, and he sank deep into her heat, filling her.

He felt their hearts engage in a sensual explosion of heat and love.

Her eyes flew open, widening.

"The bond," he murmured.

A look of amazement creased her passion-drugged features. "It's stronger than before."

"From what I've heard, it'll grow even stronger over time."

Her eyes contracted with pain, with the reminder, he knew, that time was the one thing they might not have. She closed her eyes again.

"Look at me, D."

"But . . ."

"*Look at me.* It's your eyes that strengthen me." He slid into her again and again, slowly, loving her with his body. And with his mind, his heart. His soul.

Afterward, he pulled her into his arms and held her as the hour until midnight slowly counted down.

Tighe was sitting on his bed, watching Delaney strap on her ankle holster when a knock sounded on his door. It was ten to midnight.

Hawke opened the door and stuck his head in. "We're heading out. Give us twenty minutes."

Tighe nodded, rose, and went over to the man who'd been a friend for well over a century. Understanding and deep friendship moved through Hawke's dark eyes as he met him halfway, embracing him hard.

"We'll get him, buddy. This isn't the end." But despite the positive words, worry riddled his eyes.

"I hope to hell you're right."

Hawke left, with a nod to Delaney.

When she finished tying her boots, Delaney straightened, her gaze carefully not meeting his. "I'm ready to kick some Daemon ass."

He never tired of watching her, never failed to marvel at her strength and resiliency. She was a vision of beauty and power in the jeans and long-sleeved tee she'd borrowed from Kara, the gun strapped boldly at her waist. She'd twisted her damp hair into a knot at the back of her neck, accentuating the feminine shape of her head and the long, graceful line of her throat.

Goddess, but he loved her. "You know guns won't kill him."

A savage smile lifted her mouth. "I'm fully aware of that, sport. But when I'm armed, I feel ready for anything. I could take on the world if I had to." She shrugged. "Just maybe not this world."

Tighe chuckled.

Delaney scowled. "I hate not being able to look at you."

"I'm drinking my fill of you, brown eyes."

He watched her gaze slide up his legs, lighting tiny fires along his skin as it went. "Maybe I've been a little too cautious."

"If that gaze of yours travels any higher, you may blow the whole operation, Agent Randall. You're going to make me forget everything. Everything but that sweet body of yours."

Her worry rolled over him, quieting the teasing. He went to her and took her in his arms, holding her, calming both of them as much as either could be calm when so much was at stake. If the clone didn't bite, what would they do?

Finally, he pulled away, again, careful not to meet her gaze. "It's time for act two."

With a deep sigh, Delaney nodded and preceded him out the door and down to the foyer, where Kara waited. Kara gave Delaney a big hug, then came to him, sliding her arms around him. He hugged her tight. As he held Kara, he asked, "Are you ready, D?"

"As ready as I can get."

He released Kara, then turned to Delaney, took her into his arms, and stared deeply into her eyes, all the way to her heart. The warmth rushed into him. He nearly closed his eyes to drink the sweet intensity of her love, but he forced himself to hold her gaze.

Slowly, he repeated the second batch of lines they'd rehearsed. "I have to go, D. The trap isn't working. They need me to add my power to theirs."

"Be careful, Tighe. I love you." The fear in her eyes was real. As was the love.

Pulling her into his arms, he kissed her thoroughly. When his mind told him it was time to pull away, to leave, as they'd planned, his hands wouldn't let go. What if their plan failed? What if he never made it back to her before his soul was spent?

Goddess, but he needed just one more kiss. But then he'd need another and another. With a massive force of will, he cupped her cheek and pulled away.

Tears glistened in her eyes. "Be careful."

"Always." Then he turned and left Feral House, stepping into the cool night wind.

As he ran across the circular drive at a slow jog, his body was tense and ready for the fight for his life. He just prayed he'd timed this right, that the clone would come for him before the draden, before he had to shift. Prayed that he'd come for him at all. Because if he didn't . . .

Tighe clenched his hands as he ran. He might have just held Delaney for the very last time.

Tighe? Hawke's voice rang in his head. *Was there a part of this plan you didn't tell us about? The part where Delaney runs out of the house on her own?*

Tighe slowed, his mind scrambling. *No.*

I'll get her.

Out of nowhere, a dark cloud of draden descended, blocking out the treetops. *Shit.* He was going to have to shift. As he transformed into his animal on a rush of power, Wulfe's curse rang in his head.

The damn draden are attacking the animals!

No sooner did Wulfe's words register than the draden bit right through his tiger's fur. *Dammit.* Just as they'd attacked Hawke and Kougar by the Lincoln Memorial.

Tighe's blood went cold, understanding slamming him in one fell blow. *It's the clone! The clone can control the draden.* His heart clenched with fear, his mind screaming with pain. *Goddess help her. He's controlling Delaney!*

Chapter
Twenty-nine

Tighe fought back the draden, gut clenching, terror pounding through his brain as he sent his heart outward, seeking Delaney.

A hundred times brighter than their old connection, the bond that bridged their hearts showed him the way. With draden clinging to him, he took off through the woods, following his sense of her, feeling her confusion and fear.

Goddess stone, he sent out to the other Ferals. *He's taken her to the goddess stone.*

We'll get there as fast as we can, Hawke said. *We're fighting for our lives right now, buddy. The draden have got us good.*

Abruptly, his tiger's vision went black. He careened to a stop, slamming shoulder first into a tree. Draden tore at his tiger's flesh, but the only pain he felt was in his heart and mind. Because he couldn't reach her. And the only reason he'd be getting a vision was if the clone was about to feed.

Delaney's mind fought to draw her weapon, *to fight*, but her body remained still and trembling before the monster who wore Tighe's face.

"*What have you done to me?*" She stood before him on a wide, flat rock high above the Potomac, the cool wind whipping at the loose tendrils of her hair.

As she'd waited in the foyer of Feral House, armed and ready for whatever came, she'd felt this sudden, inexplicable need to leave. At first, she'd thought it had something to do with the strange new connection she had to Tighe and feared he'd needed her, so she hadn't fought it. But the moment she was outside, her feet took off as if they had a mind of their own, and she'd *felt* him. The clone. Controlling her.

Inside her.

He reached for her now, cupping her face in his hands, shooting cold through her body as his face took on an expression she'd often seen on Tighe's. As if she were the most precious thing in the universe.

"What have you done to me?" she demanded a second time.

His mouth turned up in a smile that froze her from the inside out. "I've made you my channel key."

She didn't know what he meant by that. And was pretty sure she didn't want to know.

"I see the questions in your eyes, fair Delaney. A channel key is made by infecting a human with a bit of Daemon consciousness. And letting it grow."

She stared at him. "*You're taking over my mind?*"

"No, just a small piece of your will. Enough to use you for the key's true purpose."

Her insides quivered with dread. "Which is?"

A single, icy finger slid down the slope of her nose. "To open the channel to the dark power deep in the earth. Power I need in order to call the other half of my soul and to find the master of the witch who created me so that I might add my strength to those who work to free Satanan and the Daemons from the blade."

Her mind flared with denial. She wouldn't help him! "You can't free them from the blade. Only the Ferals can do that."

"For a time, that was true. But the dark powers are amassing, and that time is gone." He stepped back and motioned to the rock behind her. "Bare your chest for me, Delaney, and lie down in the center of the pentagram."

Her blood went cold. Her brain screamed with refusal. But her body obeyed. She tugged off the long-sleeved tee shirt, pulled off her bra, and lay on her back on the cold stone in the middle of the blue-painted star.

As she looked up at the glowing clouds against the dark sky, her mind and heart reached for Tighe. Pouring her love into that link, unable to hide her terror or her outrage that she was to be used as the instrument of his death and that she was powerless to stop it.

As the clone looked down at her, for a desperate moment, she thought Tighe had come. But then she saw the flash of a wicked blade and knew that the nightmare wasn't over at all. It was just beginning.

As the knife pierced her chest and began a downward slide, a scream launched through her head, echoing off the walls of her skull and tearing, like blades of ice, through her brain. But no sound left her mouth, no sound shattered her eardrums. The clone's control over her was total.

The knife slid down, then beneath each breast as if cutting a design in her flesh, engulfing her in a river of agony from which there was no escape. Blood ran down her sides. And the scream in her head went on, and on, and on.

Tighe lifted his head and let out a ferocious roar of misery and fury.

Tighe? Lyon's voice.

Tighe knocked into another tree, stumbling through the woods, blind, blood caking his fur from the dradens' bites. *He has her on the goddess stone. He intends to use her to access dark power. To steal my soul and help free Satanan.*

Like hell. Can you reach her?

A wild rage ripped through his tiger's body, sending him thrashing through the trees. *Not until I can free myself from this damned vision!*

We'll converge there as fast as we can.

Sweat ran with the blood, but he kept moving, following the sound of Delaney's terror.

He was cutting her.

He had to get out of the vision!

Quit feeding, shitbag. Let me get out of your head. But he watched as the knife carved . . . a pentagram. *On her chest.* He was going to be sick.

Breathe.

The vision suddenly disappeared in the same moment the draden took off. A weird frisson of energy pierced the air, but Tighe wasted no time wondering about it. He ran on all fours, parting the woods in a flash of orange fur.

Something's happening, Lyon said.

Tighe gave a ferocious roar. *He's trying to raise the dark power. I'm on my way to the goddess stone, now.*

As he raced through the forest to reach his heart, to save the woman he loved, he prayed he wasn't already too late.

Tighe reached the goddess stone at the same time as the other Ferals.

What the fuck? Jag said, still in his jaguar form.

As one, they stared at the goddess stone. Or at the spot they knew the goddess stone should be, because they sure as hell couldn't see it.

The draden swarmed the stone by the thousands, *the millions.*

And Delaney was there.

With a roar, Tighe leaped down the rocks on his tiger's paws, following the sound of the scream,

Delaney's scream, flowing down the line that connected their hearts. He felt the others close behind him as he launched himself into the draden.

The collision knocked him back on his haunches as if he'd run into a concrete wall.

What the hell? He should have gone through!

As he sprang to his tiger's paws, he saw the others picking themselves up, too.

Magic, Lyon said. *Damn powerful magic*.

I'll make it, Tighe growled. He *had* to make it. Delaney needed him.

Opening his mouth wide, he tried to grab the little suckers in his jaws, but his teeth scraped the surface of the magic and never touched the fiends themselves.

His frustration tore through the night on a furious roar. In a desperate move, he shifted to human, praying he'd draw them out of the magic to attack him.

They didn't move. The draden wall remained solid.

"*Delaney!*"

His blood boiled even as his heart felt as if it had been shot through with ice. He had to reach her. *He had to reach her!*

With a rage born of desperation, he slammed his fist into the unnatural wall and felt it sink up to his elbow.

It worked.

But the pain and tearing had him instinctively yanking back, only to stare, disbelieving at what was left of his arm. Little more than shredded remnants of flesh clinging to the bone.

"Holy *shit*," Jag murmured, taking human form. Then tried to slam his fist through, too, but his fist only bounced off as his jaguar's body had.

Lyon, Kougar, and Hawke, too, shifted and tried to punch through, but only Tighe was able to breach the wall.

Lyon's gaze met Tighe's. "Looks like this is your fight."

Tighe nodded. As he dove headfirst into that feeding frenzy, he heard Lyon behind him.

"Kill the son of a bitch."

As he pushed through, inch by inch, he felt his flesh being devoured by savage mouths, his life force being sucked from his body. When he finally emerged onto the goddess stone, he stumbled, barely able to stand.

"*Tighe.*" Delaney lay as he'd seen her in the vision, but so much worse, her eyes tight with pain and despair, and horror at the sight he must be with his flesh nearly gone. Her own flesh was open, her blood spilling over the rock too fast for her to possibly be still alive and conscious.

Opening himself to her, he felt it. The dark hold the clone had on her, the talons gripped around her heart. It was all that was keeping her alive.

And in a shattering moment, he understood. The second the clone died, so too would Delaney.

His fury swung to the one responsible.

The clone stood a few feet away, his face and chest raised to the heavens like a man inhaling air . . . or power.

Tighe tried to shift into his tiger form, his stronger form, but he was too weak to do even that. So he did the only thing he could. He launched himself at the clone. And took a fist to the face that sent him reeling back into the wall of draden. The small bits of flesh that had started to regrow were chewed off before he could push himself out of the little monsters' grasp again.

The clone chuckled, grinning Tighe's grin. "You can't stop me, Feral. I'm nearly through, and when I'm done, you'll be dead."

"You'll never get away."

"With my draden guard, who's going to stop me?"

The Ferals would stop him. He prayed to the goddess they'd be able to stop him. But he wasn't at all certain they could.

Tighe. Delaney's voice floated through his head, soft and weak. *Come to me.*

I'm here, sweetheart.

No, my tiger. Come over here where I can touch you. I need to touch you.

He wasn't sure how she could even stand to look at him, let alone touch his decimated flesh. Though second by second his body regenerated, he still looked more ghoul than man.

Lowering his center of gravity to a fighter's stance, he began to circle the clone, inching his way toward Delaney until his feet were slick with her blood.

Brown eyes. Grief swept through him, swift and terrible. She was going to die, and there was nothing he could do to stop it. *Sweetheart, I'm sorry.*

I should have been there to stop you. To protect you.

We tried. It was a good plan.

Are you in terrible pain? He'd been able to feel her pain initially, but either it had waned, or his own was blotting it out.

I feel nothing but my love for you, Tighe. I'll always love you. I'll always watch over you.

His heart cried with anguish. *Don't give up, D. I'm going to find a way to save you. I have to find a way to save you!*

Another step, and he felt it, her too-cool fingers sliding around the bones of his shredded ankle.

I love you, Tighe. Her love flowed through him on a rush of warmth. The tiger spirit inside him stirred and raised his head. Strength began to flow once more through his body. She was pouring her love into him, making him strong. Healing him.

Brown eyes, I love you. More than life.

He felt her smile enfold him through the connection between their hearts.

Tiger! Delaney called softly. *Help him.*

The animal spirit inside him leaped to its feet. With a ferocious roar, he sent power rushing though Tighe's body. *Perhaps power enough to shift.* But enough to fight?

He wouldn't know until he tried.

Let go, D. Let go, sweetheart.

As her fingers fell away, he prayed to the goddess this worked, and pulled on the energy inside him to access his tiger form.

The lights flickered, then died, then flickered

again as he fought to shift. He *had* to shift. Only in his tiger form could he possibly beat the man who had his own strength but who was whole and strong, as he wasn't.

Finally, *finally,* the transformation slid through his body, with none of the accompanying rush of joy. He'd shifted. But the draden had taken too much from him.

The clone whipped out his dagger, the light of battle in his eyes.

Tighe's vision wavered. His heavy tiger's body lurched drunkenly, and he doubted he could rally the energy to ward off the clone's attack, let alone launch one of his own.

He had to. For Delaney, he had to.

He started forward on unsteady legs, watching as the clone lifted his dagger, ready to plunge it into his brain. A single stab wound wouldn't kill him, but in his weakened state, it might be all the shitbag needed to drive him to his knees, where he would cut out his heart. And no creature survived without a heart.

I love you, D.

Don't give up on us yet, Tighe. That small power boost from your lovely tiger spirit went both ways. I've broken free of his hold. I can move again.

As the dagger began its deadly descent, Tighe bunched his hind legs, desperate to find the strength to ward off the attack. To protect Delaney.

The first explosion rang through his ears, sending him back on his haunches. Two more rang out, the clone's eye disintegrating, holes erupting in his face, before he understood what was happening.

Delaney. She'd reached her gun. Round after round exploded into the clone's face.

Giving him a chance.

Tighe stumbled forward, grabbed the clone's bloodless leg between his powerful jaws and tore it off his body, sending the demon spawn crashing to the ground, his dagger skittering away. With another powerful bite, he tore off an arm and tossed it aside. Collapsing across the clone's broken body, he pulled off the other arm, then turned and gnawed off his second leg.

But the creature's heart remained. And his head.

Tighe's own heart cried out with the knowledge that destroying them meant destroying Delaney as well.

Tighe. Move me! Out of the pentagram. He's still sucking the power. He's still trying to steal your soul.

Rallying what little strength his body had managed to renew, he changed once more into a man, then stumbled to Delaney's side and knelt in her blood.

"Oh, D." Her skin was white as the clouds. As bloodless as the clone. With shaking hands, he scooped her up and into his arms, cradling her against him as he turned to his foe.

In a squawking frenzy, the draden took off, disappearing into the dark, as if suddenly released. The Ferals rushed onto the stone to surround him.

Delaney's head lolled over his arm, as she fell unconscious. But her heart continued to beat.

The clone met Tighe's gaze, his own face staring

back at him. "You can kill me, Feral. You'll retrieve your soul. But you'll lose your heart. She's mine." He grinned, dimples flashing, evil gleaming from eyes almost completely covered in black shards.

Jag kicked the demon spawn in the head, but the clone just continued to grin.

Jag pulled out his knife. "Mind if I do the honors?"

"Don't," Tighe growled. "He's right. He's tied himself to Delaney. When he dies, so will she."

"Tighe." Lyon's palm squeezed his shoulder, transmitting a fine tension. "You see his eyes? There's only a sliver of green left. Yours are the same. When that last bit of green goes, you die. You may only have minutes. *We can't lose you.*"

His soul cried. *Delaney must live.*

Inside, his tiger paced and leaped, growling and snarling. With a jolt, he realized the spirit was trying to get his attention. He was trying to . . .

"He's trying to pull my soul back through Delaney's body," he murmured. And suddenly he understood. Pulling the soul back through her might just undo that evil connection.

Tighe's gaze snapped to Lyon's. "I need a power raising!"

"Done," Lyon barked. "Now!"

The tiger inside him gave a powerful roar, his approval flowing through Tighe like a warm river. They would raise the spirits of the beasts. And in doing so, empower the spirit of the tiger.

Please, goddess, let this work. Let her live.

Jag and Lyon were already naked from their

shifting, as was Tighe from the decimation of his flesh. Kougar and Hawke yanked off their shirts.

Tighe's flesh was quickly reknitting and almost healed again.

Lyon helped Tighe hold Delaney as he handed Tighe a knife. Tighe sliced his chest, slapped his palm to the blood, and shoved his fist into the air. The men formed a circle around the clone on the broad, flat goddess stone, and, one by one, sliced their own chests, slapping their bloody palms on top of his.

Tighe began to chant. "Spirits rise and join. Empower the beast beneath this moon." The others joined him, the rhythmic words weaving with his heartbeat and Delaney's, flowing around them, through them.

Thunder rumbled, the ground trembled as the great force of Mother Nature herself rose from the depths of the Earth, through the bodies of flesh and bone and up through their arms to the blood raised to the heavens.

"Empower the spirit of the tiger!" Tighe shouted.

A flash of lightning lit the sky, burning through the flesh of Tighe's hand, sending power twisting through his body.

His tiger told him what he had to do.

Cradling Delaney in his arms, he knelt before what was left of the clone and held his hand out to Lyon for the blade.

The clone looked up at him with cold eyes. "The Daemons will rise again," he murmured.

Tighe lifted the knife over the clone's heart. "You

won't be alive to know, will you?" He plunged the blade through the chest wall, cutting and hacking, then reached his hand in.

Inside, his tiger waited, their minds meeting in a way they never had before. The tiger flicked his nose up with a growl, urging him to complete the task. Tighe curved his hand around the beating heart and plucked it from the clone's chest, crushing it in his fist as he poured his love into Delaney.

Inside him, the tiger pulled the missing half of Tighe's soul through the woman they both loved, freeing her from the evil and, *please goddess*, healing her body and saving her life.

For a breathless heartbeat, Delaney's body jerked, then filled with air and life as her wounds began to heal at the rate of miracles.

Joy filled him, twining with the amazing rush of life flowing back through his own body, and reuniting his soul.

He could hear her heartbeat, firm and steady, as he watched her blood-coated chest rise and fall beneath the healing wounds. Her hand twitched, lifting slightly, then relaxing as she stirred.

Dark lashes fluttered, slowly rising as her gaze took in the sky. He waited, breath caught, as those dark eyes turned to him.

"Brown eyes."

She smiled at him. "Yours are green again."

Emotion caught in his throat and he hauled her up until he could bury his face in her hair. "We did it, D. We did it."

"Is he dead?"

"He is." He blinked back the moisture blurring his vision and raised his head to meet her gaze as his brothers gathered around him, their hands slapping his now-healed shoulders in an outpouring of joyous relief.

Lyon stood at his elbow, his hand glued to Tighe's shoulder, his eyes gleaming. "*Damn,* that was close. But you pulled it off. Brilliantly."

Tighe just grinned.

Delaney wrapped her arm around his neck and pulled herself up in his arms, looking down at herself. "Uh, I know you can't see a lot through the blanket of blood, but I need a shirt."

Hawke tossed Lyon his own black silk shirt. As Lyon helped her into it, Delaney groaned.

"I can really do this myself. And I'm pretty sure I can stand. I feel fine."

"I'm not letting you go," Tighe growled. *Ever.* He met Lyon's gaze. "I want the Shaman to look her over."

"I was thinking the same." Lyon turned. "Hawke, if you've still got a cell phone, call Wulfe and have him bring clothes, then call the Shaman and ask him to meet Tighe back at the house. We've got to get out of here before the humans come to investigate the gunshots."

"What about the blood?" Delaney asked.

Lyon nodded. "I'll call a Feral Circle. They'll never see it. Then the rest of us are going draden hunting." He turned to the others. "We've *got* to get that menace under control!"

As Lyon called a Feral Circle, and the others

shifted back into their animals before any humans arrived, Tighe held Delaney against his heart.

He kissed her hair. "How do you feel?"

"Fine. Which makes no sense. I should be dead after what he did to me."

Tighe smiled into her eyes, falling into the love shining in those dark depths, a love that stretched between them like an unbreakable cord. "When my soul returned to me, it passed through you, healing you."

"That's amazing."

"It was the tiger's idea. A damn fine spirit, that one."

Delaney smiled. "I love you both."

The tiger positively purred.

"It's mutual, brown eyes. Both ways." He brushed his forehead against hers.

"It's really over?" she asked softly.

The rush of grief he felt rise in her nearly brought him to his knees.

She still meant to leave him.

He felt as if she were cutting out his heart. His excuses for keeping her here were all but gone. If the Shaman gave her a clean bill of health, he'd have no more reason not to cloud her mind, as he should easily be able to do now that the clone's hold over her was gone. Taking her memories of this whole ordeal.

Taking her memories of him.

"D," he said softly. *He needed her.* But somehow he had to convince her she needed him.

*Chapter
Thirty*

"Tighe, I can walk." Delaney tightened her hold on Tighe's neck as he swung her through the front door of Feral House. "I feel fine."

He'd been carrying her constantly since he lifted her off that pentagram, as if he were afraid to let her go.

"Not until the Shaman gives you a clean bill of health."

"Stubborn man," she muttered, loud enough for him to hear. But she kissed his cheek, softly, loving that he cherished her so.

Loving him.

How am I ever going to live without him?

A glad cry rang from high up the stairs, and Delaney looked up to see Kara running toward them, her face wreathed in joy. "You did it!" She wrapped them both in a big hug. "Lyon said you'd gotten him, but I had to see for myself." Kara's gaze swung to her. "Are you okay?" The uncomplicated friendliness in Kara's eyes warmed her all over again.

"As I keep telling Tighe, I feel fine. But he refuses to let me down."

Kara stepped back, a knowing smile lighting her eyes.

The sudden tightening of Tighe's grip on her had her looking at him with question.

"What's the matter?"

"Have you met Pink?"

"No, but Kara's told me about her." She knew Pink was their cook and housekeeper. And half-flamingo.

She felt the stiffness go out of his hands. "Good. Pink, come join us."

Delaney turned to look down the hall, where the extraordinary creature walked slowly toward them. The size of a woman, she possessed a human-looking face and hands, but her legs were those of a flamingo. In place of skin, she was covered in pink feathers.

Kara had told her that Pink should have been a Feral many centuries ago, but the animal spirit had flown to her in the womb, just before the egg split, creating twins. And possibly destroying the animal spirit. Pink's twin had been killed in an attempt to free the animal, but it hadn't worked. So Pink kept house and cooked for the Ferals, safe from the prying eyes of humans.

"Let me down, Tighe. I want to greet her properly."

With a grumble, he did, and Delaney turned to the unusual woman. "Hi, Pink. I'm Delaney." She held out her hand. "Do you shake?"

The bird-woman inclined her head and held out her own.

Delaney took it, gently curling her fingers around the soft feathers. "It's nice to meet you."

Unblinking birdlike eyes watched her, then slowly lit. A smile formed on her not-quite-human-looking mouth. "I'm happy to make your acquaintance, Delaney. I wish you and Tighe much happiness."

"Thanks, but . . ." The words caught in her throat. "We're . . . only a temporary item."

Pink's expression clouded. "Tighe's a good man."

Delaney was horrified to feel tears pricking her eyes. "I know. It's just . . ." She smiled unhappily. "I'm human."

Without warning, Tighe swept her back into his arms. She forced a laugh, trying to make up for the damper she'd thrown on the mood, even as misery burned in her chest, and her eyes filled with tears.

"We need to have a talk. *Now*." As he swung her toward the stairs, he called back to Kara. "Send the Shaman up when he gets here."

"How about I call you first to make sure you're not . . . busy?"

"*Talk*, Kara. I said we're going to have a talk."

But he said nothing until Delaney was sitting in the middle of his bed and he'd paced the room a good seven times before finally swinging to face her, his body and expression as fierce and rigid as a man going into battle.

"I don't give a damn that you're human. I want you to stay."

"Tighe . . . it's impossible." She swiped at the tears running down her cheeks, but more just followed. "I have to go back. I can't stay here."

His expression turned almost hostile. "Why not?" In his eyes an emotion flared. *Pain*.

"*Oh, Tighe*." Delaney climbed off the bed and went to him, sliding her arms around his rigid body as she pressed her damp cheek to his chest. "It's not that I don't love you, because I do. But I don't belong in this world. You know that. *I can't stay*."

Tighe gripped her shoulders and pulled her away from him. The desperation in his eyes nearly crushed her heart.

"I'll make you happy, D. *I swear it*. You can carry all the guns you want, and all my knives. You can come draden hunting with me anytime, or you can stay here with Kara and Pink. *Whatever you want*."

"Tighe, you're not thinking this all the way through."

His hands caressed her shoulders. "I know I'm being unfair in asking you to give up everything for me. I have no right, brown eyes, no right. *But I need you*."

"It's because you bound yourself to me. You shouldn't have done it."

He squeezed her almost painfully. "Do you think that's what this is? The bond? You're wrong,

Delaney. I was already in love with you." His voice rose, his words turning angry. "This isn't the ritual speaking, dammit, this is my heart!"

His anger tore at her. His pain twisted inside her, merging with her own until she was almost doubled over from the onslaught.

"It's your heart, Tighe, *for now*. But you're not seeing the big picture. If you keep me here, you'll be tying yourself to a woman you won't want in twenty years. Maybe far, far sooner."

He looked at her as if he was ready to draw swords and fight it out. "*I'll always want you.*"

"No. You won't. Think, Tighe! I won't stay this way. In forty years, I'll have gray hair and wrinkles. My figure will be gone. I'll be an *old woman*."

With a snarl, he gripped her face. "And I'll have fangs. And orange eyes every time I look at you, because I'll always want you. *Always*."

The fight went out of him, his face crumbling into a mask of aching tenderness as he slid his palms over her jaw, cradling her face with infinite tenderness.

"Don't you understand?" His words were soft as silk, yet woven with a thread of desperation that tore at her heart. "I'm going to use your own words back at you, D, because they healed my soul. When I look into your eyes, I see you. I will *always* see you, no matter what changes time makes to the body you're in."

Her tears turned slowly to sobs as she slid her hands over his and held him as he held her, wanting to believe. But she couldn't.

"You think that now. But . . ."

"*Don't doubt me, D,*" he snarled. But his thumbs were feather-soft as they stroked her skin. "If you live longer than most humans, I'll still only have, at most, another seventy years with you. That's a blink of an eye in my life. For six hundred years I've made love with women. Most young-looking, I admit. Most beautiful. Scores of women, D."

"Is this supposed to be making me feel better?" She tried to laugh, but it caught in her throat, tangling with her tears.

"Other than those few short years with Gretchen, not a single one has ever touched my heart. Until you. Beauty is meaningless without love, D. *I know this.*" His hands were beginning to tremble. "It's lust. Little more than scratching an itch. *But it's not that way with you. From the moment I first saw you, it hasn't been that way with you.* It's *you* I want to spend the next seventy years with, not your breasts. Not your skin. *You,* D. Your heart. Your soul."

He bent until his gaze was nearly at a level with hers, his eyes as certain as the sunrise. His love poured into her through his gaze and rushed into her through that warm connection between their hearts, filling her. Lifting her.

He pressed his hand to her chest, over her heart. "You belong with me. And I with you. You fill me, Delaney, in a way no one ever has before. And never will again. *No one.*" He pulled her tight against him, stroking her hair, as his big body shook. "If you really want to go, I won't make you stay." His voice was hollow, his eyes bleak as he pulled her back where she could see him through the glaze of her tears.

Moisture glistened in his own eyes. "I would never do anything to hurt you, brown eyes. But, sweet goddess, D, *I want you to stay.*"

As she clung to him, she thought of all she'd be giving up if she took the risk and followed her heart. All her adult life, she'd sought revenge for her mother's murder with a drive born of a need she'd never really understood. A need to make her life right. To make her *self* right. But, she knew now, no number of arrests were going to do that. Not even if by some miracle she caught the man who'd killed her mom.

Because the thing she'd been truly lacking all these years wasn't closure. It was love.

As the sobs began to choke her, Delaney reached up and pressed her palm to his cheek. "All I want is to be with you."

"*D.*"

He swung her into his arms and laid her on the bed, following her down. The joy that flowed between their hearts, a joy mirrored in his eyes as he lowered his face and kissed her, filled her soul.

They were still kissing when a rap sounded at the door. Slowly Tighe pulled back, his eyes golden orange and shining with love. "That will be the Shaman. Anyone else, I'd let stand out there for a couple of hours while I made love to my mate."

She threw him a saucy look. "Sure he can't wait?"

Tighe grinned. "Hold that thought." He vaulted

off the bed and went to open the door as Delaney sat up and rearranged her shirt.

Kara had told her that though the Shaman looked to be about fifteen, thanks to a Mage attack in his youth which ended his growth, he was in fact thousands of years old. Apparently he could see no reason to pretend to be what he wasn't. Which probably accounted for the long hair, tight black pants, and white ruffled shirt that made her think of an eighteenth-century swordsman.

He lifted an eyebrow as he saw her adjusting her clothes, a smile hovering at his youthful-looking mouth. "Shall I come back?"

"No." Tighe ushered him into the room.

The Shaman winked at her. "Let's have a look at you, young lady. Lie down for me." For minute after minute, the Shaman touched her, passed his hands over her, and pressed his fingers into her skull. Finally, he stepped back.

"Well?" Tighe asked, his voice vibrating with concern.

The Shaman clasped his hands behind his back. "Well, it's not what I expected." Tension filled the room, hers and Tighe's combined. "Why don't you tell me what happened?"

Tighe did, and by the time he was through, the Shaman was nodding, an odd smile playing around his mouth.

"He left no dark magic behind," he said. "Nor any piece of his consciousness, now that I know what I'm looking for. I gravely apologize for missing that before."

Tighe waved away the apology. "*Tell us*, Shaman."

The Shaman turned to her. "You're completely healthy, Delaney. As strong as any other immortal."

Delaney jerked. "I'm not immortal." She looked at Tighe and found him staring at the Shaman with an expression that was nothing short of stunned.

"What are you saying?" Tighe demanded.

The Shaman smiled fully. "Passing your soul through her did more than heal her. You've shared your own immortal essence with her."

Tighe's gaze swung to hers, filled with the same hope, the same joy swirling inside her shocked brain. "Are you sure?"

"Cut her and see for yourself."

Tighe scowled. "I'm not cutting her."

Delaney leaped off the bed and pulled down the closest of Tighe's knives. "I'll cut me." She pricked her finger on the tip and watched, wide-eyed as the wound closed right up again.

Her gaze swung to the Shaman. "Are you sure this is permanent? It's not going to wear off?"

The Shaman shook his head. "It's not going to wear off. You've been altered, Delaney." He lifted a brow. "I hope this is good news?"

Her heart stuttered as she turned to Tighe. "It won't be seventy years. Are you sure you want me around forever?"

With a shout of triumph that shook every knife on the wall, Tighe lifted her into his arms and swung her around until she was dizzy with joy.

Slowly he let her feet slide to the floor as he loved her with his eyes.

"Even eternity won't be long enough."

As Tighe kissed her, she felt his love wrap around her and blossom inside her in a bloom of color and life, filling her heart and mending her soul.

And through the link that bound them, she heard the unmistakable sound of a tiger's satisfied roar.

An hour later, after the Shaman left and Tighe had made thorough love to his mate, he led her down the stairs to raid the refrigerator, the two of them grinning like a pair of guilty teenagers. Until he heard the rumble of Lyon's voice and knew from the tone, there was trouble.

He squeezed Delaney's hand. "The food may have to wait." As they entered the dining room, he saw that the others were already there, sitting silently, their expressions grim as they watched their leader on his cell phone.

Tighe held Delaney against his side as they all waited. Finally, Lyon hung up.

"That was Foxx. Paenther's missing. Somewhere in the Blue Ridge."

"Mage?" Jag asked the question all of them feared.

Lyon nodded. "That's what it looks like. Foxx sounds . . . disoriented. More than a little confused. I think he may have fallen under an enchantment as well. He's near Winchester. I told him to stay there and wait for us."

Lyon's hard gaze swung to Delaney. "The Shaman says you're no longer mortal."

Tighe pulled her tighter against him as they both watched Lyon warily.

Delaney tensed within his hold. "Apparently not." A smile flickered over her face as she glanced behind Lyon.

Kara was grinning at her with a double thumbs-up.

Lyon stepped toward them. "You're a trained FBI agent."

"I am."

"Good. I need you to work this case, if you will, without involving the human authorities in any way. You'll be accompanying Tighe and Jag. Can I count on you?"

Tighe felt her excitement, her *pleasure,* flowing down the link between them and grinned.

Delaney smiled. "Absolutely."

As Lyon turned away to issue other orders, Tighe hugged her tight with both arms.

She looked up at him, excitement shining in her eyes. "Looks like we're going to be partners."

"*Always,*" he murmured, his eyes going hot.

In those shining dark eyes of hers he saw the warrior she would always be. *His* warrior.

His love.

His life.

Turn the page for an exciting sneak peek from

PASSION UNTAMED,

the third book in the Feral Warriors series
Available September 2009 from Avon Books

Paenther fought his way back to consciousness like a man hacking a path through a dense, fog-shrouded jungle. Little by little, he parted the misty enchantment that encased his brain, impressions flying at him through his senses. Cold, rough stone dug into the bare flesh of his back as he lay with his arms pulled taut above his head. He flexed his muscles and tried to move, but harsh metal bit into his wrists as the sound of chains clanked against the rock.

Icy disbelief clawed through his mind. His pulse began to race.

He was chained. Naked.

Finally, *finally,* his vision tore free of the enchantment. His eyes snapped open, and he stared around him at the unlikely sight. He was alone.

In a cave.

High above him, dozens of daggerlike stalactites dripped from the roof. Floating around them were small flames encased in luminescent bubbles. A sight he hadn't seen in nearly three centuries. A sight that filled him with cold dread.

Mage lightwicks.

He fought against his bonds in furious desperation as he struggled to remember what had happened.

The beauty. Innocence and wisdom shining from eyes the color of a summer sky. He'd buried himself inside her and found a passion and release more intense, more incredible, than any he'd ever known. Until, at that moment of raging perfection, she'd revealed herself. As damning copper rings appeared around the blue of her eyes, marking her as a Mage, he'd felt the net of enchantment snare his mind.

The memory stopped his breath, cramping his guts. For the second time in his life, he'd been captured by a Mage witch.

Fury charged through his body, a yell of denial roaring through his head as he struggled to free himself.

This couldn't be happening. He had *not* fallen into another Mage trap! He'd barely survived the first one.

Goddess, I have to get out of here.

He studied his cage with a strafing gaze. It appeared to be a room, an uneven room roughly fifteen by fifteen feet, with a steel door that had been left open. Through the doorway, he glimpsed more stone, telling him he was probably in one of the extensive caverns that riddled the Blue Ridge. The air was damp and cool, but he'd never minded the cold and didn't feel it now.

The rock slab beneath him appeared to be high off the ground, yet attached to the wall like some kind of wide, natural shelf. The wall curved just enough to shield him from the mineral-laden water dripping from the stalactites into the puddles on the floor.

As he tipped his head back to look behind him, he caught the odd sight of a showerhead sticking out of the rock. Plumbing? Was this actually the Mage stronghold, then, and not simply a prison?

He turned to look in the other direction behind him, and froze. Hanging from wooden hangers, from a single peg on the wall, were three softly colored dresses in a shapeless, long-sleeved style he recognized all too well. *Hers.*

Fury ripped through his mind as he remembered, in painful clarity, lifting the hem of one of those soft, worn dresses and sliding his hand beneath to encounter only warm flesh and damp heat. A heat the witch had invited him to drive himself into. And he had. It was an act he'd regret for the rest of his life.

He wondered just how long that would be, now.

His muscles corded as he fought the chains with every ounce of strength he possessed until his skin was damp with sweat. But the chains didn't budge. He was pinned fast, his arms trapped above his head, his legs spread and tethered.

Ah, goddess. If only you'd stopped me. There

was no fate worse. He'd have sold his soul to have escaped this.

Heaven help him. His soul was probably the very thing the witch wanted. To finish what the Mage had started all those years ago—tearing him loose from his animal once and for all.

He caught her scent, the delicate, damning smell of violets. She stepped into the doorway, the ethereal beauty who'd shown him heaven between her thighs, then captured him in her net of bewitchment. Lust slammed into him all over again.

Even as hatred seared its way through his blood, his gaze drank in the sight of her. She was slender, with few curves revealing themselves beneath the soft, shapeless blue dress. But her short hair accentuated a long, graceful neck and features that were too fine, too delicate for a coldhearted witch.

Mage or not, she stole his breath.

She watched him, her eyes wary, as she gently stroked the rabbit in her arms. At her side, a doe pressed her head against the witch's hip, while several excited squirrels chased one another around her ankles.

He'd thought she was human.

Closing his eyes against the sight of her, he prayed that grave error didn't turn out to be the last mistake he ever made.

At the soft sound of her movement, he opened his eyes and watched her cross the room, leading her small menagerie to a cage in the corner. The rabbit and squirrels ran inside, and she fastened the door, then tied the docile doe loosely with a rope attached to the wall. Empathy for the creatures jolted him. Creatures she'd captured as surely as she'd captured him.

The animals seemed to like her. Pets, no doubt. A growl rumbled low in his throat. He would never be *her pet*.

The hatred inside him was so raw, so pure, if his gaze could kill, she'd be dead. Goddess, he couldn't remember the last time he'd let his cock do his thinking for him. No woman had pierced his icy control in centuries. The fact that this one had should have rung a thousand warning bells that she wasn't what she seemed.

"*Witch*," he snarled. "What do you want from me?"

She rose from her animals with the grace of a dancer and turned to him. There was a delicacy about her that tried to tug at his protective instincts. But like everything about her that pulled at him, he knew it was a lie. If he ever managed to free himself from the shackles, he'd carve the heart out of her chest just as he had Ancreta's.

"What I want doesn't matter." Even her soft voice, rich with a regret he didn't believe, held a musical lilt that stroked his senses. "I'm sorry to have brought you here."

"Then let me go."

"I can't." She came toward him, stopping at the foot of the stone platform where he was chained. To his consternation, she watched him, her gaze sliding over his flesh. His body rose, hardening, as if her hands and not her gaze caressed him.

The faint scent of her arousal stole across his senses, tripping a wild rage inside him. How many times had Ancreta forced him to rise for her, then impaled herself on his unwilling body before beginning the torture of trying to free him from his animal?

Placing her palms on the waist-high rock, the witch pulled herself up and knelt between his legs with a swish of soft cotton.

Paenther went feral, his fangs erupting, his claws unsheathing as his eyes turned to the glowing green of a jungle cat.

"You touch me, you die."

The witch laced her fingers together tight enough to turn her knuckles white. The sympathy and remorse in her blue eyes almost seemed real. "I've been where you are. I wouldn't wish it on my worst enemy." She leaned forward, her voice strong and low, and laced with steel. "I know you don't believe me, but you aren't my enemy."

"You *are* mine," he bit out.

She sighed. "I know." Sitting back on her heels, she loosened the knot of her hands. "I'm sorry. I have to touch you, but I won't touch you *there*. Not unless you want me to."

"I'll kill you first."

With a single nod, she splayed her cool palms lightly across his bare thighs. With that simple touch, sensation rippled across his flesh, a heady, electric heat that sent the blood surging through his veins. He fought the desire that blasted him, clawing to hang on to the icy control that had molded his life, but his mind betrayed him as thoroughly as his body. All he could think of was the way her silken thighs had felt beneath his hands as he'd spread her in the woods, as he'd entered her.

The scent of violets washed over him. The sight of her mouth, ripe and unsmiling in that delicate face, reminded him of the taste of her kiss, like clear, sweet raindrops. Even knowing what she was, even knowing she'd lured him into her trap with a siren's song of lust, he couldn't stop wanting her.

Her palms slid along the tops of his thighs, across his flesh as if he were an animal to be petted. It was all he could do not to purr. Without consciously willing it, his fangs and claws retracted.

"You hid your Mage eyes," he snarled instead.

Her mouth twisted in a wry, frustratingly engaging shadow of a smile. "You wouldn't have come with me otherwise."

Paenther tried to growl, but the feel of her hands was doing things to him in parts of his body that had nothing to do with sex. Almost as if she were soothing the rage burned into his soul by Ancreta all those years ago.

"You're beautiful," she murmured. "Your skin is warm as the sun. Your hair like black silk." Her words flowed over him, as irritatingly pleasing as her touch. "The animal inside you purrs."

Paenther froze. She knew he was a Feral. Dammit, he hadn't even tried . . . Closing his eyes against her, he called on the magic deep inside him and tried to shift, praying his panther's paws would be able to slide free of his shackles.

Nothing happened.

As he opened his eyes, the witch's copper blue gaze met his. "The manacles steal your power, warrior. You can't shift as long as you wear them."

"How did you know I was Feral?"

"I knew the first time I saw you. I felt the animal inside you. Just now, I felt you call to the power he gives you."

He scowled. "You couldn't possibly have felt that."

She watched him with those eyes as deep as the oceans but said nothing.

Witch.

Hatred curled in his gut. Ice congealed in his heart. His only reason for being in these mountains at all was to find Vhyper. Something had happened to his friend during a ritual a few weeks ago. He'd been cut by the Daemon Blade, as they all had. But unlike the rest of them, Vhyper had changed. Some of the Ferals thought the evil in the blade had stolen his soul.

Paenther refused to believe he couldn't be saved. He fully intended to save Vhyper, just as Vhyper had saved *him* all those long years ago. But he had to find him first, and getting trapped and chained in a Mage witch's lair sure as hell wasn't the way to go about it.

His body went rigid as a thought occurred to him. He hadn't been alone. What if Foxx had been captured, too? He forced himself to look into the siren's face, guarding himself against the tug of her beauty, steeling himself for her answer.

"How many of us did you catch?"

"Just you, warrior. Your companion got away."

He stared at her, wanting to feel relieved yet not trusting her at all. Still, maybe Foxx *had* escaped. He'd call Lyon, and they'd initiate a rescue. He hated the thought of his unbridled lust's putting his brothers in danger, but knowing the others would come, that he wasn't doomed to spend the rest of his life there, helped calm his storm-tossed mind.

His thoughts evaporated as the witch leaned over him, her dark, sleek head dipping toward his body as if she intended to take him in her mouth.

The growl that erupted from his throat was that of an animal, dark with warning, even as part of him longed for the feel of her wet tongue stroking his length. But her lips landed well to the right of his heavy erection, brushing a light, damp kiss on his hipbone.

Paenther sucked in a hard breath, sweat beading at his temples. Even that small brush of her lips sent heat rushing through his body. His arms shook as they strained against their bonds, his driving need shifting from retribution to pulling her on top of him and burying himself in her heat.

How could he want her so badly when he hated her so violently? She was a fire in his blood. A need raging out of control.

The heady musk of her arousal thickened in the air, and he knew he wasn't the only one feeling the desire. She lifted her gaze, heat a living thing in her eyes. The woman was a potent, dangerous blend of false innocence and a siren's temptation. His body burned to possess her again.

She bent down, her mouth trailing soft, damp kisses along his hip to his thigh, her lips inches from the base of his hard, throbbing shaft. He wanted her to touch him with a need bordering on desperation. But he would never admit it. Never.

What is she doing to me?

Avon Romances
the best in
exceptional authors and unforgettable novels!

At Avon Books, we know your passion for romance—once you finish one of our novels, you find yourself wanting more.

May we tempt you with . . .

- **Excerpts** from our upcoming releases.

- Entertaining **extras**, including authors' personal photo albums and book lists.

- Behind-the-scenes **scoop** on your favorite characters and series.

- **Sweepstakes** for the chance to win free books, romantic getaways, and other fun prizes.

- Writing **tips** from our authors and editors.

- **Blog** with our authors and find out why they love to write romance.

- **Exclusive content** that's not contained within the pages of our novels.

Join us at
www.avonbooks.com

AVON

An Imprint of HarperCollins*Publishers*
www.avonromance.com